Imitation of Wife

D0967342

Imitation of Wife

La Jill Hunt

URBAN
BOOKS

www.urbanbooks.net

Urban Books, LLC
300 Farmingdale Road, NY-Route 109
Farmingdale, NY 11735

ISBN 13: 978-1-60162-928-9
ISBN 10: 1-60162-928-1

First Trade Paperback Printing June 2020
Printed in the United States of America

10 9 8 7 6 5 4 3 2 1

Distributed by Kensington Publishing Corp.
Submit Orders to:
Customer Service
400 Hahn Road
Westminster, MD 21157-4627
Phone: 1-800-733-3000
Fax: 1-800-659-2436

Imitation of Wife

by

La Jill Hunt

Prologue

The last place Tricia King wanted to be was at a basketball game. It didn't matter that it was the state championship, nor did it matter that her son was the captain and star player of one of the high school teams that were playing. Tricia had no desire to attend, and until her husband insisted, she hadn't even planned on being here.

Tarik, or Tank as everyone called him, had been playing basketball for the past ten years, since the age of 7. In the beginning, she would attend his recreation league games when his father was unable to attend because he was out of town working. But after Titus's job changed and he was home more, basketball became their father-son activity. That was fine with Tricia because it meant she didn't have to be bothered, especially since Titus made sure he was the one on sidelines at every game and practice. As Tank got older, his skills and talents on the court, along with his height, made him a standout and led every team he played on to victory: middle school, AAU, and now high school. Although she and Titus had a nice amount put away for Tank's college savings, the scholarship offers had been pouring in for a while. Thankfully, they wouldn't have to pay a dime for his college education. She planned on purchasing a new Lexus she'd been eying for a while and maybe sending her mother on a cruise, unbeknownst to Titus, of course. The fact that basketball had afforded her son to go to college without them having to foot the bill still wasn't enough to motivate her to go to the game that had the entire city, except her, excited.

"But why do I have to be there?" she said to Titus the morning of the game after he informed her that her not going wasn't an option.

"Because it's the last high school game of your son's career, Tricia. Damn, you'd think you'd want to be there. You haven't been to any of his games this year," Titus said. It wasn't as if she'd planned on missing all of his games. It was just that each week she'd told herself that she'd make the next one, and before she knew it, the playoffs had begun.

"And he's been fine," she responded. "Tank doesn't care if I'm there. You're the one making a big deal out of this, not him."

"Tricia, I'm telling you, you need to go to this game tonight. Tank's worked so hard for this. The school has chartered buses and everything. It's going to be a big deal. The press is going to be there—"

"I don't give a damn about the press. They aren't going to be there for me."

"I didn't say they were."

"You know how much I hate crowds, Titus, and isn't that game five hours away? I'm not riding on a damn bus for five hours. I'm sure someone will broadcast the game since it's such a big deal or go live on social media. I can watch from right here."

"It's only four hours away, and you don't have to ride the bus with the other parents. We can drive." Titus shook his head. "Listen, I don't ask a lot of you. But you are going to this game to support our son. So get ready."

She thought about the plans she'd made for the day: appointments to get her hair, nails, and feet done, and a full-body massage, after which she planned to stop by Total Wine and pick up a couple of bottles of cabernet, then come home and enjoy the Hallmark channel while she ordered takeout and relaxed. All of those things sounded so much better than driving five hours and then sitting in a crowded gymnasium full of loud people yelling at her son and his team.

But Titus was right, this was Tank's last basketball game in high school, and though she wanted to be selfish, she also knew how important this game was for her son. So she relented and agreed to go. It really was bittersweet because this game solidified the fact that her son was growing up and would be leaving home.

Tricia spent most of the five-hour car ride playing games on her cell phone while Titus drove the entire way, listening to old-school hip-hop in between talking to his friends and relatives on the phone about the game they were headed to. When they arrived, the line into the coliseum where the game was being held was wrapped around the building.

As they made their way inside, her anxiety increased, and by the time they made it to their seats, it was on level ten. Most of the other parents had on blue and gold, the school colors, or shirts with the mascot and their son's name and number. Her last-minute decision to attend hadn't warranted a wardrobe change, and her outfit, which consisted of a simple Mickey Mouse graphic T-shirt and jeans, certainly was less spirited than everyone else, including her husband, whose own shirt had Tank's picture on it.

People walked up and spoke to Titus and congratulated him on Tank's success as if he were the one winning the games instead of their son. There were even a couple of sports reporters who asked to speak to him. Titus laughed and smiled, enjoying making small talk. Tricia kept glancing at him, hoping he would just sit down. She was relieved when the game finally began.

It was a close game the entire time, and while everyone else seemed to enjoy it, Tricia didn't. Between her rowdy

husband, who spent most of the game on his feet screaming along with the rest of the crowd, and the anticipation
while watching her son and his teammates play their
hearts out, her nerves were shot, and she was ready to go.
She was on sensory overload. But she fought the urge to
leave and stayed. At the very end, when Tank hit the winning shot, she was elated. He did it. Her son was a state
champ. Everything he'd been working and sacrificing for
had paid off, and she was happy for him.

The crowd went wild, and it was she, not Titus, who
rushed down the bleachers, pushing past everyone as
she called her son's name. His face lit up with surprise as
he ran over and hugged her, making her glad that she'd
come. Then Tank looked over and saw his father and ran
to give him a hug. Tricia stood watching the two men in
her life cry while embracing one another. It was a proud
moment for them.

Moments later, Tank began calling out for someone.
Her son took off toward a gorgeous young lady standing
near the bottom of the bleachers, smiling at him. Tank
swept the girl into his arms, kissing her as he lifted her
off the ground. All eyes were on them until, suddenly,
two men began screaming at one another then shoving
each other. Tricia reached for Titus, but instead of him
protecting her from the chaos that was ensuing, he took
off toward it. The next thing she knew, her husband was
shoving one of the men, blocking him from a woman
grabbing at Titus's arm. Seconds later, security was
pulling them apart before taking them away.

"What's going on? Who is that?" Tricia asked Tank,
who looked just as confused as she did.

"I don't really know, but I think one of the guys was
Peyton's dad." Tank frowned. "Mr. Blackwell."

"Who the hell is Peyton?" Tricia demanded.

"She's my girl," Tank said as if she should've known the answer to her question before asking it.

"Tank! Get to the locker room now! Come on!" the coach yelled as another set of security guards began rounding up the players and instructing everyone to clear the arena.

"Wait, that's my son," Tricia tried to explain.

"I understand, ma'am, but we need to make sure these players are safe, so everyone needs to get out now. You can wait around back by the buses with the other parents," the guard told her as he pointed toward the nearest exit.

"I didn't ride the bus with the other parents," she snapped. "And I need to find my husband."

"Then you can find him outside. But either you leave now, or you will be arrested," he threatened.

Instead of cussing him out like she wanted to, Tricia just turned and followed the rest of the crowd out the door. When she got to the parking lot, she called Titus to see where the hell he was. It took three tries for him to finally answer. He said they were holding him in the security office and for Tricia to wait in the car. By then, she was hot, tired, and angry, so she didn't say anything. She went to the car, which was parked near the charter buses, and waited.

Thirty minutes later, Tank and his team walked out. Tricia hopped out of the car as she waved toward him and called his name, but he didn't answer. She was about to walk over to him when Titus came running out and stopped him just before he got on the bus. Even though she was too far away to hear what they were saying, Tricia could tell that it was a heated exchange, based on their body language and the look of anger on her son's face. The coach said something to both of them, then Titus headed toward the car where she was waiting.

"What the hell was that about, Titus?" Tricia demanded as soon as he got to the car.

"He's upset right now because security made everyone leave before they were given the trophy, and they didn't get to cut down the net," Titus said as he started the engine. "I told him he'll be fine, and Coach explained that there will be a victory celebration at the school."

"That's not what the fuck I'm talking about," she snapped.

"What?" Titus asked as if he had no clue what she was referring to, which made her even angrier.

"You jumping into that fight and getting hauled off by the police, that's what." She frowned.

"I didn't get hauled off by the police. It was just security, and I didn't jump into a fight. I was trying to break up the fight and got swept into the commotion, that's all. Everything was straightened out when we got into the security office." His phone began ringing, and he answered it. "What's up, Tony? Yeah, my boy did good. Thanks, man, I appreciate that. No doubt, you know I'm hella proud of him."

Tricia sat back in her seat and took out her own phone, turning her attention to her game since it was clear Titus was finished with this conversation, even though she wasn't. For the remainder of the four-hour ride home, she listened as he took call after call from people congratulating him. The only conversation they shared was when she told him she was hungry, and he asked what she wanted to eat.

When they finally arrived home, Titus went into his man cave after taking a shower, and Tricia settled on the sofa in the den to watch television before going upstairs to bed. She didn't realize she'd fallen asleep until the sound of the toilet flushing woke her up. She sat up, looking at her watch, and saw that it was eight in the morning. The drive and the game must've worn her out, because she hadn't even heard her son come home. Her attention went to the corner of the room, expecting to see Tank's basketball and gym bag, but it wasn't there: a clear indication that he wasn't home. It wasn't her son in the bathroom. It was Titus.

"Titus, where's Tank?" she called out.

"What?" Titus walked into the den, rubbing his eyes.

"Where is Tank? I didn't hear him come in last night, and his stuff isn't by the doorway." She pointed.

Titus looked over then shrugged. "You just didn't hear him. He's probably upstairs asleep and took it with him."

"I would've heard the alarm when he opened the door. He didn't come home, I'm telling you."

Titus turned and yelled, "Tank!" When there was no answer or response, he headed up the staircase toward Tank's room.

Tricia stood up and walked over to the bottom of the stairs, waiting for him to confirm what she already knew. Her son wasn't there.

"I told you." She shook her at Titus, who was walking back downstairs. "I knew his ass didn't come home."

"Calm down, Tricia. He probably was out with his teammates and fell asleep. The boy did just win his state basketball championship. It's fine."

"It's not fine. I don't give a damn if he won the Super Bowl. He doesn't get to stay out all night, especially without calling and getting permission," she said with a glare. Then she asked, "Wait, did you tell him he could stay out all night without discussing it with me first?"

Communication was not her family's strong suit, and it wasn't unusual for her husband and son to make plans without her. Over the years, it seemed as if Titus didn't feel the need to discuss any parental decisions with her. When she'd complain about it, he'd apologize and say it was no big deal and explain that most of the time, the discussions they had were at a time when she wasn't around. He never took into consideration that that mostly happened because the two of them were always together and hardly ever at home, where she spent most of her time, while they were always at the gym working out, at basketball practice, a game, or hanging out somewhere else. The two of them were tighter than a fresh set of braids done by an African stylist.

"I need for you to rethink that question you just asked. No, Tricia, I didn't give him permission to stay out all night. I ain't even know the boy wasn't here until you said something. Don't you think if I'd given him permission, I would've said something?"

She paused, and instead of pointing out that he probably wouldn't have said anything to her, she picked up her phone off the coffee table and dialed Tank's number. It rang once then went to voicemail. She sent a text, demanding that he call her back, then told Titus, "Go call him."

"Uh, didn't you just do that?"

"Yes, but he'll probably answer for you before he does me. You know how the two of you are."

"That's not true, but fine," Titus said and walked out. When he didn't come back after a few minutes, Tricia went into the man cave and found him watching television

"Well?" She put her hands on her hips as she stood in front of him, blocking his view of the screen.

"He didn't answer for me either." He leaned to look past her.

"Did you text him?"

"I did."

"Did he get it?"

"I'm assuming he did." Titus shrugged.

His nonchalance made her angrier by the second. "Isn't one of the big deals the two of you are always bragging about your iPhone is that you can see when someone reads your text message?"

Unlike the two of them, she was the only one in the household with an Android phone, another little idiosyncrasy that made her an outsider to their all-boys club. She knew Titus could track her son through his phone and probably knew exactly where he was. He was way too calm about their son's absence not to know.

"Yeah, the message has been delivered, but he hasn't read it yet," Titus said, looking at his phone. "Let me see if any of his friends know where he is. I'm sure he's fine."

"Why are you so damn calm? You should be pissed."

"Tricia, look, I'm just as upset about him not coming home as you are. The boy just won the state championship last night, and he probably went out to celebrate with the team. Now should he have called? Yeah, he should have. My main concern is that he's safe, and once that's confirmed, I'll talk with him, and he'll have to deal with the consequences of his actions. He ain't getting a pass."

"You'll deal with the consequences." She rolled her eyes. "We are supposed to deal with them."

"Fine, we." Titus shrugged. "I'll take a quick shower and go find him."

"You don't know where he is, remember?"

"I'll find where he is, Tricia."

"He's probably with that girl he was kissing after the game. And when the hell did he get a girlfriend anyway?" Tricia asked.

"I didn't know about that shit until last night. And no, he ain't with Peyton. That I'm sure of."

Titus's response was not what she expected. She assumed he'd known about the girl and thought he would've been satisfied with her considering how pretty she was. Instead, he seemed bothered, which meant that, whoever she was, there was a problem with her. From the way she was kissing her son, she was probably some little trick who was probably planning to trap their son. If Tank had been with his teammates or friends, he would've at least called and checked in. He hadn't, which probably meant that he was somewhere else that they wouldn't approve of. Unlike her husband, she knew how predatory teenage girls could be. Not only was Tank good-looking, smart, and athletic, he was well-mannered and had a bright future. There was no telling what that girl was plotting for her son.

"How do you know he ain't with her? He said that was his girlfriend, and she was all over him. The way she was slobbering all over him was ridiculous," Tricia scoffed.

"Because I know he's not with her, and Peyton, she's not like that."

"You don't know that, Titus. You and Tank may be close, but you said yourself you ain't even know he had a girlfriend until last night. So he don't tell you everything. They seemed pretty close until all hell broke loose," Tricia told him. "Wasn't her father one of the ones you were fighting with? Was that why y'all were fighting?"

"What? I told you I wasn't fighting anyone. I was trying to help."

"That's another thing, Titus. Why the hell were you more concerned with helping someone else than making sure your wife was safe during all of that commotion?" Tricia asked. "You force me to go to the damn game, and then what? You forgot I was there with you?"

"I'm not even going to continue this conversation with you right now, Tricia. I'm going to get dressed then go find my son." Titus shook his head as he walked past her and headed up the stairs.

"Our son," Tricia tossed over her shoulder. "He's probably with that skank."

"She's not a skank," Titus yelled back down the steps. "I'll take care of it."

On the floor near the sofa was a folded piece of paper that Titus must've dropped. She picked it up and read what turned out to be the incident report from the coliseum, listing the names and information of all parties involved. The vision of her son and the girl kissing flashed in her head. If her son was anywhere, it was with that fast-ass girl. Any other time, Titus would be all involved and have so much to say, but this didn't seem to even matter to him. *Typical man.*

Tricia may not have had a lot to say when it came to her son and basketball, or school, or pretty much anything else, but she wasn't going to just sit back and allow some skank to trap Tank and ruin his future and their lives with a baby. *Bump that. She's probably got him laid up somewhere, throwing it on him right now while Titus is upstairs acting like it's no big deal. He might not recognize how trifling these high school heffas are, but I do.*

"It looks like Peyton's dad. Mr. Blackwell." Tank's voice echoed in her head as she stared at the paper in her hand. *The father is fighting at a high school basketball game, and the daughter is acting like a thot in heat. These folks are probably ghetto project negroes looking for a come-up, and it damn sure ain't gonna be my son.* Tricia grabbed her purse, typing the address into her phone as she rushed out the door.

Chapter 1

Sylvia

Sylvia Blackwell was in the middle of arguing with her husband, Garry, when the doorbell interrupted their heated conversation. It wasn't even nine o'clock on a Sunday morning, and they weren't expecting anyone, especially the woman who was standing on their doorstep when she opened the front door of their home.

"Um, come in," Sylvia said, moving to the side so her unexpected guest could enter. She recognized Tricia King from a photo that her sister, Janelle, found on social media while cyberstalking her ex-boyfriend Titus, who was Tricia's husband. They'd never met, nor spoken to one another, and now she was at her house. Sylvia's heart raced, knowing that Tricia was probably looking for Janelle, especially after the incident last night after the basketball game. As soon as Titus laid eyes on Janelle and saw she was in danger during the fight that was erupting, he immediately ran to her rescue like some kind of action-movie star saving his love interest. If Tricia had seen her husband's actions, that might be the reason for her pop-up.

"I'm looking for the Blackwell residence. I'm sorry. This has to be the wrong house." Tricia looked around as if she was confused. "I was looking for Garry and Peyton Blackwell."

Although Tricia looking for Garry and Peyton was a bit odd, Sylvia was a bit relieved she wasn't there for her sister.

"I'm Garry Blackwell." Garry stepped forward and said, "Peyton is our daughter. What's going on?"

Tricia looked him up and down, still seeming a bit confused, and said, "You were in an altercation last night after my son's basketball game?" It sounded more like a question than a statement.

"Yeah, I was." Garry nodded. "It was an unfortunate event, and I owe your son and his team an apology for that, but I went to the game looking for my daughter and—"

"Is he here?" Tricia asked.

"Excuse me?" Garry asked.

"My son. Is he here with your daughter?" Tricia clarified.

Sylvia stepped closer to her husband, offended by Tricia's question. "Why would you think that?"

"Because he didn't come home last night, and he's not answering his phone. And he mentioned that they've been seeing one another," Tricia stated. "I guess your daughter is supposed to be his girlfriend."

"What do you mean seeing one another? Girlfriend? Since when?" Garry's question was directed to Sylvia, who was just as surprised by this revelation as he was. She knew Peyton had to have a reason to sneak to the game, but she had no idea it had anything to do with Titus's son.

"I don't know anything about this." Sylvia's eyebrow raised. "But to answer your question, your son isn't here."

"And my daughter isn't anyone's girlfriend," Garry added.

"Well, can you ask your daughter if she knows where he is?" Tricia asked.

"Where who is?" Aunt Connie suddenly emerged from the kitchen. Her attention went to Tricia. "Good morning."

"Hello." Tricia's tone was stoic.

"Aunt Connie, this is Tricia King." Sylvia told her, "She's uh . . ."

Sylvia didn't know how to introduce her. The day had barely begun, and it was getting more and more awkward by the minute. The turmoil from the night before was overflowing, and before she could wrap her mind around one thing, another one popped up. First, Jordan went missing, and they tracked her down five hours away at a basketball game. Then when they arrived, not only did they find her there but also Peyton, who'd snuck off with Janelle. Then Garry got into an altercation with Sherrod, the guy Janelle had been dating, who also turned out to be the friend of her newly discovered stepdaughter's deceased mother, Randi. Now Tricia was standing in her foyer, looking for her son, who apparently had been dating their daughter without their knowledge. It was too much, too early.

"I'm Tarik's mother." Tricia said, "I came to see if he was here."

"It seems that Tarik didn't come home last night, and he and Peyton are friends," Sylvia explained. "But I've told her that he's not here."

"Does Peyton know where he is?" Aunt Connie asked.

"That's what I was asking." Tricia sighed, then added, "And based on the way she was all over my son last night, I think she's more than a friend."

"I don't know what you're referring to, but I can promise you my daughter wasn't all over anybody," Garry snapped. Sylvia placed a hand on his arm, squeezing it gently.

"Listen, why don't you just run upstairs and ask Peyton if she knows where Frank is," Aunt Connie suggested.

"Tank," Sylvia, Garry, and Tricia all said simultaneously.

"I'll go talk to her," Sylvia volunteered, but at that moment, both Peyton and Jordan came walking down the steps. Sylvia was taken aback since Jordan's room was downstairs and she rarely even ventured to the second floor of their home.

"What's going on?" Jordan asked.

"Mrs. King?" Peyton's eyes widened when she saw Tricia standing beside Aunt Connie.

"Peyton, when's the last time you talked to Tank?" Garry asked her.

"Um, I talked to him last night after the game. He was pretty upset about what happened," Peyton said. "They didn't even get to cut the net off the rim like they were supposed to because of—"

"Sweetie." Sylvia shook her head slightly at her daughter, hinting for her to stop talking. "Tank didn't go home last night. His mother is worried."

"He's probably with somebody from the team partying. We did win the state championship last night, remember?" Jordan shrugged and folded her arms. "Not that they got the chance to celebrate and enjoy the moment like they should have. Someone stopped that from happening."

"Not now, Jordan," Garry warned.

"I'm just saying," Jordan said. "You kinda ruined his moment."

"Wait, you thought Tarik was here at my house?" Peyton frowned.

"Who is Tarik?" Aunt Connie leaned and whispered to Jordan.

"That's his real name," Jordan told her.

"Oh, okay, I see. Peyton baby, why don't you run upstairs and get your phone and see if you can call Frank," Aunt Connie said.

"Tank," they all said again.

"Okay. I'll be right back," Peyton said and hustled up the stairs.

"I can't believe him," Tricia mumbled as she exhaled loudly. "If he's not here, where the hell is he?"

Sylvia realized that there was a hint of concern under her somewhat-cold exterior and thought about how she felt herself less than twenty-four hours before when she was facing the same situation. Unlike Tricia, though, she wouldn't consider showing up on a stranger's doorstep, especially with an attitude dressed in jeans and cheap boots, looking like she was ready to fight.

"I'm sure he's fine," Aunt Connie said. "Both Peyton and Jordan here snuck off yesterday, and we found them. And Peyton went off for a couple of hours the other week and we couldn't find her, and she showed up at home."

Sylvia gave Aunt Connie the same warning Garry gave Jordan moments before. "Not now, Aunt Connie."

"He probably just needs to cool off, that's all." Jordan shrugged. "I do that all the time. I take a time-out."

"Has he ever gone missing before?" Sylvia asked.

"No, never." Tricia shook her head. "My son isn't a kid who runs away, and he doesn't need a time-out."

Jordan went to react, but Aunt Connie placed her hand on her shoulder, whispering loud enough to be heard, "Don't justify that comment with a response, baby. She's just worried about her son and ain't thinking before she's speaking."

The tension was noticeably uncomfortable, and something needed to be done. Sylvia was trying to remain cordial, especially since Tarik was missing, but she was already dealing with the stress of her own family drama, and her patience was thin. Her empathy was limited, and Tricia's attitude wasn't making it easier. She wanted this woman to leave but didn't want to be rude and make an already-awkward situation worse.

"I'll be right back," Sylvia said. She was up the stairs and about to enter her bedroom when she heard Garry behind her.

"Syl, where are you going?" he hissed. "You can't leave that woman downstairs."

"I said I'd be right back," she whispered as she kept walking. "I have a phone call to make."

"Who the hell are you calling?" He followed her into their bedroom.

Sylvia picked up her cell phone and pressed her sister's name.

"What?" Janelle answered after the third ring.

"Nelle, wake up. We have a situation," Sylvia told her.

"You're calling Janelle? That's the last person you need to be calling right now considering who's downstairs," Garry said.

"Shut up, Garry. You're the last person who needs to be talking to me right now considering everything," she snapped at him. He sulked but didn't say anything else.

"What the hell is going on? What time is it?" Janelle groaned.

"Nelle, I need you to call Titus right now," Sylvia told her. "Call him on three-way. I need to talk to him."

"I'm not calling him. Why do you want him?" Janelle asked.

"Because his wife is downstairs crying in my living room," Sylvia said, trying not to yell.

"Shit. What?" Janelle squealed. "What the hell for? Why is she there? Is she looking for me?"

"No, she's not looking for you. She's looking for her son. Now call him."

"What? Tank is at your house?"

"Janelle." It was taking everything for Sylvia not to snap, and she was two seconds from losing it. "I don't have time to play damn twenty-one questions. Get Titus's ass on the phone now."

"Fine, hold on," Janelle said, and then the phone went quiet.

"Go downstairs and check and see what's going on," Sylvia told Garry.

"I'm sure Aunt Connie has it all under control," he said. "They don't need me down there."

Although her husband was probably right, she told him, "Well, I don't need you up here either."

"Hello?" Titus's voice came on the line. "Syl, what's going on? Tricia's at your house?

"Yes, she is. She came over here looking for your son," Sylvia told him.

"Oh my God. I told her to relax and I would handle it." Titus sighed.

"Wait, do you know where he is?" Sylvia asked, wondering why he seemed so calm while Tricia was so agitated by their son's disappearance.

"No, not really," Titus said.

"What the hell does that mean? 'No, not really.' Have you talked to him?" Sylvia was now talking through clenched teeth, angered by Titus's lack of concern. His wife was out trying to locate their son, and he was acting as if it were no big deal.

"No, I haven't talked to him, but I don't think he's run away anywhere. His clothes are still in his room, and he knows he has a news interview at three o'clock this afternoon. Besides, the entire school will be celebrating the team at school tomorrow, and he ain't missing that. He's probably with a couple of his teammates," Titus told her. "I'm heading out now to go find him."

"What made her go to my sister's house to look for him?" Janelle spoke up. She'd been so quiet that Sylvia forgot she was on the phone.

"She found out Peyton and Tank are dating," Titus told her. "Look, I'm sorry about her showing up like that. I know you probably thought—"

"Call your wife, and get her the hell out of my damn house, Titus," Sylvia snapped before hanging up.

"What did he say?" Garry asked. "You should've let me talk to—"

"Don't." She turned and held her palm up toward him as she walked past. "We still have unfinished business from this morning. This situation happening right now doesn't change anything. I still want you to leave."

Chapter 2

Sylvia

By the time Sylvia returned to the foyer, thankfully, Titus had already phoned his wife, and she was ready to leave, barely saying, "Thank you," as she walked out the door. Within seconds of the door closing behind her, Peyton and Jordan quickly disappeared, and Aunt Connie was back in the kitchen. Sylvia headed back up the steps, and when she got to the top, she was at an impasse and had a decision to make. She could either go left, where the hallway led to her bedroom, where she knew Garry was probably waiting. Or she could go right into Peyton's bedroom. She looked from one side to the other before making her decision.

"Peyton?" Sylvia knocked and opened the door at the same time.

"Yes?" Peyton answered.

Sylvia walked in. Peyton was sitting Indian style in the middle of her bed, scrolling on her phone. "Did you reach Tarik?"

"No, he's still not responding to my calls or texts." Peyton sounded frustrated. "Or anyone else's. None of his friends knows where he is."

"I'm sure he's just somewhere cooling off," Sylvia said, sitting on the side of the bed.

"I feel really bad. He's embarrassed, and he didn't even do anything wrong. This wasn't even his fault," Peyton whined.

"That's true. He has no reason to be embarrassed," Sylvia agreed.

"I don't even understand what happened. Why was Dad fighting that guy?" Peyton's thick eyebrows furrowed as she stared at Sylvia, who really didn't have an answer.

"I'm still trying to figure that out myself, baby, and that's a valid question, but I'm more concerned about why you felt the need to sneak off to the basketball game instead of asking for permission." Sylvia's head tilted to the side, her eyes blinking slowly as she waited for Peyton to speak.

Peyton's eyes dropped to her colorful bedspread, and her voice was barely above a whisper. "Because I knew you'd say no."

"You don't know that."

"I do. The answer is always no, even though I'm seventeen and an honors student who's leaving for college within a few months. I knew if I said I wanted to go watch Tarik—who's also a great guy and an honors student—play in the championship game, it would still be no. So I asked Aunt Nelle to take me," Peyton explained. "This game was the moment of Tank's life, and I wanted to be there for him."

"You could've come to me, Peyton," Sylvia told her. "You can come to me about anything."

"No, I couldn't have."

Peyton saying she felt as if she couldn't talk to her was a surprise. Sylvia believed that she and her daughter had a great relationship. Over the years, she'd made sure to keep an open dialogue about everything: school, friends, body changes, boys, and even sex.

"Peyton, we talk about everything," Sylvia pointed out.

"We talk about some things. Other stuff we talk around. There's a difference," Peyton told her.

"What do you mean?" Sylvia frowned.

"We have discussions about grades, or college, or fashion. We laugh about movies, TV shows, and yeah, we love our celebrity gossip. But when it comes to dating or guys, it's always been this negative vibe and a warning. 'You don't need to be thinking about boys, Peyton. You don't have time to be wasting on these knucklehead boys,'" Peyton mimicked. "God forbid I say I want to go on a date, or worse, if Tank had come over to the house like he'd been trying to do for months. That would've been a disaster."

Sylvia shook her head. "See, that's where you're wrong. Had you come and explained to me and Daddy who Tank was and allowed us the opportunity to meet him, we may have been open to your dating him. Instead, you decided to sneak around, and look what happened."

"I was wrong for doing that, and I apologize." Peyton sighed. "But, Mom, you know even if you would've been cool with meeting Tank, Dad wouldn't, and you always side with him, no matter what. It's always his way or no way."

"That's a lie, Peyton, and you know it." Sylvia stiffened, and her anger began to rise.

"It's not. Remember when you said I could wear makeup, and we went to Sephora and bought stuff and had so much fun? Then Daddy came home and lost his mind. All of a sudden, you agreed that all I really needed was lip gloss, mascara, and eye liner."

Peyton was right about that situation. But it wasn't that Sylvia had been siding with Garry. It's just that she'd seen his point when he pointed out that Peyton was beautiful enough without needing all of the makeup she was wearing at the moment. The salesperson at Sephora who'd given them a demo had been generous and given Peyton a dramatic look, which included lots of eyeshadow, foundation, lashes, and highlighter. When

Garry saw her, he was very vocal about their daughter's glamorous appearance. Peyton was disappointed but seemed to understand when Sylvia told her she only needed a simple look.

"Peyton, I know you know how much your father and I love you." Sylvia sighed.

"I do." Peyton nodded. "And before you say it, I already know, you make the decisions you do to protect me."

At that moment, Sylvia's mind went to her husband and why he'd kept so many secrets from her in an effort to protect her and their marriage. How he'd withheld the truth, and even after everything was revealed, she'd accepted his reasoning. She'd acquiesced with no question. Could there be some truth to what Peyton was saying?

Tap, tap, tap.

"Breakfast is ready," Aunt Connie stuck her head in the door and announced.

"I'm not really hungry," Peyton said.

Sylvia knew that didn't matter to Aunt Connie. When it was time to eat, it didn't matter whether you were hungry. It also didn't matter what you felt like eating.

"Be downstairs in five minutes. You don't want it to get cold." Aunt Connie smiled then disappeared from the doorway.

"But—" Peyton went to protest. Sylvia quickly shook her head, and Peyton's mouth snapped closed.

"We'll finish this discussion later." Sylvia stood up. "And you know there will be consequences."

"I know." Peyton sighed. "Real talk though, this is all Jordan's fault if you look at it. She's the one who was with that man Daddy was fighting," Peyton said. "She's been nothing but trouble since she got here."

Sylvia frowned. "No, ma'am. I'm not gonna let you do that. Jordan and her actions don't have nothing to do with the fact that you decided to sneak off without permission, young lady. That damn sure wasn't on her. Now bring your behind on."

Peyton had sense enough to simply mutter, "Yes, ma'am."

The two were heading downstairs when Sylvia heard her cell phone ringing from the bedroom. "Go ahead, I'll be down in a minute."

"I can wait for you, Mom," Peyton offered.

"Go eat," Sylvia told her before rushing down the hallway to her bedroom. By the time she reached her phone, it had stopped ringing. In addition to missing the call from Lynne, her best friend, Sylvia also had three missed calls from Janelle. Despite calling her sister earlier to help out with the Tricia situation, Sylvia still had some choice words for her sister about her decision to take Peyton out of town without saying anything. Now wasn't the time, though. She tossed her phone back on the bed and went downstairs.

"You want me to make your plate?" Aunt Connie offered when Sylvia entered the dining room. Peyton, Jordan, and Garry were already seated, all three looking forlorn and picking at their food. Sylvia looked at the grits, eggs, sausage, bacon, and homemade biscuits sitting in the middle of the table and wondered how her aunt had managed to prepare all of it in a short period of time.

"No, I got it," Sylvia answered, picking up one of the empty plates and putting a small amount of each item on it. Had she allowed her aunt to do it, it would have been piled with more than she would've been able to eat, that was for sure. It was a risk she knew not to take.

The tension in the room was deafening. Not even Aunt Connie's small talk was enough to engage everyone in a full conversation. Peyton and Jordan mumbled one-word answers to any question directed at them, while Garry and Sylvia remained quiet while purposely avoiding looking in each other's direction.

"When we leave church today, I was thinking we could stop by that new grocery store they built. I heard they have a nice produce section," Aunt Connie said. It was as if the tension became thicker, and everyone became focused on their plate.

After a few seconds, Sylvia looked over and said, "We aren't going to church, Aunt Connie. We all had a late night, and uh, we have some things to handle with the girls."

Surprisingly, Aunt Connie didn't fuss. She just shrugged and said, "I understand. I had a nice conversation with Ms. Jordan when she came in my room and let her know what she did was unacceptable. Ain't that right?"

Jordan nodded and said, "Yes, ma'am."

"Well, just because y'all are being heathens and skipping service doesn't mean I am. Let me get on up so I can get ready for service," Aunt Connie stood and announced. "Peyton, Jordan, y'all clear the table and put the food away. Garry, feed Gypsy and then make sure you take her out so she won't have an accident."

"I can drop you off," Sylvia volunteered, "and pick you up."

"No need, baby. I'll get there and get home. You take care of everything going on here." Aunt Connie gave her a reassuring nod.

Jordan stood and picked up both her and Aunt Connie's plates and headed into the kitchen.

Peyton glanced up and said, "I can do the kitchen by myself. I don't need help."

"I know you can, and I didn't ask you if you needed help. You and your sister will do it together," Aunt Connie told her. Peyton exhaled loudly.

Garry looked as if he was going to say something, but instead, he whistled and called out, "Gypsy."

The small Pomeranian hopped into the dining room and ran over to Garry. While everyone's attention was on the dog, Sylvia used the distraction to quickly exit the uncomfortable atmosphere and go back to her bedroom. She needed to think and somehow process everything. She thought about going to church with Aunt Connie just to get away from the house. But there was no sense in running away. Her troubled marriage and children would still be waiting when church was over, so there was no point. Her head was pounding, and after taking a much-needed Extra Strength Tylenol that she found in the medicine cabinet, she lay back on her bed and closed her eyes.

Chapter 3

Janelle

As if last night weren't crazy enough, Titus's wife showing up at Sylvia's house was even more perplexing. Janelle was both baffled and nervous in addition to being tired as hell. After getting home after two in the morning from the basketball game, she'd tossed and turned most of the night, and when she finally drifted off to sleep, Sylvia called to tell her about her unexpected guest. There was no way she could go back to sleep now, so she got up. She needed a drink, and a strong one. She also needed to talk to someone, so she dialed her best friend Nivea's number. When Nivea didn't answer, she called her other friend Natalie.

"What's up?" Natalie answered.

"I need a drink. Actually, I need several drinks," Janelle told her.

"So early? Wow, what's going on, chick?"

"I'll tell you when we get to Brutti's. Where the hell is Nivea? I called her, but she didn't answer," Janelle said as she pulled out a pair of her favorite jeans and a sweatshirt.

"I don't know. I haven't talked to her since Friday. She's been low-key this weekend. Maybe she finally hooked up with Sherrod. You know she's been chasing him for the past couple of weeks." Natalie laughed.

At the sound of Sherrod's name, Janelle froze. She almost told Natalie that couldn't be where Nivea was because she and Sherrod were together the night before at the state basketball championship where he'd been involved in an altercation with her brother-in-law, something she still couldn't believe happened. Instead, Janelle simply said, "Maybe."

"You know she's gonna be mad if we go to Brutti's without her. We're gonna have to hear her mouth," Natalie warned.

"Then she should've an—" Janelle's response was interrupted by a beep. She looked at her phone and saw that it was Aunt Connie. Her heart began racing, wondering if something had happened at Sylvia's house with Tricia. She waited a few moments before finally clicking over and nervously saying, "Hello."

"Good morning. I know you're up," Aunt Connie said.

"Yes, ma'am," Janelle told her.

"I'm gonna need to ride to church with you this morning. I'll be ready in about an hour after I make breakfast then finish getting dressed," Aunt Connie told her.

"Uh, I, uh, wasn't planning on going to church this morning, Aunt Connie. I didn't get home until late last night. Actually, it was more like this morning," Janelle explained, slightly relived that was the reason her aunt was calling and not for anything else.

"I know what time you got home. But you're up now."

"Aunt Connie, can't you ride with Sylvia?"

"She ain't going this morning. She's got stuff around here to deal with."

"Is, uh . . . Does she still have company?" Janelle couldn't resist asking. Her aunt hadn't mentioned anything about Tricia, and Sylvia hadn't called her back yet, so she was curious.

"No. Titus's wife is gone. I know that's who you're talking about. Poor woman is worried to death about her son. Too worried to be concerned with anything else, right now, thank God. That's why you need to be going to service, because Lord knows y'all dodged a bullet this morning, because things could've gone way differently," Aunt Connie told her. "And we need to go lift that young man up in prayer so he can come home safe. Hell, we especially need to lift our own family up in prayer because the devil is busy, and his ass needs to be handled. So I'll see you in an hour." Aunt Connie hung up before Janelle could say anything else. It probably didn't even occur to her aunt that she'd cussed and talked about the Lord in the same sentence.

"Janelle, you there?" Natalie's voice came through the phone. Janelle had forgotten that her friend had been holding on the other end.

"Yeah, I'm here. My bad," Janelle told her. "But brunch has been changed to a late lunch."

"What? Why?" Natalie asked.

"I have to go handle the devil's ass first." Janelle put her jeans and sweatshirt back and reached for a dress instead.

"Well, hopefully by the time you're finished handling that, Nivea will have surfaced, and she can join us," Natalie suggested.

"I'll text you when I'm headed to Brutti's," Janelle told her.

An hour later, she pulled into the driveway of her sister's house. After parking, she sent Aunt Connie a text, letting her know she was outside. Under normal circumstances, she would've tapped on the door to the kitchen before using her key to walk in. But today definitely wasn't normal. Sylvia hadn't answered her calls or responded to any of the texts she'd sent, which meant that despite their phone call with Titus earlier, she was pissed. Janelle knew she owed her sister an apology and an explanation for taking Peyton to the game without permission, and she would give one. But for now, she decided to give her a little space.

A tap on her window caused her to jump. She turned to see Garry standing next to the car, looking like he'd just lost his best friend. "What you sitting out here for?" he asked after she rolled down the window.

"Waiting on Aunt Connie. We're heading to church."

"You can wait inside, though. It's no biggie."

"I'm good. She's probably coming out any second. She told me to be here in an hour. Am I blocking you? Do you need to get out?"

"No, you're fine." He shifted his weight from one foot to the other. It was chilly out, but he had on a short-sleeved shirt and wasn't wearing a jacket.

Janelle frowned then asked, "What are you doing out here?"

"Walking the dog." Garry pointed to Gypsy playing in some nearby bushes.

"You sure aren't walking her very far."

"True." There was an awkward silence for a few seconds until he said, "Last night was something else, huh?"

"Is that what we're calling it? Something else?"

"Sylvia is done."

"Oh, trust me, I know she is. I tried calling her, and she's not answering. I figure I'd just talk to her when I bring Aunt Connie back after church. Maybe by then, she'll—"

"No, Nellie, it's over," Garry interrupted her. "She's done . . . with me."

"What do you mean?" Janelle asked, noticing the tears in his eyes. She'd known Garry over twenty years, and the only time she'd seen him cry was when Peyton was born.

"I mean, Sylvia wants a divorce. She told me she wants me to leave. Last night was the last straw. That fight with Sherrod . . ." His voice drifted off.

Janelle was speechless. She knew her sister was frustrated and to her breaking point, but she wasn't expecting this. After Sylvia's initial forgiveness of Garry's acceptance of Jordan into their home, Janelle thought their marriage would survive, although it would take some work. She was proud of the way Sylvia was handling the situation and admired her strength. She'd always been the stronger of the two sisters. But maybe she'd been wrong. Had she been looking at things at face value instead of truly seeing how heavy the weight was of everything Sylvia was carrying? Garry, the affair, Randi's death, Peyton, Gypsy the dog, Aunt Connie, Sherrod, the fight after the game, and then this morning Tricia showing up on her doorstep. It was more than any woman should have to deal with. *And I didn't make anything any better by helping Peyton sneak away to the game. I have some fault in all of this too. I owe Sylvia one hell of an apology.* "Damn."

"It's my fault," Garry said, causing her to realize she'd spoken her last word out loud instead of in her head.

"What are you gonna do?" Janelle asked.

"Go in the house and talk to his wife," Aunt Connie said as she walked over to the car. "That's what he need to be doing instead of standing out here in the cold chatting with you." Instead of coming from the front door, she'd come from the opposite side of the house without either one of them seeing her.

Garry hurried to open the car door and help her inside. "She doesn't want to talk to me." He shook his head right before closing the door.

"How you roll down this window?" Aunt Connie asked. Janelle hit the button, and when it lowered, she said,

"She ain't the one who needs to be talking. You do. Just make sure that whatever it is you telling her betta be worth her hearing. Now I'm gon' praise the Lord. See you when I get back."

Garry put his hands in his pockets and took a step back as Janelle started the car. She rolled the window up as they pulled out of the driveway.

"You really think Sylvia wanna hear anything he has to say, Aunt Connie?"

"Nope, she don't. And I don't blame her either. But that don't mean he shouldn't try. Talking is the one thing that fool need to be doing. If I were him, I'd be singing like a canary and telling my wife anything she wanna know and then some. That's been his problem this whole time and what caused some of this mess he's got everybody in now."

"Some?" Janelle raised an eyebrow.

"Don't act like you ain't do your part, Nellie. What were you thinking about taking Peyton all that way without saying nothing to her mama and daddy?" Aunt Connie glared at Janelle.

"I didn't think it was that big of a deal, Aunt Connie. I swear," Janelle explained. "It was just a basketball game. Had the fight not happened, it would've been harmless."

"And did you know about the boyfriend?"

"No, I didn't know. I didn't know about any of that other stuff until we got to the game, I swear," Janelle said adamantly. "None of it."

"Out of all the boys that child could be dating. Out of all the men you could be dating." Aunt Connie shook her head, making Janelle feel even guiltier than she already was.

"None of it, Aunt Connie," Janelle said again.

"So, explain to me what you saw happen last night. And the pharmacist, how is he involved in all of this?"

Janelle told her aunt her version of what happened and exactly what Sherrod had explained when they spoke in the parking lot afterward. "That's all I know."

"This is a whole mess," Aunt Connie said. "Is he seriously going to fight for custody? Can he do that? He's not Jordan's father. Garry is."

"I don't know." Janelle shrugged as she pulled into the church's crowded parking lot. Her phone rang, and she glanced at the Apple Watch on her arm. As if he felt himself being discussed, Sherrod was now calling. Janelle dismissed the call and focused on trying not to hit the well-dressed pedestrians heading toward the front doors of the church. "I'll drop you off in front, Aunt Connie."

"Okay, that's fine. But wait a few seconds before pulling to the door. That's Myrtle Ford. Let her get inside first. I don't feel like being bothered with her bourgeois ass this morning, and if she sees me, she's gonna try to talk to me," Aunt Connie said, causing Janelle to laugh.

"Aunt Connie, now you know that ain't Christian-like."

"Neither is what you and Titus do, so I guess we going to hell together," Aunt Connie said with a smirk, then opened the car door and hopped out. Janelle didn't know whether to be offended or amused, so she just shook her head.

After parking, she sat in the car for a few moments. Sherrod called again, then sent a text asking her to call. She thought about calling him but decided not to. Not until she'd talked to her sister. She didn't want to complicate things any more than they already were.

She got out of the car and hit the lock on the remote. As she walked through the parked cars, she spotted a familiar face sitting in one of them, and she stopped in her tracks. At first, she thought she was mistaken, but as she began walking closer, she had no doubt who it was. She had almost made it to the small green Honda when the door opened and he stepped out. Janelle reached into her purse and grabbed her cell phone, dialing the number by heart as fast as she could. Before the voice on the other end spoke, she did.

"Titus, I found Tank."

Chapter 4

Tricia

"Where the hell is he?" Tricia demanded.

"I'm going to pick him up now, Tricia. He's safe. That's the only thing that matters," Titus said. "We'll be home in a little while."

"What matters is how I'm gonna go upside his head when you get here," Tricia said, grateful that her son had been located but still pissed that he'd pulled his little disappearing act.

"See you in a bit," Titus said, then ended the call.

Once she arrived home, instead of retreating to the den where she spent most of her time, she went upstairs and into Tank's bedroom. His bed was made although still rumpled where he'd probably sat on it before leaving for the game. There were pictures of him and various teammates from over the years hanging on his wall, along with ribbons and shelves of trophies. It seemed as if she blinked and he had grown up before her eyes. Tank had always been independent, but now it seemed as if he didn't need her for anything, especially with Titus being so hands-on. Her son was now a young man she didn't even know.

On his desk was a pile of letters and envelopes from countless colleges. Tricia flipped through them until she spotted one that Tank had circled and put a red star on. It was from Mission College, the college Titus was attending when Tank was born. Tank hadn't made a decision about what school he'd be attending. Out of all the offers he'd received and scouts he'd met with, Mission should have been the last school he should be considering, she thought. With his stellar grades and basketball talents, Tank was Ivy League material, or another top school, not some middle-of-the-road black college.

The ringing of her cell phone interrupted Tricia's snooping. Seeing her mother's number on the screen, she took a deep breath before answering. "Hey, Mama."

"Good morning, Tricia. I was just calling to see how Tank's game went."

"They won. As a matter of fact, he made the winning basket," Tricia bragged.

"Is that right? Well, good for him. Where is he so I can congratulate him?"

"He's out with Titus. They should be home in a little while, and I'll have him call you," Tricia said, not mentioning that Tank had been missing overnight. There really was no need, especially since he'd been found and was on his way home.

"Those two stay in the street. I don't know what Titus gon' do when Tank go off to college. I guess you and him gonna have plenty of time to spend together and get on each other's nerves." Her mother laughed.

"Probably."

"Y'all can always make another baby. Start over again."

"That's one thing we won't be doing, Mama. I'm almost forty."

"And? Plenty of women over forty are having babies these days."

"Not me." Tricia thought she was imagining things when she heard crying in the background. "Mama, who is that?"

"That's Bethany whining. Her mama is trying to ween her off the pacifier, and she has not been a happy camper."

Bethany, Tricia's 2-year-old niece, was the daughter of Violet, Tricia's youngest sister. Tricia also had another sister, Felicia, and an older brother, Wyatt. Unlike Tricia, all of her siblings still lived in the same town where Tricia had grown up, four hours away. They also all had major drama in their lives, something Tricia avoided by avoiding them.

"Mama, please don't tell me you're still the drop-off babysitter for Violet. I told you to start telling her no. Now here it is Sunday morning, and you gotta deal with an overgrown baby crying about a pacifier," Tricia groaned as she walked out of Tank's bedroom and into her own. Sitting on the side of the bed, she slipped her sneakers off and slid her feet into a pair of slippers.

"I ain't babysitting, Tricia. Calm down. Your sister is here too. She's actually been staying here and will be home for a little while."

"What? Why? Where is Maurice?" Tricia said, referring to Violet's husband.

"They're having problems right now." Her mother's voice lowered.

"What kind of problems?" Tricia asked.

Her mother whispered, "She left him."

Tricia wasn't surprised to hear the news her mother just shared. Violet and Maurice dated on and off for years before marrying. But they constantly fought about the dumbest things: an outfit Violet wore, the way some girl spoke to Maurice in the store, some random item one of them purchased. Maurice was a truck driver, and Violet was a nurse. Their lavish wedding was the talk of the town. When Violet got pregnant, the last thing Tricia thought her sister needed was a baby, but everyone else was elated. She knew their marriage wasn't going to last, and it seemed as if she was right.

"And she ain't have nowhere else to go except your house? How convenient," Tricia said.

"I told her to come home. She's gonna need help with the baby."

"You act like she's got a newborn, Mama. Bethany is a toddler. And help doing what? Isn't Violet working at the same middle school where Felicia works?"

"Yes, but still."

"Bethany goes to day care every day. Her mama don't work overnight or weekends," Tricia pointed out. "And Felicia got that big ol' house. Why can't Violet stay with her?"

"Tricia, it's just temporary. You would think she asked to come and stay with you the way you're acting. I probably shouldn't have even said anything to you and let Violet tell you herself."

Tricia couldn't remember the last time she'd spoken to either one of her sisters. They weren't close at all. She and Wyatt kept in contact mainly because he checked up on Tank every now and then.

"Okay, now you're trying to be funny, Mama."

"I'm just saying if she don't bring it up next weekend, don't you bring it up."

"Next weekend?" Tricia frowned.

"You said you were coming for my luncheon."

"That's week after next, Mama." A sigh of relief escaped Tricia's mouth. She'd been putting off her visit home for a while, but this trip would not only allow her to celebrate her mother's birthday, but to make sure the plans for her retirement were handled correctly.

"Okay, whenever, just don't say nothing. And make sure Titus don't say nothing either."

"I won't, and I'm sure he won't either." Bethany's screams in the background became too much for Tricia to deal with. "I'll talk to you later."

"Tell Tank I'm proud of him, and make sure he calls me."

"I will," Tricia told her before hanging up. Noticing the time, she wondered what was keeping Titus and Tank. She'd expected them to be home by now. Plus, she was starving. Normally on Sundays, Titus and Tank would go grocery shopping while she slept in, and they would pick up something for her from IHOP or Denny's on their way back home. She would eat while they put away the groceries, then they'd head out, leaving her home to relax and enjoy her day. It was doubtful that after the events of the morning they would be bringing her food, so Tricia decided to just order Uber Eats. After placing her order, she sent Sylvia a quick text thanking her again and letting her know Tank was found.

"What took you so long?" Tricia asked an hour later when Titus and Tank finally made it home.

"You ordered food?" Titus asked, staring at the IHOP bag on the sofa beside her in the den where she was sitting. "Did you order us anything?"

"No," Tricia admitted.

"Good thing we stopped and got something. Tank, come in here and speak to your mother."

Moments later, Tank eased into the den, his eyes lowered. "Hey, Ma."

"Don't 'hey, Ma' me. Have you lost your mind? What the hell is wrong with you not coming home? Do you know how worried we were?" Tricia screamed at him.

"Yes, ma'am. I'm sorry."

"Where the hell were you?"

"I spent the night at my friend's house. I should've called and told you where I was, but I fell asleep," Tank said. "Then this morning, my phone was dead, and I didn't have a charger."

"What friend? Your friend didn't have a charger?" Tricia waited for her son to answer those questions before she fired off any more of the hundreds she had to ask.

"Palmer and no, he didn't." Tank shrugged. "I really thought I'd be home before you got up. You normally aren't up this early. I'm really sorry."

"Who the hell is Palmer?" Tricia tried to recall the familiar names of Tank's teammates.

"He's the team manager," Tank told her.

Tricia looked over at Titus to confirm this information, but he seemed to be more concerned with texting than the conversation she was having with their son. Her anger increased, and she moved to the edge of the sofa, preparing to stand, when suddenly the doorbell rang.

"I'll get it," Tank offered.

"You'll stay your ass right here. Don't move," Tricia told him.

"I got it." Titus quickly headed out of the room.

"Tarik DeVaughn King, what the hell is wrong with you?" Tricia went back to yelling at Tank, who looked as if he'd rather be anywhere than standing in front of her. "You are grounded, do you understand me?"

"I'm sorry, Mom. I was irresponsible, and I know better. I should've made a better decision," Tank said. "I honestly didn't think you would panic, for real, and I really was trying to make it home before you woke up but—"

"Man, do you know how worried we've been?" Coach Darby, Tank's basketball coach, walked in and announced. He was a tall, older, but handsome gentleman, and he always seemed to talk louder than necessary, in Tricia's opinion.

"I know, Coach," Tank said sheepishly. "I'm sorry. I didn't mean to upset anybody."

"No one's upset, Tank. I told you, we all make mistakes, even me," Titus said. Tricia had to bite her tongue to keep from responding. Mistake or not, she damn sure was upset, and he should've been too.

Coach Darby put his arm around Tank's shoulders. "Your dad's right. We all make mistakes. I'm gonna need for you to perk up, because we've got a lot to celebrate. I've called a team meeting in an hour because I've got some news to share."

"News? What kind of news?" Tank asked excitedly.

"I'll announce it at the meeting," Coach Darby told him.

"Go get ready," Titus told Tank, who wasted no time rushing out of the den. His rapid footsteps were so loud they could hear them as he ran up the stairs.

"I told Tank he was grounded," Tricia said. "He didn't come home at all last night, remember?"

The two men looked at her, and for a second, neither one said anything. Coach Darby's eyes went to Titus, and he said, "He'll be dealt with and punished, Tricia. Team meetings are mandatory. This isn't a social event."

"He's right." Coach Darby nodded. "Players are required to attend."

"Isn't the season over?" Tricia mumbled.

"Coach, I talked to Tank about this, but I do wanna formally apologize to you, the players, and the coaching staff about what happened last night after the game. I was out of line, and not only did I embarrass Tank, but also myself and the entire team," Titus said to the coach, ignoring her question.

"Hey, tensions were high, and you just got pulled into the altercation. I understand. Hey, what did you tell Tank? Mistakes happen. You've been a valuable asset to the team over the past few years, and that was out of character. We not gonna let that incident overshadow Tank's victory. That's all we need to be focusing on right now." Coach Darby smiled. "That, and that he's fine."

"You're right, Coach. I appreciate that." Titus nodded.

"A'ight, Titus, I'll see you and Tank at the gym," Coach Darby said. "Mrs. King, nice to see you again."

Tricia didn't say anything, and both the Coach and Titus looked confused and uncomfortable.

"I'll walk you out," Titus announced, and the two men exited just as Tank had earlier.

Tricia got up. She still had plenty to say to Tank about the little stunt he pulled. She'd barely made it to the top of the stairs when she heard Tank yelling.

"Mom?" he called out as he rushed out of his room dressed in a pair of basketball shorts and a tank top that was clinging to his body. He apparently was still wet from his shower when he put it on.

"What?" Tricia answered.

Tank frowned and asked, "You went to Peyton's house this morning?"

Stunned by his question, Tricia responded, "Huh?"

"This morning? You went to Peyton's house?" Tank reworded the question.

"I did." Tricia nodded.

"What? Why? Why would you do that?" he groaned and shook his head.

"Because my son was missing, and I was looking for him," Tricia told him.

"Oh my God. I can't believe you. You just popped up over there. How did you even know where she lived?" Tank began pacing back and forth in the hallway.

"You're damn right I popped over there. And don't worry about how I know. The question is, why the hell didn't I know that you even had a girlfriend?" Tricia couldn't believe he had the nerve to be questioning her when he was the one in trouble.

"I was going to tell you when the time was right. Jesus, I haven't even been to her house yet, or even met her parents," Tank said. "I thought Peyton was joking when she texted and told me that."

"Oh, now your phone works, huh?" Tricia rolled her eyes.

"I put it on the charger, and my texts came through. So yeah," Tank told her. "You shouldn't have gone over there."

"You should've brought your ass home, and I wouldn't have gone looking for you," Tricia yelled. "Don't tell me what I should or shouldn't have done. Have you lost your mind?"

"Whoa, what's going on?" Titus came running up the steps.

"She went to Peyton's house looking for me. Her parents don't even know we're dating, and she pops up, asking if I'm there. They're pissed," Tank explained to Titus.

"I'm pissed!" Tricia yelled.

"Me too!" Tank commented.

"I don't give a damn what you are!" Tricia went to grab Tank, but he moved too fast, and she missed.

"Okay, let's all calm down. All this yelling ain't helping. Tank, apologize to your mother, and go finish getting dressed so we can get over to the school for this meeting," Titus told him.

"Sor . . ." Tank didn't even get the full word out as he turned and stomped off to his room.

"This is some bullshit, Titus." Tricia sighed and walked down the hallway into their bedroom.

Titus followed. "Tricia."

"His attitude is fucked up, and he's the one who's in trouble. I can't deal with this." Tricia sat on the edge of the bed. She was so angry that sweat began forming on the bridge of her nose and on her temples.

"He apologized, Tricia. I get it, and you have a right to be upset. I was too."

"Was?" She looked Titus up and down.

"Am," he quickly corrected himself. "But let's just give him a little space."

"Space? He had space when he was at Pedro's or Palmer's or whoever's house last night instead of his own. And now he got the nerve to be questioning where I went. He's lost his damn mind." Tricia exhaled loudly.

"Fine, maybe space isn't the right word. Let's let him have his moment. I talked to him already, and I'll talk to him again, I promise." Titus nodded. "We'll get through this. He's a good kid, Tricia. A damn good kid who made a bad choice last night. And I have to take some fault in that because of the fight. Some of this is on me. But you know Tank is a good kid."

Titus was right. Tank was a good kid. Any other kid would've been out somewhere partying and drinking to celebrate their win. Tank was asleep at a friend's house. *Maybe I am overreacting, but I don't care.*

"Still, the way he just spoke to me was disrespectful," Tricia pointed out.

"You're right, and like I said, I'm gonna talk to him about that. But come on, Tricia, you would've been mad too if you found out your mama popped up over your boo's house." Titus laughed.

"Whatever." Tricia fought the urge to smile.

"Say what you want, but that's something she would've done too. You say you and your mama are nothing alike, but you might be wrong," Titus said. "We'll be back in a little while. You want me to put something on the grill tonight for dinner or order something?"

"Some steaks would be cool," Tricia said.

Titus walked over and kissed her cheek. "Steaks it is."

Tricia grabbed the remote and turned on the TV, which was just as big as the ones in the den and in Titus's man cave. Turning to the Lifetime channel, she tried to relax, but couldn't. She was still bothered. Tank had been surprised when he found out that she'd gone over to Peyton's house. Titus, on the other hand, didn't seem surprised at all.

Chapter 5

Janelle

Although she'd been in church, Janelle had no clue what the sermon had been about. She'd been too distracted by thoughts of Titus, who she'd seen briefly when he arrived to pick up Tank, and Sherrod, who'd been calling and texting nonstop. Both men had her mind in a mental whirlwind, and she couldn't focus on anything Pastor Franklin had said. As the service ended, she hoped Aunt Connie wouldn't ask her opinion about it.

"Hey, Janelle. It's good to see you."

Janelle turned around to see Willie Barnett smiling at her. "Good to see you too, Deacon," Janelle said as she gave him a brief hug. He was a nice-looking, likable man in his late sixties. He was also very stylish and prided himself on being the best-dressed man in the congregation. Suits, ties, pocket squares, and snakeskin shoes with matching belts, Deacon Barnett stayed sharp. His Cadillac Eldorado was just as clean as his Sunday attire every week.

"Your aunt told me you brought her to service this morning. I offered to take her home, but she said y'all have some place to be."

Lying to the deacon, especially while standing in the middle of the Lord's house, wasn't something Janelle felt comfortable doing, but she had to back up Aunt Connie's story. "Yeah, we have a couple of errands to run." Janelle nodded.

"I understand, I understand. Would've been nice to take her to lunch and on a nice drive, though. I keep inviting her out, but she keeps declining."

Janelle saw the disappointment in his handsome face and felt sorry for him. "That sounds like it would've been nice, Deacon."

"Maybe you can talk to her and suggest that she accept an invite one of these days."

"I'll try," Janelle told him. "You know she's a tough cookie to crack."

"You got that right. But I'm determined to soften her up." He winked and gave her another quick hug before rushing off.

Janelle walked out into the vestibule and spotted her aunt near the exit.

"What took you so long?" Aunt Connie asked. "You know I'm trying to get out of here before Loretta and the other women start talking me to death about joining some committee I don't wanna join. I done tried to be polite and smile while waiting for you, but it can only last for so long."

"Lord, Aunt Connie." Janelle shook her head. "I'll go get the car."

"I can walk with you." Aunt Connie slipped her coat on and followed Janelle out of the church. As they were getting into Janelle's car, a horn honked. Deacon Barnett slowly drove by in his shiny Cadillac and waved. Janelle waved back, and Aunt Connie frowned.

"Aunt Connie, why are you so mean to him? He's nice."

"He's aggravating, and he's old," Aunt Connie told her as she put on her seat belt.

"Old? Y'all are about the same age."

"Exactly. Hell, I'm old too."

"He really likes you. Don't you want a nice friend to go out on dates with?" Janelle asked.

"Yes, but I don't want an old one. Willie is gonna have to take his zoot-suit-and-shiny-shoe-wearing, funeral-car-driving, AARP ass and find someone else, because I am not the one."

Janelle laughed. Aunt Connie was truly a character, and an entertaining one at that.

"Aunt Connie, how do you feel about coming and staying with me for a couple of days?"

"With you? For what?" Aunt Connie asked.

"I mean, I was just thinking with everything going on at Sylvia and Garry's, maybe you wanted to get away while they figure everything out," Janelle explained.

"Well, thanks for the offer, Nelle. That's real nice of you, but I'm praying I'll be getting back to my own house in a couple more days," Aunt Connie told her. "They should be finished with the remodeling by the end of the week."

"Okay, well, just so you know, if you ever wanna come and hang out with me at my place, you're always welcome. It's been kinda fun hanging out with you the past few weeks. We love you."

"And I love y'all. Even though between you and your sister there's more drama than one of those housewives shows on TV." Aunt Connie sighed.

As she drove toward her sister's house, Janelle couldn't help thinking that, once again, her aunt was right: her life had more drama than a reality show.

"Syl, can I come in?" Janelle knocked on Sylvia's door. She listened but didn't hear anything, so she slowly turned the knob and opened the door. "Syl?"

"What do you want, Janelle?" Sylvia's voice came from the sitting area of her bedroom.

Janelle walked in and saw her sister on the small love seat in front of the fireplace, typing on her laptop. A glass of wine sat on the coffee table in front of her, and soft jazz was playing. Had Janelle not known what had gone on over the course of the past twenty-four hours, she'd have thought that Sylvia was relaxed and enjoying a typical Sunday afternoon.

"I wanted to talk for a few," Janelle told her, "and make sure you're okay."

"I'm fine," Sylvia said, still typing, not even looking up.

"I also wanted to apologize for taking Peyton without telling you. That was dead-ass wrong, and I'm sorry." Janelle eased over and sat on the opposite end of the love seat. Under normal circumstances, she would've picked up the glass and taken a sip. Lord knows she felt as if she needed a drink even more than she had earlier. Instead, she just promised herself plenty of mimosas later, once she'd made up with her sister. "I got caught up in being the cool aunt she felt comfortable talking to. You know how Peyton and I are. I love her like she's my own child. But even with that, I was wrong. And I told Peyton that she was wrong for asking me to take her. So like I said, I'm sorry."

"I'm fine, Nelle." Sylvia glanced up, then went back to typing.

"You're not fine, Syl. And no one expects you to be fine. Last night was crazy, and then this morning with Tricia. I mean, I'm sorry about that too. I feel like I got you in the middle of this, and you shouldn't be." Although technically it wasn't her fault that Titus's wife showed up at their house, Janelle still felt responsible somehow, and since she was already apologizing for the Peyton situation, she added it in for good measure. When Sylvia didn't respond, Janelle reached over and closed the laptop.

"Stop it. What are you doing?" Sylvia whined.

"I'm trying to talk to you and say sorry. You're being rude and not even listening."

"I heard you." Sylvia picked up the glass and sipped her wine.

"And?"

"And what?" Sylvia asked.

"Talk to me, Syl. Why are you being like this?"

"Being like what, Janelle? You said what you had to say, you gave your apology, I said everything's fine. It's whatever. Last night was a whole mess, but the girls are safe."

"And Tank is home safe too," Janelle volunteered, hoping hearing something positive would lighten the tension a little.

"I know. Tricia sent me a text and told me."

Janelle frowned. "Why is she texting you? How did she even get your number?"

Sylvia placed her laptop on the coffee table next to her now-empty wineglass. "I gave it to her."

"You what? Why would you do that?" Janelle couldn't believe Sylvia.

"Because she was an emotional wreck because her son was missing, and I understood exactly how she felt because I felt the same way last night." Sylvia rolled her eyes at her, then added, "Wait, how did you know Tank was found?"

Janelle cleared her throat nervously as she prepared to answer the question. "Um, because I was the one who found him."

"What? Where?" Sylvia gasped.

"At church. He showed up there, trying to surprise Peyton."

"Church? You're lying."

"Nope. He was right in the parking lot. I called Titus, and he came and picked him up."

"That's crazy." Sylvia shook her head. "At church of all places. His mother is probably going upside his head right now."

For a second, Janelle thought about asking her details about Tricia, but she didn't. She reminded herself of the same thing she had for years: there was no point in comparing, because she was his wife.

Instead, she changed the subject. "Speaking of church, did you know Deacon Barnett was tryin'a holla at Aunt Connie?"

"For months." Sylvia finally laughed. "But she won't budge. I don't know why. He's handsome, nice, and paid."

"And he can dress and smells good," Janelle added.

"He does smell good." Sylvia nodded.

"I asked Aunt Connie if she wanted to come hang at my place for a few days."

"Why would she do that? Did she say she wanted to leave?"

"No, she didn't. I was trying to help, honestly."

"Help who?" Sylvia frowned.

Janelle moved a little closer and stared into her sister's face. "You. And I should've offered for her to stay a long time ago. You've been dealing with a lot, and I could've let her stay with me to lighten your load, at least a little."

"Load? Aunt Connie? Girl, please, she may have a whole lot to say, but she's a whole lot of help. She lightens my load. And quiet as it's kept, I probably need to talk to her about moving in with us for good." Sylvia sighed.

"Wait, what?" Janelle knew Sylvia didn't mind her staying at their home every now and then, but she was shocked to hear her talk about making this a permanent situation.

"Yeah, after Garry moves out, I'm probably gonna need her to help."

"So, you really are done, Syl?" Janelle asked, using the same term Garry had earlier.

"You seem surprised. You were there last night. Garry was a complete madman. I've never seen him act like that before. Did you recognize that man who attacked Sherrod? Hell, did you even know Garry knew Sherrod, or that he had been keeping Jordan from seeing Sherrod for weeks?" Sylvia asked, but before Janelle could answer, she continued. "Nope, and neither did I. It's one secret after another. And honestly, I'm sick of being married to a man who thinks it's fine to communicate with his wife on a need-to-know basis."

"I'm sorry, Syl."

"Don't be. The last thing I need is people feeling sorry for me. I'm going to be fine." Sylvia shrugged.

Janelle didn't want to upset her sister, so she didn't press the issue. She also figured now wasn't the time to bring up the letter Sherrod told her about last night. Instead, she decided it was probably best to leave. She'd apologized, and Sylvia had forgiven her for the role she'd played in Peyton's disappearance. Besides, she still had plans to meet up with Natalie for mimosas, even if they weren't bottomless.

"I'll call you later?" Janelle said as she stood.

"Sure." Sylvia nodded.

Janelle went downstairs, pausing to check on Peyton before she left. "Hey, kiddo, you okay?" she asked as she walked into her niece's room. Peyton was lying across the bed, her hands tucked under her chin, watching television.

Peyton sat up and said. "Yeah, I'm okay. Tank finally texted me. He's fine. He thought I was gonna be at church this morning and was waiting there for me. That's cute, huh?"

"It is." Janelle nodded. "But he still should've let his parents know where he was. The same way you should've yesterday."

"I know. He's at a team meeting but says he has something important to ask me. You think he's gonna propose?" Peyton smiled.

"You better pray to God he doesn't." Janelle laughed. "Your mom would kill him."

"Is she still mad?"

Janelle gave her a look, letting her know she knew the answer to her own question. "Well, I'm gonna go ahead and get out of here."

"Thanks, Aunt Nelle. I love you."

Janelle had almost made it to her car when she heard someone calling her name. She turned around and saw Jordan running out of the front door toward her.

"Miss Janelle, wait!"

Janelle stopped and waved. "Hey, Jordan."

"Hey," Jordan said. "Here, please."

Janelle looked at the cell phone Jordan was holding toward her. "Huh?"

"It's for you."

Janelle took the phone out of her hand. The caller ID read Pops. She hoped Garry wasn't about to try to talk to her about Sylvia, because now wasn't the time.

"Yeah?" she said into the phone.

"Janelle?"

"Sherrod?" Janelle sighed. She'd avoided him all day, but now with Jordan standing in front of her, she had no choice but to talk.

Chapter 6

Sylvia

When she heard someone knocking on her bedroom door, Sylvia didn't move from where she was sitting. She figured Janelle would once again open the door and waltz in as she had earlier. Instead, the light tapping continued. Sylvia walked across her bedroom. "Nellie, stop playing and bring your ass in. I thought you were leaving." She snatched the door open.

"Oh, I . . . My bad."

Sylvia looked at Jordan standing in the doorway, looking as uncomfortable as she now was. "Jordan, I thought you were Janelle."

"She's gone. But I can come back."

Sylvia shook her head and moved aside, motioning for Jordan to come into her room. "No, come in. It's fine."

Jordan hesitated for a moment, then stepped inside. Sylvia followed, then closed the door. She saw Jordan looking around, and it dawned on her that this was probably the first time that the girl had ever been in there. Every time they'd ever really interacted had been downstairs, where Jordan's bedroom was located.

"What's up?" Sylvia asked, wondering what prompted Jordan to come looking for her. Since arriving at their home after her mother's death, Jordan hadn't been receptive to any of the attempts Sylvia made to connect with her. Other than Garry, the only person Jordan seemed to even like was Aunt Connie.

"I, uh, I just wanted to, uh, tell you something," Jordan said, her eyes looking down at the floor.

"Okay."

"Um, well, first, I'm sorry about what I did yesterday. Sneaking off without permission and not letting anyone know where I was going. I shouldn't have, uh, I mean . . ." Jordan's voice cracked, and she sounded like she was about to cry.

"Hey." Sylvia's voice was soft. She reached out and touched Jordan's shoulder. "Come over here, and let's sit and chat."

Jordan nodded and accompanied her as she went back into the sitting area to the love seat.

"Now, let's start over, and this time, how about you look at me while you're talking? I know it hasn't been that long since you got here, but you know me well enough by now to know I don't bite and my breath don't stink," Sylvia told her.

Jordan looked up at her and smiled slightly.

"That's better."

"Okay, well, like I said, what happened yesterday was uncalled for, and I'm sorry. Like, I didn't think anyone would come looking for me. And I definitely wasn't expecting you to show up at the game. Then the fight . . ." Jordan shook her head. "This is all messed up."

"Well, I appreciate your apology, Jordan, and you're right, it's messed up. Your dad and I went into a panic when we didn't know where you were," Sylvia explained. "It didn't matter where you were. We were going to find you and show up."

"I see," Jordan mumbled.

"You're going to have to accept the fact that we care enough to make sure you're safe. That's not a bad thing, either," Sylvia said.

"I was safe, though," Jordan told her.

"And how were we supposed to know that when we didn't even know where you were?" Sylvia asked.

Jordan shrugged. "I don't know."

Sylvia angled her body so that she could face Jordan. "Jordan, I know your life has literally been turned upside down the past few weeks. When I lost my mom, I felt like someone ripped my heart out. You not only lost your mom, but you had to move to a new city and live with strangers."

Jordan's tear-filled eyes met hers, and she softly said, "Strangers?"

Sylvia nodded. "Yeah, strangers. Because even though we are family, the situation is strange for all of us, right?"

"Very right."

"But you're not going through it alone."

"He's not a bad person," Jordan whispered.

"Who? Your dad?" Sylvia asked.

"No," Jordan answered. "Sherrod."

Sylvia was caught off guard by Jordan's statement, so she simply said, "Okay."

"I know Dad doesn't like him, and I don't want you to think any bad things about him. I heard him talking on the phone and asking about a restraining order. I don't want that to happen." Jordan swallowed hard. "The only reason he took me to the game was because I threatened to run away and never come back. He made me promise that if he took me, I wouldn't run away again."

"Sweetie, I don't know him. But he probably still should've let us know," Sylvia said.

Jordan shook her head. "In theory, maybe. But I just need for you to know he's not a bad guy. He loved my mom, and they were best friends, and he loves me. He's smart and nice, and he says I can come and live with—"

"Oh my God, Mom. Guess what?" Peyton's voice called as she rushed into the room.

"What?" Sylvia answered. She heard Peyton coming toward her.

"You're not gonna bel—" Peyton stopped midsentence, and her eyes went from Sylvia to Jordan. "Oh."

"What? What's going on?" Sylvia asked.

"Nothin'." The excitement was gone from Peyton's voice, and she turned to walk away.

"Peyton, where are you going?" Sylvia called behind her.

"I need to go take Gypsy out," Jordan jumped up and said.

Sylvia knew she was using the dog as an excuse to leave but didn't say anything. She definitely wanted to hear what Jordan was about to tell her before Peyton walked in. As Jordan walked past Peyton, she noticed the slight frown on Peyton's face.

"I didn't know she was in here. What was that about?" Peyton asked.

"She just wanted to talk about last night and apologize, that's all. We were just talking," Sylvia said. "What did you want to tell me?"

"Oh, it's not important." Peyton shrugged.

"It was important enough for you to come running up in here. What is it?" Sylvia asked.

"Tank got invited to play in the McDonald's All-American Game," Peyton told her. "That's all."

"Wow, are you serious?" Sylvia asked. "That's amazing. Wow."

Peyton's excitement returned. "I know, right? I'm so happy for him. He really deserves it, though."

Even though Sylvia had never seen Tank play, she had seen his father on the basketball court several times when he played in college, and he was good. Being selected for the McDonald's team meant that Tank was recognized as one of the nation's top high school players.

"Well, I'm happy for him."

"And guess what else?" Peyton grinned. Sylvia didn't have a chance to guess before Peyton blurted out, "He asked me to go to his prom."

Sylvia's first thought was to remind Peyton that prom should've been the last thing that she and Tank should've been discussing considering the stunt she pulled the day before and his own disappearing act. But seeing the joy in her daughter's face and remembering their conversation earlier, Sylvia smiled and said, "Well, that is exciting."

Peyton nodded as she sat beside Sylvia and said, "I know I have a punishment coming, and a big one, Mom. But please don't say no."

"I didn't say no, Peyton. I will say that I can't give you permission to go to prom with a young man I haven't met." Sylvia gave her a knowing look. "You're right. You are going to be punished."

"Understood. So once I'm off punishment in twooooo . . ." Peyton raised an eyebrow and waited for Sylvia's reaction. Sylvia pursed her lips and shook her head, so Peyton quickly changed what she was about to say. "Threeeee weeks, I can invite him over?"

"Ma'am, you are pressing your luck here. I would quit while I was ahead," Sylvia said. "I wouldn't make plans for that to happen within the next month."

"But it can happen, right? That's safe to say?" Peyton leaned against Sylvia's arm.

"I'll consider it." Sylvia sighed.

"Thank you, Mommy. I love you." Peyton threw her arms around her neck and kissed her cheek.

"That's not what you were saying last night and this morning," Sylvia reminded her.

"Why you gotta bring up old stuff, Mom? Aunt Connie says, 'In life, we must forget the mistakes of the past and press on to greater achievements in the future,'" Peyton told her.

Sylvia frowned. "I hope you know that's not an original quote, Peyton."

"It's not?" Peyton looked surprised.

"Honey, you'll learn that most of Aunt Connie's wisdom is plagiarized." Sylvia smiled, then asked, "Wait, you said Tank invited you to his prom. What about your prom?"

Peyton stood up and said, "Oh, well, about that. He agreed to be my date two weeks ago."

Sylvia's mouth dropped open. "Peyton Janelle."

"I was going to tell you, I promise. No more secrets." Peyton crossed her heart.

"I hope not."

The excited look on Peyton's face faded into a frown, and she asked, "But what about Daddy? Are you going to tell him?"

"We'll discuss it," Sylvia told her. "But that's not what you need to be concerned with right now. Because he and I will also be discussing your punishment."

"I know, I know," Peyton groaned. She gave her mother another hug and rushed out of the sitting room. "Oh, sorry, Daddy. My bad."

"Uh, it's okay, baby," Garry said.

A few seconds later, Sylvia looked up to see him standing in the area between the bedroom and the area where she was sitting, looking as if he was unsure if he should come in.

"What was that about?" he asked.

"What?" Sylvia asked.

"Peyton. She rushed out of here smiling and referred to me as Daddy instead of Dad. Not the usual mood of someone in as much trouble as she's in." He leaned against the wall.

"She knows she's being punished for her actions. She's excited because Tank asked her to prom." Sylvia picked up her laptop and went back to working on the proposal she'd been trying to finish all day. She hoped Garry would sense that she wasn't in the mood to deal with him and go somewhere else.

"Whoa? What? I hope you said no."

Sylvia glanced up. "Why would I say that?"

"Because that's absolutely crazy, Syl, that's why. We can't let her."

Sylvia felt the same anger from earlier that morning quickly return. Once again, Garry found it necessary to intervene and decide what could or couldn't happen. Frustrated, she slammed her laptop on the table and stood up, taking Garry by surprise.

"Shut up, Garry. Just shut the hell up," she yelled.

"Syl."

"Stop calling me that. Don't 'Syl' me. I'm so tired of this, of you. Our daughter found it necessary to sneak and have my sister take her to a damn basketball game because she was afraid to tell us the guy she likes was playing in it. A nice guy, not some thug on the street. And Jordan is walking around here damn near about to have a panic attack because you're making calls about restraining orders. Something else you're planning to do without discussing it with me. It's like you feel like you have total control of everyone and everything around here. I don't even feel like your wife. I'm damn sure not your equal," Sylvia said to him as she stood. "At least that's not how I'm treated."

"Sylvia, that's not true," Garry said. "All I was saying—"

"Fuck you, Garry. I don't care what you were saying. I'm tired of listening to what you say. You never ask. You just say." She continued walking toward him. "If Peyton wants to date Tank, then good for her. I'm all for it."

"Will you just listen to what—"

"No, I'm not listening to shit you have to say right now. I'm tired of listening, Garry," Sylvia snapped. "No, I'm tired of listening when you want me to listen. See, when it comes to certain situations, you have so much to say, but when it came to Jordan and Randi and now Sherrod, you didn't say nothing. So until you find it necessary to talk and have me listen to everything, I ain't listening to shit."

They stood face-to-face. Garry just stared. He didn't speak, and he didn't move. It was one of the rare times Sylvia had seen him speechless. He was breathing so hard that she could see the rise and fall of his chest. He was looking at her as if she were a stranger, and she wondered if he had somehow mentally blacked out. She'd read an article once about a man who'd been arguing with his wife and he blacked out and killed her with his bare hands. Garry had never put his hands on her except in a loving, affectionate manner. But just in case that was all about to change, Sylvia took a step back.

Finally, Garry spoke. "Well," he said, "I was only saying the idea of Peyton going to prom was a bad idea because your sister is his father's mistress, and we all have history."

He turned and walked out of the room. Sylvia closed her eyes and realized the reality of what he'd said. She's been so caught up in Peyton's excitement that she hadn't considered the obvious. And despite not wanting to, she had to admit that Garry may have been right.

Chapter 7

Janelle

By the time Janelle arrived at Brutti's, the restaurant where she was meeting Natalie, she needed more than a mimosa. She needed a drink, and a strong one. Her unexpected phone call with Sherrod ended with her agreeing to his coming to her house later to talk about something that now she wasn't so sure was a good idea.

"Hey, girl. You look cute," Natalie, who had arrived at the restaurant before Janelle, said as they greeted one another with a hug.

"Thanks. You do too. How long is the wait?" Janelle asked, noticing that even though it was past two o'clock, the time that brunch ended, the dining room was still packed.

"Actually, the hostess said it won't be that long because people are leaving," Natalie told her. "How was church?"

"It was good. Can we wait at the bar?"

"I'm sure we can. Let me let her know," Natalie said before walking over to where the server was standing.

"Let me get a Cîroc and cranberry, please," Janelle ordered a few minutes later as they took their seats at the bar.

"Wow, I thought you were exaggerating when you said you needed a drink. You need a *drink* drink," Natalie teased. "I'll take a pineapple martini."

"Coming right up," the bartender told them.

"Where is Nivea? Is she coming?" Janelle asked.

"I don't know where she is. I've been trying to reach her since you called this morning, but she hasn't responded to my calls or texts. I told you she's probably boo'd up somewhere."

"With who, though?" Janelle asked. As far as she knew, her friend wasn't seeing anyone.

"I don't know. The only person she's really been mentioning is that dude Sherrod she ran into, but last time she spoke about him, she said he wasn't really responding to her too tough. But you know how she is. We won't know for sure until all of a sudden, her relationship status changes on social media, and he shows up on her arm at some event we all happen to be at."

Janelle was both bothered and relieved at the same time. On the one hand, it bothered her that she was seeing the guy her friend may or may not be interested in. On the other, she was glad to hear that Sherrod wasn't responding to her. As if her life weren't already complicated enough with her friendship with Titus, the situation with Sherrod was proving to be just as difficult for a lot of reasons.

"You're right," Janelle said as she took a long sip of the drink the bartender placed in front of her.

"Now tell me what's got you so stressed today. Is it Aunt Connie?" Natalie asked.

"No, it's not Aunt Connie."

"Is Sylvia trying to make you wear an ugly bridesmaid's dress?"

"No. I wish that were the case. I'm not even sure if there's going to be a vow renewal anymore."

"What? Why? I thought she and Garry were working things out. Is it because of Jordan? I figured that was a little too much for Sylvia to deal with at one time."

Natalie shook her head. "It's sad, because I really like her and Garry. They're such a strong couple."

"Time will tell." Janelle sighed.

"Well, on a positive note, I'm glad it's Syl who's got you drinking instead of Titus, because that's who I thought you were going to be venting about." Natalie laughed. Janelle gave her a guilty look, and Natalie shook her head. "Nellie, please don't tell me it 'just happened' again."

"No, nothing like that. I promise. Well, something did happen, but not that," Janelle said, finishing her drink.

"Well, what is it?" Natalie asked.

"We're gonna need more drinks." Just as she was about to order another round, the server walked over.

"Ladies, your table is waiting."

They paid the bar tab, and as they were heading over to their table, Natalie pointed. "Hey, isn't that Jarvis?"

Janelle turned to see Jarvis walking on the opposite side of the restaurant toward the door. "Yep, that's him."

She wasn't surprised that he was there. He was actually the one who first brought her to Brutti's, because it was one of his favorite brunch spots. Janelle hadn't seen nor talked to him since her birthday weekend, mainly because she'd been enjoying spending time with Sherrod. Truth was, until she spotted him, she hadn't noticed that they hadn't spoken.

"Jarvis!" Natalie called out.

"What are you doing?" Janelle hissed.

"I'm just speaking to the man, that's all. What's wrong?"

Janelle saw Jarvis turn to see who had called his name. When he saw them, he paused for a few seconds before finally waving.

"What if he's on a date?"

"I don't care. I can speak to her too." Natalie laughed as they arrived at the table and sat down. "And you shouldn't care either. Aren't you the one always saying that you and he are just cool?"

"We are, and you're right. We are just cool. But that don't mean I wanna speak to him while he's on a date."

"Well, you can relax, because I don't think he has one."

"How do you know that?"

"Because he's walking over here and there's no one with him."

Before Janelle could turn around and confirm what Natalie said, Jarvis was standing right next to their table.

"Good afternoon, ladies. How y'all doing?" He smiled.

"We're good." Janelle said, "How are you, Jarvis?"

"I'm well. It's good to see you two. It's been a minute." He made sure to direct his comment to Janelle.

"It has, hasn't it?" Janelle smiled at him dressed in a Nike hoodie, jeans, and sneakers, standing so close that she could smell his cologne. There was no denying that he was one of the best-looking men she'd ever dated, and there'd been a few in her lifetime. But despite Jarvis having all the qualities most women sought in men, there was something understated about him that automatically let her know that there would never be more between them than enjoyable dates and great sex. As much as she liked that, recently she'd wondered if that was enough.

Jarvis looked at her as if he was waiting for her to give some kind of additional information, and when she didn't, he looked over at Natalie. "Well, you two enjoy yourselves. I'm about to get outta here and get home so I can catch this game. It was good seeing you."

"You too, Jarvis." Natalie nodded.

"Bye." Janelle waved. And just as quickly as he appeared at their table, he turned and vanished.

"What the hell was that?" Natalie frowned.

"I don't know. I thought it was me, but you sensed that too, huh?"

"Normally he would've pulled up a chair, talked shit for a minute, and at least bought us a drink," Natalie pointed out. "Are y'all beefing?"

"No, not at all." Janelle shook her head. "Like he said, it's just been a minute since we've talked, that's all."

"Any particular reason why?"

Janelle looked over at Natalie. They'd been friends for years, almost as long as she'd been friends with Nivea. But the truth was Nivea and Natalie had been friends for much longer. She wasn't sure what Natalie would have to say if she told her she'd gone out with Sherrod, even if nothing really happened. And considering that at that moment she wasn't too sure if she and Sherrod would even be a sure thing, there was no point in even mentioning it.

"Nope." Janelle shrugged.

"Well, I would just like to point out once again that Jarvis is one fine-ass brother." Natalie sighed, repeating the same thing she'd said over and over since Janelle and Jarvis had met.

"Once again, point taken," Janelle said as she picked up the menu.

The waitress came over and took their food and drink orders, and Natalie didn't waste any time reminding Janelle of what they were supposed to be discussing.

"What happened but didn't happen between you and Titus?"

Janelle leaned her head back in a dramatic fashion. "Oh God, Nat, you're not going to believe this."

Natalie's mouth remained open as Janelle told her about everything that had taken place over the course of the past two days, including the fight at the game, but leaving out the fact that Sherrod was the guy Garry was fighting.

"You lie!" Natalie gasped when Janelle told her about
Tricia showing up at Sylvia's house looking for Tank. The
waitress, who was placing their food on the table at that
moment, thought she'd done something wrong.

"I swear to God. Sylvia called me in a panic. So I called
Titus," Janelle told her, picking at her plate full of French
toast and bacon.

"And what did he say? Was he scared? I betcha he was
nervous as shit."

"He was cool as a cucumber and said he'd take care of
it."

"That's it?"

"That's it. I swear, it was like Syl and I were the nervous
ones," Janelle told her. "Titus always acts like that,
though. Nothing shakes him. He's the most nonchalant
man in the world. I don't think I've ever seen him upset,
and we've been friends for almost eighteen years."

"I feel you, but all of that might change if his son starts
dating your niece. That's a little too close for comfort for
all of y'all," Natalie pointed out.

"I doubt if that will happen. You know how Garry is.
Trust me, he's going to shut that down before it even
starts. I definitely ain't worried." Janelle laughed. Her
cell phone chimed, alerting her that she had a text.

"Damn, I see why you needed a stiff drink. Hell, I need
one after hearing all of this."

"I told you. And I didn't even mention that while his
mother was at Sylvia's looking for Tank, when Aunt
Connie and I got to church, there he was. So I had to
call Titus again," Janelle said, taking her phone out and
reading the message.

"Yeah, I'm def gonna need something stronger than
these mimosas," Natalie said. "Nellie, you okay?"

"Yeah," Janelle said. "It's Nivea."

"Where the hell is she? What did she say?"

"She says she's coming over later because we need to talk."

"Talk about what?" Natalie asked.

"I don't know," Janelle said, wondering the same thing and praying it wasn't what she thought it was. "Waitress, can I get another drink?'

As soon as Janelle got into her car to leave Brutti's, she called Sherrod.

"Hey, tonight isn't a good night. Can we reschedule?" she asked.

"Sure, is everything all right?"

"Yeah, something just came up that I have to deal with." For some reason, she felt the need to let him know it had nothing to do with another guy, so she added, "Girl stuff. Nivea has something going on and is coming over."

"I get it, and it's fine," Sherrod told her.

"How are you holding up?"

"I'm hanging in there. You know I spoke with Jordan, and she's flipping out because she thinks she's never going to see me again. I told her not to worry, and we'll figure everything out. I made her promise not to run away again. But, Janelle, I hate that she's going through this because her dad is being an asshole. What he did last night was totally uncalled for, and he fucked up big time. He'd better get ready because I love Jordan, and I'm ready to fight for her."

"I'm glad you told her not to leave again." Janelle sighed. "I know you're pissed, and you have every right to be. I don't know exactly how all of this got to this point, but I know Garry, and I've known him a long time. I'm just surprised."

"Well, he's gonna be surprised too, because not only am I filing for full custody of Jordan, I'm filing assault charges, too," Sherrod told her.

Janelle didn't know how to react. But she knew she had to do something. "Listen, Sherrod, please don't do anything until we talk face-to-face."

"Janelle, this shit can't wait."

"Please, Sherrod, this situation is messed up, but I know we can figure this out. Just don't do anything yet."

"I'll talk to you later," Sherrod said, then hung up.

As she drove home, her head began pounding as she tried to think of how to handle this situation. Calling Sylvia and telling her what Sherrod said he was going to do would be pointless, considering how angry she was at Garry, but Janelle ordered Siri to call her anyway. The last thing she wanted was for her sister and brother-in-law to be blindsided by this in case Sherrod decided to move forward.

"Hey," Sylvia answered.

"Hey, Syl, I need to tell you something."

"What is it?"

"I know you are dealing with a lot of shit right now and you've had the day from hell, but I just talked to Sherrod. He talking about filing assault charges against Garry and seeking full custody, too."

The phone was quiet. Janelle looked down briefly to make sure she still had a signal.

"Hello, Syl?" Janelle said.

"I'm here."

"Okay, so . . ." Janelle again waited for her sister to say something.

"Good."

"Huh?" Janelle was confused.

"Good for him. He should."

"You don't mean that."

"Yeah, I do. Garry shouldn't have put his hands on that man. Now he has to deal with the consequences, for that and everything else. So good," Sylvia said.

This wasn't the reaction she expected. She knew Sylvia was mad, but she thought she'd be a little more concerned. "Well, I guess that's it."

"I guess. Tell Sherrod I wish him luck," Sylvia said.

Chapter 8

Sylvia

"Straight home after school," Sylvia said as Peyton opened the door and hopped out of the car. She'd told both her and Jordan that they were grounded for a month and would not be able to go anywhere other than home and school. They would also share household chores, which they would have to complete together. The latter part of the punishment was Aunt Connie's idea. She thought that would help the relationship between the two girls somehow. Sylvia wasn't so sure.

"I have track practice until five thirty," Peyton said, pointing to the duffle bag she had taken out of the back seat along with her backpack.

"Fine, I'll pick you up then."

"I can get Meagan to bring me home. It's right on the way, and she doesn't mind." Peyton tossed her shoulder-length hair as she adjusted both bags.

"No, I'll pick you up. When I said no social activities for a month, that includes car rides with Meagan too. See you then."

"Fine," Peyton replied with a hint of an attitude and closed the door.

Although she was tempted to roll down the window and yell an embarrassing threat, Sylvia just drove off. She and her best friend Lynne were meeting for coffee, and at this point, caffeine was way more important than having the last word. She'd spent most of the night tossing and turning. At one point, she expected Garry to come back into the bedroom to at least change for bed. But after their argument, he'd left the house. Sylvia thought he had stayed out all night until she heard a noise coming from the den as she and Peyton were about to walk out of the house. She peeked in, noticing the large blanket-covered body sprawled on the sofa, and realized it was him snoring. For a split second, she considered waking him up and telling him to go get in their bed since she was leaving the house. But she quickly changed her mind. Sleeping on the sofa in the den was something he probably needed to get used to since it was where he would be until he found somewhere else to go.

"He's moving out?" Lynne asked as they sat across from one another at Starbucks.

"Either he goes or I go," Sylvia said, then took a sip of her much-needed Cinnamon Dolce Latte with an extra expresso shot. "And you know I ain't going nowhere."

"Lord, what is Aunt Connie saying about all of this?"

"Well, she hasn't really said too much, which means she's not too happy, because she always has something to say."

"About everything," Lynne added.

"Everything." Sylvia nodded. "I asked if she would consider staying a little while longer after her apartment is finished in a couple of months."

"You want her to stay longer? Well, I wasn't expecting that." Lynne gave her a surprised look.

"I know, but believe it or not, she's been a big help in a lot of ways."

"You just like them home-cooked meals every day." Lynne laughed.

"True, but it's more than that," Sylvia explained. "She's good for the girls, especially Jordan. She seems to gravitate toward Aunt Connie, and she can get through to her in ways that we can't. I know the reason Jordan came to talk to me yesterday was because of her. She listens to and trusts her. I don't want to take that away from her."

"Wait, I thought you said they were leaving." Lynne frowned.

"I said Garry was leaving. I didn't say Jordan had to." Sylvia pinched a corner of her muffin and popped it into her mouth.

"Don't you think he's gonna have something to say about that?"

"Probably." Sylvia shrugged. "Why are you looking at me like that?"

"I'm just surprised, that's all. I mean, I just assumed one of the biggest obstacles in this whole ordeal that you've been dealing with is Jordan, and now here you are saying you want her to stay. But you want him to go." Lynne picked up her own muffin and took a bite.

Sylvia shrugged. "I know it sounds crazy, but yeah."

"Does this mean you want a divorce?"

That was the question Sylvia had been pondering all night. She really didn't know what she wanted. All she knew was that she was angry: angry at Garry for his actions, but she was also angry at herself for a lot of reasons.

Just as she was about to answer Lynne's question, Sylvia glanced over and saw a guy standing in line, looking at her. He looked familiar, but she couldn't quite place where she knew him. They nodded politely at each other, and Sylvia turned back to look at Lynne.

"Lynne, I forgave him for the affair, I accepted his outside child, I gave him another chance, and we've tried everything." Sylvia sighed.

"Everything? Are you sure?" Lynne gave her a questioning look.

"Everything. We even tried therapy." Sylvia nodded. "You know I've tried, Lynne."

"I know you have. I just want you to consider that ending a marriage is sometimes worse than holding on to it. You know what I'm saying? You were there when I dealt with my divorce, and I can honestly say that sometimes I wonder if I made the right decision. After the smoke cleared and the hurt healed, I still love Hamp, and I wish I had tried everything," Lynne said with tears in her eyes.

Sylvia reached across the table and grabbed her hand. "Aw, Lynne, I know you do. And he still loves you too. It's not too late."

"Honey, that ship sailed five years ago. He's moved on with his life. You see his Instagram and Facebook pages. He stay having a young thot in his pics." Lynne shook her head and used one of the napkins on the table to dab at the corners of her eyes.

Sylvia felt bad for her friend. Lynne Hampton had been great friends for almost ten years until they divorced due to Hampton's gambling addiction. It got so bad that he'd lost almost all of their savings, and they nearly lost the house. The final straw was the day Lynne walked out of work to find her car missing. She panicked, thinking it had been stolen, only to find out that it had been repossessed. Hampton had taken out a payday loan without her knowing. Although Hampton was apologetic, Lynne said she couldn't live with someone who constantly risked her livelihood and everything that she'd worked so hard for, so she left him. It took her a long time to recover, not just financially but emotionally as well. They found a way to become friends again after Hampton finally went through rehab, and Sylvia knew her best friend was still in love with him, despite him actively dating, as she pointed out. Sylvia still hoped that Lynne would eventually find love again, if not with Hampton, then with someone else.

"I'm telling you he does that to get your attention. And look, it's working." Sylvia smiled.

"Whatever, but speaking of attention, there's a fine dude who's been checking us out. You see him?" Lynne nodded toward the direction she was talking about.

Sylvia turned slightly and saw she was referring to the same guy she had locked eyes with moments before while they'd been talking. "I know him from somewhere, I think."

"I hope so because he's walking over here," Lynne whispered.

"Good morning."

Sylvia smiled politely as she quickly tried to pinpoint who he was. "Good morning."

"How are you?" Lynne volunteered in a voice that was a little too friendly.

"I'm okay." He nodded, then he asked Sylvia, "I know this may seem a bit awkward, but can I talk to you for a few minutes?"

Sylvia looked at Lynne, who, by the wide grin on her face, seemed to think the question was directed at her. She turned back to the guy and looked closely at his face, noticing a slight bruise under his eye. It was then that she realized why he looked familiar.

"Sherrod," Sylvia said.

"I promise I won't take up too much of your time. To be honest, I'm running a little late for work."

"Sure." Sylvia nodded as she stood, then told Lynne, "I'll be right back."

She followed Sherrod to a nearby table, and they sat. Before speaking, he set down the cup of coffee and small bag he was carrying. "I guess this is kind of odd, considering the events of this past weekend."

"You could say that." Sylvia nodded.

"I'm sure you've heard a lot about me, most of it pretty negative. Garry doesn't care for me, and I gotta be honest, the feeling is mutual," Sherrod told her. "Things came to a head Saturday night, and he crossed the line."

Sylvia remembered Janelle telling her that Sherrod was pressing charges against Garry and started to tell him that she had no opinion one way or the other at this point. "Look—"

"But last night, I had to take a step back and look at the situation from all sides," Sherrod continued. "And I had to realize that I have some fault for what he did. Jordan was with me without permission, and I was wrong. And I'm sorry. I had my reasons though, and I hope you understand that."

Sylvia raised an eyebrow. Jordan had stressed that he was truly a nice guy, and from what Sylvia was seeing right now, she was right. "I appreciate your apology."

"I love Jordan, and I have since the day she was born. I loved her mother just as much. Losing Randi has been hard for both of us, but especially Jordan. When Garry snatched her and brought her to live with you all, she felt like she lost both parents," Sherrod said.

"Snatched?" Sylvia frowned.

"Essentially, that's what he did. He knew Randi had a plan in place and left instructions for Jordan to be placed in my care if anything happened. But he wasn't trying to hear it. He forced her to come and live with him."

Sylvia remembered the day she stood in the hospital and Garry told her that Randi was dead and Jordan was his daughter. She then remembered him explaining that Jordan had nowhere else to go. The truth was that Garry possibly could have continued to keep this all a secret, but he hadn't. Jordan had come to their home, and that's where Sylvia wanted her to remain.

"So, now what?" Sylvia asked.

"I'm not going to just walk out of her life. Jordan needs me, and I need her. I'm not going anywhere." Sherrod looked at Sylvia. "Let your husband know that fight Saturday night was nothing compared to the one he's about to have in court."

"I understand."

He stood and picked up his items. "Thanks for talking with me. Jordan is a handful at times, but she's a good kid. She deserves to be where she's happy, loved, and with her family."

"Sherrod, thank you for letting me know all of this. I understood everything you said. But I also want you to know that, even though she's only been with us a short while, I've grown to care for Jordan also, and so has my aunt."

"Aunt Connie." Sherrod smiled.

"And I can't explain why Garry has made the decisions that he has, but I can say that he loves Jordan too." Sylvia stood. "And we are her family."

Sherrod didn't say anything else before walking off. Sylvia watched him walk out the door as she went back to her seat.

"What was that about? What did he want?" Lynne asked.

"He wants custody of Jordan, and he's ready to fight for it."

"What are you going to do?"

"I guess I'm gonna need to hire an attorney. One who handles divorces and custody cases."

"Damn," Lynne said, saying exactly what Sylvia was feeling.

The house was quiet when Sylvia returned later in the afternoon. She and Kenny met with several clients on site, and she was surprised that she was able to remain focused, considering everything that was going on in her life. Although her personal life was in shambles, her business was doing extremely well. Her plan was to respond to emails, send out invoices, and then take a quick nap before picking Peyton up from school. She walked upstairs and into her home office, and as soon as she sat at her desk, she got a phone call.

"Hey, Sylvia, it's Amanda Channing."

"Hey, Amanda," Sylvia said. Dr. Amanda Channing was the head of the women's ministry at their church.

"I was calling because I have the scholarship application package for Peyton, and she also asked me about volunteering for the food pantry," Amanda said. "I looked for her yesterday."

"Okay, yeah, we missed service yesterday. But I appreciate the call. I will let Peyton know."

"Thank you so much. She's a really amazing young lady, and I am so proud of her. You and Garry have done an awesome job raising her."

"Thank you, Amanda. It's a tough job, but someone has to do it."

"And I also wanted to let you know I've been praying for you guys. I know it hasn't been easy the past couple of weeks," Amanda said. "Just know if you need me, my door is always open, and that's why I'm here."

Sylvia paused for a few moments, then said, "Well, that means a lot, Amanda. I'll keep that in mind."

In addition to being head of the women's ministry, Amanda was a licensed therapist and the director of the family counseling center at the church. When they'd agreed to counseling, Amanda was the first person she'd thought of. But Garry said he didn't really feel comfortable discussing his personal life with someone they were familiar with. Sylvia felt the opposite. She really liked Amanda and felt like she would not only help them navigate through their issues, but be a little more supportive because she knew them. The therapist they'd been seeing was one referred by their medical insurance company. He was nice, but he wasn't exactly what Sylvia felt they needed.

"Sylvia? You still here?"

Sylvia realized that she'd zoned out and missed something Amanda said. "Huh? What was that? I'm sorry."

"I asked how things were going."

Out of nowhere, a lump formed in Sylvia's throat, and she felt hot. She tried swallowing and clearing her throat, but her body betrayed her, and a quiet sob escaped her mouth and tears began to fall. Before she could catch herself, the emotions she'd been holding on to for weeks erupted, and she began weeping. She was overwhelmed and crying so hard that she could hardly breathe.

"It's okay, Sylvia." Amanda's voice was soothing in her ear. "It's perfectly okay. Let it go. Just let it go."

Hearing that she had permission to let go and cry freely was a welcomed surprise, and Sylvia continued shedding tears. Each time she thought that she was done, they started all over again. Eventually, she stopped trying to stop and let them flow: tears of anger, disappointment, fear, sadness, and grief. By the time she was finished, she was both exhausted and embarrassed.

"Oh God, Amanda, I'm so sorry."

"What are you apologizing for? You did nothing wrong. All you did was answer my question."

Amanda's reassuring reaction made her feel a little less awkward. She'd probably had to handle plenty of emotional breakdowns in her line of work.

"I guess I did," Sylvia said, reaching into her purse and fumbling for the pack of Kleenex. She pulled one of the tissues out along with a compact mirror.

"Listen, I would love to sit down and talk with you and Garry if you're willing. Or maybe even just you by yourself if you'd feel more comfortable. Either way is fine," Amanda said.

As she opened the small mirror, Sylvia looked at the woman staring back at her, eyes red and swollen, face full of worry and stress, and she hardly recognized her. This was not how she expected life to be. She should have been finalizing plans for her vow renewal, securing reservations with their travel agent for the multiple-destination trip to Europe they planned to take after dropping Peyton off at college, and looking forward to being an empty nester with Garry. Instead, she was now considering becoming a parent and fighting for custody of a child who didn't even want to live with her and possibly facing a divorce. It was too much, and she didn't know how she was going to handle any of it. Maybe Lynne had been right when she suggested that she hadn't tried everything. There was one more thing she hadn't tried.

"I'd like that," Sylvia told Amanda. "When is your next appointment?"

Chapter 9

Tricia

"Congratulations, Tricia."

"I saw your son's team on the news."

"State champs, that's huge."

It seemed as if everyone at Tricia's job heard about the game. She spent most of the week thanking people she rarely spoke to and barely knew. For the past three years, she'd worked as an admin at a small accounting firm. Her workspace was located in the back of the office, tucked away from everyone else, which she enjoyed. It made avoiding social situations and meaningless conversations with coworkers easier for her to do. She was also able to work undisturbed. Her desk was where she would remain from the time she arrived at work until she'd venture out for lunch alone at whatever nearby restaurant she chose for the day. Tricia was a loner, and thankfully, most of the people she worked with recognized and respected that, including her boss. She didn't bother anyone, and they don't bother her, not even to include her in the occasional office celebrations for birthdays, baby showers, et cetera, unless it was the only major one, which was the company Christmas party. Tricia came to work to do just that: work and collect a check, not make friends. She arrived on time, did her job, kept it professional, and went home.

Even though she was somewhat annoyed, she managed to remain pleasant in her responses to everyone who mentioned Tank's basketball victory. Her son had been featured on the local news and all over social media. He wasn't the only one. Titus also made an appearance when they showed the brief video footage of the brawl. Luckily, his name wasn't mentioned, and the film was so grainy and fast that none of the men were recognizable. That didn't stop her from watching it over and over, trying to figure out exactly what prompted his participation in the altercation. She still didn't understand. But she'd resolved to accept his explanation of attempting to break up the fight and somehow getting caught up in the mayhem. She also accepted that his enforcing the punishment they'd discussed for Tank was not going to happen either. It seemed to be business as usual in their household.

"The season is over, Titus. He's not supposed to be going anywhere," she said when he strolled into their bedroom after eleven o'clock. He and Tank had just arrived home fifteen minutes earlier. "I told him to be home by four o'clock."

"He wasn't out having fun, Tricia. He hit the weight room and the court after school. Regular season is over, but he still has to be ready for the game next month. You do realize that being selected for the All-American team is the biggest opportunity of his life, right? He'll be playing with and against the nation's top players," Titus said as he undressed and grabbed a pair of shorts and a T-shirt to put on after he showered for bed.

"That's what you said about the state championship game, Titus. It was the biggest game of his life. He has to have some kind of consequences for his action. He's around here keeping the same routine, and you're helping him. What the hell?"

"His car is parked, and he's not driving. The boy is going to school and practice, that's all. What more do you want?" Titus shrugged.

Tricia stared at him. "Tell him he can't play. Isn't that what a punishment is? Missing out on something you really want to do?"

Titus stared with a look of disbelief. "That ain't happening. Every college basketball scout in the country will be at that game. He's gonna be right there playing."

"Why? He's already got plenty of scholarship offers. He doesn't need any more. At this point, he just needs to pick a school," Tricia pointed out.

Titus shook his head and walked across the bedroom floor toward the bathroom. "And he will, after he plays in this All-American Game. Calm down, Tricia. Tank and I have a plan for his college future, the same plan he and I have been working on for the past seven years. I get it, you're pissed. He needs to be punished, and I have his keys, he can't drive. That's fine for now. That's punishment enough for right now."

"Says who?" Tricia called after him.

"We'll figure it out," Titus said before closing the bathroom door.

Later that night, she was half asleep when she felt his arm groping for her. She moved closer to the edge of the bed. "Stop. We took care of your needs last week, remember?"

"Cool," Titus said and rolled over. There used to be a time where he would whine and complain when Tricia would reject him in bed. Now it seemed as if he'd finally gotten used to it. She had no problem fulfilling her sexual duties one or twice a month, which mostly occurred when she happened to be in the mood. Still, Titus would still try every so often, and rarely, if ever, would she oblige. Sex with her husband was satisfying, but she just felt as if it was too much work at times and she would much rather be asleep.

As Tricia sat at her desk, deciding where to treat herself for lunch, her cell phone rang with a call from a number she didn't recognize. It was the third time whoever it was had called, and they didn't leave a message. She decided that if they called again, she would block the number.

"Heading out?" Mr. Dolbert, her boss, stopped at her desk and asked.

"Yes, sir." Tricia stood and nodded as she reached for her purse.

"Okay. I was wondering if you'll be taking any additional vacation days. I know you have a few scheduled in a couple of weeks, but I'm sure you'll be traveling to watch your son play in the All-American Game. I just want to make sure that you let HR know in case we need to get a temp in," Mr. Dolbert said.

Tricia shrugged. "I hadn't planned on going, honestly. So no."

The look Mr. Dolbert gave her was the exact same one Titus had given her the night before when she suggested Tank couldn't play in the game. "Uh, well, uh, all right then."

"Thanks for double checking, though." Tricia shrugged. "I'll be back in an hour."

"Okay."

Tricia hadn't even thought about going to the game, which was being held in Atlanta. Her nerves could hardly handle the anxiety and crowd of the state championship she was guilted into attending. Attending one even bigger was definitely something she didn't want to do. Just the thought of it made her uneasy: the crowd, the traffic, the chaos.

By the time she arrived at her SUV and climbed in, her pulse was racing, and she had to take deep breaths. As her body slowly began to calm, Tricia realized that although she was hungry, there was something else that she desired way more than food. She wanted to shop.

The mall was located less than ten minutes from the office. As she walked into the entrance of Saks, she calculated how much time she had to split between the shoe department and designer bags and still be able to grab something from either the food court or a drive-through on the way back to work. She would still be a few minutes late, but she knew Mr. Dolbert really wouldn't care. He probably wouldn't even notice her tardiness if she timed it so that she arrived after he'd gone to lunch himself.

"Can I help you?" a saleswoman asked.

Tricia held up a black Kenneth Cole flat and asked, "Do you have this in an eight?"

"I'll check and be right back."

While she waited, Tricia glanced over the multiple high-heeled sandals and strappy stilettos. Although she loved shoes, heels weren't her thing. Not only because she was a larger, plus-size woman and her ankles hurt like hell when she wore them, but also because she didn't go anywhere fancy enough to wear them. Her work wardrobe consisted of slacks and the occasional skirt, which she'd pair with a simple blouse and whatever cute, overpriced designer flat or low-heeled footwear matched her ensemble. On the weekends, she mainly wore leggings and T-shirts. And of course, there were her bags, all designer: Gucci, Prada, Louis Vuitton, Chanel, and so many others. She spared no expense when it came to buying them, and she had a closetful.

"Where the hell is she? What's taking so long?" Tricia asked no one as she became increasingly impatient. One of the main reasons she preferred to shop in the middle of the day was because not only was it less crowded and there were fewer people she had to deal with, but it was quicker to make purchases.

The saleswoman finally came back after several minutes. "I'm so sorry, but we don't have them. I can order them for you and have them shipped to your home or here to the store."

Irritated because she waited all that time only for the woman to tell her the shoes weren't in stock, Tricia gave her a look that was as nasty as the tone of her voice when she said, "No, if I wanted to do that, I would do it myself. Thanks for nothing."

"I'm sorry. I didn't mean to take that long. I was double-checking to see if we had them in another size, and then I wanted to check online before I offered to order them," the poor girl tried to explain.

Tricia looked her up and down, staring at her pretty brown face, petite body, and expensive hair extension, then said, "Not all big women wear a size eleven. I didn't ask for a bigger size."

"No, that's not what I was saying at all. These run a little small, so—"

"I don't have time for this." Tricia walked off. She was highly annoyed and decided she didn't even want to bother looking for a new bag. She quickly went to the food court and ordered one of her favorite meals, consisting of hibachi shrimp fried rice, chicken wings, two egg rolls, and a large Dr. Pepper. While she was eating, Titus called.

"You want me to pick up Popeyes or Chick-fil-A for dinner?" he asked.

"Whichever one y'all want," Tricia told him. His work hours were much earlier in the day than hers. She would still be asleep when he left the house and still be at work when he got home early in the afternoons. Since he would be hungry when he got home, Titus would pick up something for dinner unless he felt like cooking.

"I'll probably just grab a smoothie for me and Tank before we hit the gym today," Titus told her. "But I can grab something for you and have it waiting when you get home."

"In other words, y'all won't be home until real late again tonight." Tricia exhaled loudly so Titus could sense the attitude she had.

"Not that late, Tricia." He sighed.

"Hold on." Her phone beeped, and she held it out to see who was calling. It was the same number that called before. "Do you know anyone with this number? They keep calling and not leaving a message."

"Nope," Titus said after she read the number aloud. "Did you call the number back?"

"Obviously I didn't if I'm asking if you know the number," Tricia snapped as she blocked the number. "Don't worry about getting me food. I'm fine."

"You sure? I told you it's no big deal. I don't wanna hear you complaining about having to deal with traffic on the way home and then having to stop for food. You know how you are."

"I said I'm fine. I'll see you when you get home, whenever that is," Tricia said, looking at the food on her plate and deciding to eat the leftovers for dinner.

"It won't be that late, Tricia."

"Bye, Titus," she said and ended the call.

It was already dark when Tricia pulled into the driveway of their house. She hit the garage door opener on her sun visor and was about to pull inside when she slammed on the brakes just in time before the front bumper of her SUV made contact with the black Acura that belonged to Tank parked in the space where she normally parked. The other space of their two-car garage was occupied by Titus's motorcycle, a weight bench, and four basketballs.

"Damn it," she said as she reversed and parked in the driveway. After climbing out, she opened the rear door and grabbed her purse and the plastic bag holding her leftovers. She pushed the door with her hip to close it, then hit the lock.

"Excuse me," a male voice called out as a shadowy figure in the darkness walked toward her. They lived in one of the safest neighborhoods in the city, but that didn't mean it wasn't possible for crimes to happen. She'd seen hundreds of stories on the ID channel of suburban housewives who'd been raped and murdered. Now she was about to become one.

Tricia looked around, trying to determine whether she would be able to escape from whoever it was she assumed was about to attack her. She hit the unlock button and took a step back toward her car, thinking that if she could get in fast enough, she could drive off and maybe run him over in the process.

"Go away. I've got a gun," she warned, hoping the approaching predator wouldn't call her bluff and catch her in her lie.

"Whoa, whoa." The man stopped, and she could see him lift his hands. "I'm sorry. I'm not here to hurt anyone. I'm here about Tarik King."

"What about him?" Tricia frowned, taking another step backward. Her movement triggered the flood-light attached to the garage, and suddenly light was everywhere. The shadowy figure she now saw was a guy wearing glasses and dressed in a suit. He looked more like a minister than the serial rapist she thought he was seconds earlier.

"Are you his mom? How are you? I'm Everett Matthews." He smiled nervously. "I'm so sorry I frightened you. Please don't shoot."

Tricia relaxed enough to ask, "Who are you again?"

"My name is Everett Matthews. I'm with Burke University, and I'd like to talk to you about Tarik."

"*The* Burke University?" Tricia asked. Burke University was one of the top Ivy League universities, comparable to Harvard, Yale, and Cornell.

"Yes, ma'am, *the* Burke University." He nodded.

"Well, Tarik isn't here. He's still at school practicing with his dad and his coaches. You need to go there and talk to them, Mr. Matthews," Tricia told him and started walking toward the house.

"Everett. And uh, well, see, I've tried talking to him and his dad as well, but I haven't been that successful." Everett fell in stride beside her. "That's why I'm here. I don't want to talk to Tarik. I want to talk about him with you."

Tricia stopped and turned around. "Me?"

"Yeah. I've tried calling you a couple of times but couldn't reach you. Then I couldn't get through at all. So I took a chance and drove over," Everett explained.

Tricia remembered the number she blocked. "Oh, well, you ain't leave a message, so I ain't know who you were."

"I understand. And I apologize for that."

"His dad and coaches are the ones to talk to about basketball, not me."

"I don't want to talk about your son's athletic career. I'm here to discuss his academic future," Everett said. "Can we go somewhere and chat?"

Fifteen minutes later, they were sitting across from one another at the Panera not far from the house. Everett asked if she'd like anything to eat or drink, but Tricia said no. She really wasn't sure if she should even be there talking with him, but he seemed harmless, and she was curious about what he had to say about Tank.

"Are you some kind of admissions recruiter?" Tricia asked.

"No, I'm actually a Burke graduate, and I'm the president of the black alumni association. We identify students we believe would make great Burke students and help them. We mentor them, offer scholarships and financial assistance, and make sure they're taken care of while on campus. Tarik would be exceptional at Burke," Everett said. "We would love to help him get a degree for free."

"I don't understand," Tricia said. "This doesn't have anything to do with basketball?"

"Don't get me wrong, if he'd like to play for the university, I'm sure the basketball coach would have no problem with that. But the scholarship we're offering him from the alumni association would be a full academic scholarship. He has the grades, the test scores, he's a leader at his school and in the community. He's exactly what we're looking for."

"And you told Tank, I mean, Tarik all of this, and his dad?" Tricia blinked.

"About a month ago when I was in town. I travel quite a bit for work, but I do stop and reach out to those students we identify."

"And what was their response?" Tricia couldn't believe this was her first time hearing about any of this, and it wasn't coming from her son or her husband.

"They both said Tarik had no interest in our university. Neither really gave an explanation, but I got the vibe from Tarik that even though he hasn't made an official announcement, he's made a decision. I even invited him to come visit and tour, all expenses paid, but he said no."

"Wow."

"They didn't say anything to you at all?" He frowned. "You don't know what his decision is?"

Tricia shook her head. "As far as I know, he was waiting until after the All-American Game."

"That makes sense. I just hope he understands the huge opportunity this would be for him and seriously considers it. I just decided to make one last effort while I was in town and talk to you instead."

Tricia's eyes lifted from the single spot on the table she'd been staring at while Everett talked. "I appreciate that. Burke University is a great opportunity."

"Your son is academically gifted. His teachers say he's a math and science whiz. Our engineering or pre-med programs are stellar and the best in the country. Not only would Tarik graduate with a free degree from an Ivy League university, but he'd easily walk into a career making at least six figures. So many times, our young black men, especially those in athletics, feel like they have to attend the school that's gonna give them the most playing time. But they can have more."

Everett's words were so sincere. Tricia could see that he was really trying to look out for Tank, and she appreciated that he made an effort to talk with her. "Thank you, Mr. Matthews," Tricia said. "I'll talk to Tank."

"Everett, please."

"Everett."

"Here's my card." He reached into the pocket of his blazer and handed her a business card. "Please call me if you have any questions. And like I said, we'd love to have him come and tour the school."

"I will." Tricia nodded. "I'll follow up with you in a few days."

They walked to the parking lot, and he waited for Tricia to get into her car before he got into the Mercedes he was driving. She waved as she backed out. As she drove home, her mind was a myriad of thoughts. On the one hand, she was ecstatic that her son was being recruited by a prestigious college. On the other, she was angry at the thought of Tank being offered this opportunity months ago and it not being mentioned to her at all. They complained about how Tricia bitched all the time, but they failed to realize that it was the only time they seemed to pay her any attention.

As soon as she walked into the house, she called Titus. He didn't answer the first four times, but on the fifth attempt, he finally picked up. The sounds of basketballs bouncing, yelling, and sneakers squeaking could be heard in the background.

"Yeah?" he answered. Instinctively, as if he instantly could sense her anger, he asked, "What's wrong now?"

"Titus, first of all, why is Tank's car in my spot?" she snapped.

"What? That's why you're blowing up my phone?"

"I'm blowing up your phone because you ain't answering."

"Tricia, Tank has an eight-hundred-dollar amp and stereo system in that car that he won't be driving because you insist that he be punished. It doesn't make sense for it to be parked out front for weeks. It's safer in the garage," Titus said. "I gotta go."

"Titus, wait. I'm not done talking."

"What is it?"

"You and Tank met with a guy from Burke University, and they offered him a scholarship?" Tricia took her food out of the bag.

"What? Man, I'm not—"

"You don't think that's something you should've told me, Titus? Something that important? What the hell?" she said, opening the microwave door and putting her Styrofoam container inside.

"Tricia, Tank has met with a lot of colleges over the past year, and Burke was one of them, but he doesn't wanna go there. So it was a moot point." Titus sighed.

"Moot point for who? Damn sure not me," Tricia yelled and slammed the microwave door so hard she looked to make sure it hadn't shattered.

"Moot point for Tank considering he's the one who gets to pick his damn school and not you," Titus replied. "I'm gone."

Tricia stood in the middle of the kitchen. She was so angry that she almost screamed. Titus knew being hung up on was one of her biggest pet peeves, even though she had no problem hanging up on him whenever she felt like it. She knew for him the conversation was over, but she had plenty more to say. But she was tired, and it would be hours before he and Tank got home.

Tricia took the card Everett gave her out of her purse and stared at it. According to Titus, talking about Burke to Tank was pointless, but she would talk to her son and make sure he understood all of the points.

Chapter 10

Janelle

"Hey, wanna grab some sushi?"

Janelle looked up from her computer and smiled at her coworker Dexter who was standing in the doorway of her office. "Thanks, but I'm actually meeting someone."

"Oh, really? Teacher bae?" Dexter asked coyly.

Janelle shook her head and laughed. "No, not teacher bae."

"What happened to teacher bae? I liked him." Dexter faked a pout.

"Nothing happened to him. We are still cool." Janelle shrugged. She grabbed her blazer from the back of her chair and slipped it on.

"Just cool? Wait, what did I miss? See, this is why we need a lunch date. We are long overdue for one. We haven't had a sit-down since you were out sick with the flu. Clearly, I missed some things," Dexter said.

"We will definitely do lunch one day this week, I promise." Janelle playfully pinched his cheek as she passed him. They'd been friends since what had been their first day of work, years ago. At that time, Dexter was fresh out of law school and preparing for the bar. Now he was a junior partner and one of the best attorneys at the firm. Dexter was also a great lunch buddy and listening ear when she needed one. Had she not already had plans, Janelle definitely would've taken him up on his offer.

"Don't make me come and find you," Dexter warned. "You may not be meeting teacher bae, but whoever it is you're meeting must be special, because you're looking cute."

"Dexter, dear, I always look cute." Janelle winked.

The midday traffic was surprisingly light, and Janelle made it to her destination a few minutes ahead of schedule. Just as she parked her car, Natalie called.

"What's up, Nat?"

"Nothing much. What are you doing?" Natalie asked.

"I'm actually about to walk into a lunch appointment," Janelle said, checking her reflection in the rearview mirror. Hearing Dexter comment that she looked cute did make her feel a little more confident. When she chose the simple wrap dress to wear under her blazer and paired it with her colorful heels, she had no idea she'd even be meeting anyone for lunch.

"A lunch appointment or a *lunch* appointment?" Natalie's emphasis let Janelle know exactly what she meant.

"No, fool, just a lunch appointment."

"Okay, cool. Oh, Taryn called and said she can take us for mani-pedis Saturday at two. I tried calling and texting Nivea the other day, but she's still MIA. Did she come over the other night?" Natalie asked.

"No, she didn't. I waited for her and everything, but she didn't show up and finally sent a text that she fell asleep and would catch up with me another time," Janelle said, recapping Nivea's failure to show up and the excuse she gave. Even though she still didn't know what Nivea wanted to discuss, she was relieved she hadn't shown up. Had it been that pressing of an issue, Nivea would've at least wanted to talk about it over the phone, which she hadn't.

"That was weird. That's all she said?" Natalie asked.

"That's it. I guess it wasn't as important as she thought it was."

"Girl, knowing Nivea, she probably wanted to ask if she could order something on your Amazon account and pay you later."

"Probably. But Saturday is fine. I'll call you later," Janelle said, noticing the time and hopping out of the car.

"A'ight, girl. Chat later."

"You look nice." Sherrod smiled as Janelle walked toward him.

"Thank you. So do you."

"You're saying that to be polite, but thanks anyway." He gave her a brief hug.

They hadn't spoken to one another since Sunday. All week Janelle had been waiting for the call from Sylvia telling her that Garry had gotten some kind of summons or documentation, but there was no mention of it. She'd been pleasantly surprised when he sent her a text asking if they could meet to talk. She could tell by the look on his face that he was just as happy to see her as she was to see him. Even though they'd only known each other briefly, she realized she enjoyed spending time with and getting to know him and that she missed talking with him.

"How much time do we have?" he asked as they began walking.

"About an hour or so. What about you?" Janelle asked.

"I actually don't go into the store today. It's my day off."

"Nice." She nodded.

"So, what do you have a taste for?" The shopping center where Sherrod asked to meet had a multitude of restaurants to choose from.

"Panera works for me." Janelle pointed to the sign of the nearby restaurant.

After ordering soup and sandwiches, they found an empty table and sat across from one another. For some reason, Janelle felt a slight twinge of nervousness, so she took off her jacket in an effort to relax a little.

"How's your week been so far?" Sherrod asked.

"It's been okay. Work had been kind of hectic, which believe it or not is a good thing because it makes my day go by faster. How about yours?"

"Same. You know we're in the middle of flu season, so it's been pretty busy." He nodded.

"You know I know about flu season."

"Yeah, I recall you whining like a baby," he teased. "Good thing I came to your rescue when I did. We probably wouldn't be here having this conversation because you would be gone to glory."

"Oh my God, that sounds like something Aunt Connie would say." Janelle laughed.

A server brought their food over to the table, and they made a little more small talk as they ate. Janelle wondered if it was a coincidence or if they both were purposely avoiding the many obvious subjects at hand. Her curiosity was cured by what Sherrod said next.

"I talked to your sister."

"What? When?" Janelle asked, surprised by his statement, mainly because she hadn't even spoken to Sylvia.

"Monday morning. I ran into her at Starbucks, and we had a nice talk," Sherrod said, then continued to tell her about the conversation he had with Sylvia days before.

Janelle listened, recalling how, when she told Sylvia about Sherrod's plans to file charges, her sister had seemed nonchalant about the entire situation. Now after hearing this, she still had no idea where her head was at.

"So, you changed your mind?" Janelle asked as she stirred her soup.

"No. I can't abandon Jordan. She needs me. But I'm just coming up with a plan that will put me in the best position to do what's best for her. One thing your sister pointed out was that Jordan needs a support system, and that's the one thing I don't have in place right now. But I'm working on it," Sherrod answered.

"What do you mean?"

"Well, for starters, I'm going to need a good attorney."

At the word "attorney," Janelle looked up at him. "You want me to help you fight Garry and my sister, Sherrod? You know that I can't do that."

"I'm not asking you to help me fight them, Janelle. I wouldn't put you in that position. All I'm asking is that you point me in the right direction. It doesn't have to be at your firm."

"That's still helping you."

"Instead of looking at it like you're picking sides and helping me, look at it like you're helping Jordan. No matter what happens, don't you want her to be in the best situation?" Sherrod asked.

"And what makes you think that's not with Garry and Sylvia?"

"And what makes you think that it is?" Sherrod shot back at her. "They're in the middle of separating right now and have their own issues to sort out, don't they?"

"Who told you that?" Janelle frowned. It was one thing for her to know about her sister's marital problems, but she didn't know how she felt about anyone else commenting on them.

He stared at her and said, "From what Jordan told me, he and Sylvia aren't even speaking, and there's so much tension in the house that she can't even sleep at night. She's scared and has started sleeping with Aunt Connie."

Janelle quickly came to their defense. "Every marriage has problems, Sherrod. And no matter what I can tell you right now, their main concern is the well-being of their children. They will work it out."

"Are you sure? What if they don't? Then what will happen to her?"

Janelle didn't have an answer to his question. She didn't even want to think about what was going to happen if Garry and Sylvia inevitably split. Peyton had one foot out of the house anyway, so although she'd be hurt by her parents' decision, she would be okay. But Jordan had a few more years in the nest. She'd recently lost her mother, and in reality, Sylvia just might have a better chance at winning custody than Garry.

"Sylvia will make sure Jordan is—" Janelle started.

"Janelle, Jordan doesn't want to be there. She wants to be with me," Sherrod stated. "And her mother agreed. But just think about it. You asked me to think about it before filing those assault charges, and I did. Now I'm just asking you to do the same thing. If not for me, then for Jordan."

Janelle inhaled, then said, "I'll think about it, Sherrod. But I'm not making any promises. This situation is hella complicated as it is."

"You're right, and I thank you for agreeing to think about it." He reached across the table and grabbed her hand. "Now that we've tabled that discussion, I have something else for you to think about."

"What?" Janelle gave him a suspicious look.

"I want you to consider going out with me again. I know it's crazy with everything going on right now, but—"

"Sherrod, I don't know," Janelle said softly. "And not just because of the Jordan-Sylvia-Garry situation."

"Is it the teacher guy who was at your birthday party?" he teased.

"God, no, not him either," Janelle told him.

"Okay, then it must be him." Sherrod released her hand and sat back.

"Who?"

"You know who. The guy who grabbed you while Garry and I were fighting. The one who you can't keep away. The one who's married to someone else." Sherrod shrugged.

Janelle looked down at her half-eaten lunch. "No."

"Hey, I don't want you to think I'm judging you, because I'm not. I'm just trying to understand why a woman so beautiful and smart, with so much to offer the right guy, would be caught up and settling for less than she deserves."

Finally she looked up. "I'm not settling. Yes, Titus and I are . . . were . . . I mean, he's just my friend. We've been friends for years, even before he was married to someone else. We just somehow gravitate toward one another. But I'm not with him. I know what I want and what I deserve. Please don't get that twisted."

"And what is that?"

"What is what?"

"What do you want? And what do you deserve?" Sherrod asked.

Janelle thought about his question. At one point in time, she wanted to fall in love and get married and have a family when the time was right. But after one failed relationship after another, she began to think it wasn't possible, so she changed the items on her list of wants and found happiness in other ways. She enjoyed spending time with her family and friends, she loved her job, and she loved being independent and having the freedom to travel the world. She reminded herself that her friends who were married with children couldn't do the things that she could.

"I want and I deserve to be happy, Sherrod. And I am. And my concern for dating you has nothing to do with Titus or any other man."

"Then what is it? Is it me? Is it because you aren't feeling me anymore?" Sherrod stared at her.

"It's not you, Sherrod. You're still as amazing to me today as the day you showed up on my doorstep to nurse me back to health." Janelle gave him a reassuring smile. "I'm worried about how Nivea would feel if we became serious."

"Nivea?" Sherrod said so loud that the people sitting nearby looked over at them. He quickly apologized. "Sorry. What the hell does Nivea have to do with us?"

"It's kind of breaking girl code to date the guy who happened to be the first love of one of your best friends, Sherrod," Janelle said.

"First love? Whose first love?" He seemed confused.

"Nivea's first love. You. You said it yourself that you were her first," Janelle reminded him.

"That was in high school, Janelle. And yeah, I was the first person she had sex with, but I wasn't her first love. The crazy thing is she had sex with me because the guy she was in love with at the time didn't believe in having sex with virgins, crazy at that sounds. I didn't even know her ass was a virgin until after it was over." Sherrod laughed.

"Are you sure?" Even though Janelle didn't have a reason not to believe him, she wasn't sure if he was telling the truth, especially since that wasn't the way Nivea had portrayed them to be.

"I'm positive. So as I see it, there's no reason for us not to pick up where we left off, right?" He smiled as he grabbed both her hands this time and held them tight.

Janelle looked at his handsome face, not knowing what to say. He was right when he said their lives were complicated. There was also the possibility of their dating making both of their situations worse. *I really need to talk to Sylvia and Nivea. It's the right thing to do.*

"Sherrod . . ."

"Fine, what about this? One date, this weekend, no pressure, no strings. Just you and me hanging out as friends."

"One date?" she repeated. Agreeing to one date as friends seemed like such an easier decision for her to make.

"That's it, Saturday night."

"Fine, one date."

Sherrod put her hands to his lips and kissed them. She realized that she was just as happy about her accepting his invitation as he was. In the back of her mind, she knew she still needed to talk to her sister and best friend. *Okay, and I will. But for now, it's just one date.*

Chapter 11

Sylvia

Sylvia had just drifted off to sleep when she heard movement downstairs. Her eyes fluttered open, and she sat up in bed. Her first instinct was to call out to Garry, who would normally be sleeping in the sitting area of their bedroom, but she remembered that he wasn't home. He decided to accept a last-minute travel assignment for work and wasn't scheduled to return home until late Saturday afternoon. Having no choice but to go and check herself, she got out of bed and eased into the hallway. *Maybe it's the dog.* She heard the noise again and realized it wasn't the dog, but the door.

"Mom?" Peyton whispered in the darkness behind her, causing Sylvia to clutch her chest in fear.

"Jesus, Peyton. What the hell?" Sylvia hissed.

"You heard something downstairs too?" Peyton scurried toward her on her tiptoes.

"Yes. Go back in your room."

"I'm not letting you go down there by yourself."

"Fine. Stay behind me, though," Sylvia said as she slowly began to descend the staircase. Her heart raced, and she squinted to see if she could see any type of movement as she reached the bottom.

"You think it's Jordan sneaking out?" Peyton asked, startling her.

"Shut. Up. Peyton." Sylvia emphasized each word, wishing she had grabbed something to use as a weapon in case she needed it. Garry's gun was locked in the top of the hall closet, but she didn't know where he kept the key. He'd tried to tell her several times, but she refused to listen. She couldn't fathom having to ever be in a situation where she would need to use it, and if she did, would she really have time or be in a state of mind to find the key, unlock it, and take it out to use? Now she wished she had listened. Not that she knew how to use a firearm, but at least she could have it as an option.

Click. Another sound came from near the kitchen. Peyton grabbed Sylvia from behind. The thumping in her chest was so hard, Sylvia was certain whoever was in her home could hear it. The creaking of another door echoed through the room, and Sylvia turned around.

"Who's out there?" a voice yelled, and then the lights in the foyer came on.

Sylvia and Peyton screamed, and so did someone else. She turned to see Jordan standing at the top of the stairs near the light switch, brandishing a broom like a Samurai sword.

"What the hell is going on? What is all this screaming?" Aunt Connie asked as she rushed in through the kitchen door. Gypsy was right on her heels.

"Oh my God, Aunt Connie, what are you doing? What is going on?" Sylvia gasped.

"I'm fine. I was just taking Gypsy for a walk, that's all," Aunt Connie told her.

"Everything okay in here? Connie, you all right?" They all turned around to see the man who now stood behind her aunt. No one moved or said anything at first. It was as if they were all in a state of shock and didn't know how to react.

"Deacon Barnett?" Peyton was the first person to speak.

"Good evening, everyone." Deacon Barnett nodded toward them. It was the first time Sylvia had ever seen him not wearing a suit and hat. But he was still matching from head to toe in a blue jogging suit, blue sneakers, and a blue baseball cap. She wanted to laugh but didn't want to make him feel any more uncomfortable than he already looked.

"We thought someone was breaking in," Sylvia explained as she folded her arms across her body, suddenly aware of her own bedroom attire, which consisted of a T-shirt and a pair of Garry's old basketball shorts. "We heard the noise and came to check it out."

"And what were you gonna do, sweep him to death?" Aunt Connie smiled at Jordan, who was still standing at the top of the stairs holding the broom.

A wide grin spread across Jordan's face until she saw Peyton giggling. She quickly turned and walked away.

"Well, Deacon Barnett, thank you for checking on us, but as you can see, we are fine. You can be excused," Aunt Connie dismissed him.

"Y'all have a good night." He tipped his baseball cap and backed his way into the kitchen. A few seconds later, Sylvia heard the door close behind him.

"Let me make sure that door is locked," Aunt Connie said as she turned toward the kitchen.

"Uh, ma'am." Sylvia rushed behind her.

"Don't start. It's not what you think." Aunt Connie sighed. "I promise you, ain't nobody up to no good."

"I didn't say you were."

"Gypsy was acting anxious, and Jordan was asleep. I didn't want the dog peeing in the house, so I decided to take her out. As chance would have it, I walked to the entrance of the neighborhood, and here he comes driving by and saw me." Aunt Connie shook her head. "He offered me and Gypsy a ride home, insisted on walking me to the door, and that's when we heard all this screaming."

"It was fate." Peyton smiled.

"It was foolishness," Aunt Connie corrected her. "Now, let's all get back to bed."

"Aunt Connie, why do you let Jordan sleep with you?" Peyton asked as they were going up the stairs. "She does have her own room."

Aunt Connie stopped and said, "Because we enjoy one another's company, that's why. And for the same reason I let you sleep with me when you want to. Any more questions?"

Peyton shook her head and said, "No, ma'am. Good night."

Sylvia gave her daughter a hug and kissed the top of her forehead. "Goodnight, baby. I love you."

"Love you too, Mom." Peyton went into her room and closed the door.

"You hurt her feelings, Aunt Connie," Sylvia mentioned just as Aunt Connie was about to go into her room.

"How? I answered her question."

"I don't think she meant anything by it."

"And I didn't mean anything by answering it." Aunt Connie shrugged.

Sylvia decided that it wasn't worth any more energy. She went into her own room and climbed back into bed. Her adrenaline was still flowing, and she couldn't sleep. She thought about Deacon Barnett running in like he was there to save the day, and she began laughing. She had to tell someone. She grabbed her cell phone and dialed Garry's number.

"Hello? Syl?" he answered. "What's wrong?"

Sylvia tried to talk, but she was laughing to hard. "Ga . . . Garry."

"Sylvia, calm down and tell me what's wrong. Stop crying." Garry's voice was panicked.

"I . . . I'm . . ." She gasped.

"Syl, where's Peyton? I'm gonna call her so she can help. Where are you?"

For some reason, Garry's concern was making her laugh even harder. "No, no. I'm fine," she somehow managed to say.

"Wait, are you laughing?"

"Yes."

"Oh God, I thought something happened. What the hell is so funny?"

By the time Sylvia finished telling Garry about the robbery false alarm, Jordan with the broom, and Aunt Connie's secret midnight pop-up rendezvous with Deacon Barnett, they both were gasping for air.

"Stop playing! Deacon Barnett, for real?"

"I'm not playing. And, Garry, he was still matching, even in that sweat suit." Sylvia laughed.

"He still gotta coordinate, Syl. In church and out."

"I see. And he was definitely that." It felt good to laugh, especially with Garry. Their conversations had been tense and brief, mostly about the girls and their schedules. There hadn't been any mention of them separating, his leaving the house, or anything about their marriage. After her breakdown on the phone with Amanda, she'd gone and had one therapy session and had another one scheduled. But she hadn't mentioned any of that to Garry either. She figured it was something they would talk about face-to-face once he got home.

"I'm glad that there really wasn't any real danger, though, Syl." Garry sighed. "This is why you need to know where the key is for the gun safe."

"No, I don't. We're fine. But I have to confess, I did think about it while I was creeping down those steps."

"I bet you did."

"Well, that's all I wanted. It was funny, and I knew you would laugh." Sylvia pulled her comforter tighter around her.

"I'm glad you called, because I needed a good laugh."

He sounded discouraged, and Sylvia almost asked him if everything was okay, but she didn't. They shared a good laugh, but she wasn't at a place where she felt like she even wanted to know if he was or not. And she didn't want to make him think that she was, so asking would be giving them both some sort of false hope.

"I'll talk to you tomorrow then," Sylvia told him.

"Yeah, I'll call you in the morning. But, Syl, we need to talk when I get home this weekend. Just the two of us, away from the house."

"I don't have a problem with that. I have some things I need to tell you anyway."

"Okay, sounds like a date then. We can go to dinner, your pick."

"My pick? Wow, I hope your pockets are deep."

"After almost twenty years, you already know there ain't no depth when it comes to you, Syl. Good night."

"Good night, Garry," Sylvia whispered. She put her phone on the nightstand and turned over in the bed. As she closed her eyes and drifted off to sleep, she giggled again at what happened earlier, and she realized she was looking forward to going to dinner with the man who was still her husband.

Chapter 12

Tricia

"Are we renting a car next weekend or driving your truck?" Tricia asked Titus as she walked into his man cave. It was one of the rare nights that he and Tank, who was upstairs doing homework, were home.

"What are you talking about?" he asked, his eyes still glued to the television. "We don't leave for Atlanta for another few weeks. It's not next weekend."

Tricia paused. "Are you trying to be funny, Titus? Because you're not."

"I'm not trying to be anything."

"Titus, we're going to my mother's for her birthday," Tricia told him.

"I thought you were going. I hadn't planned on it. And Tank definitely can't go," Titus told her. "He has two-a-days starting next week."

"I don't even know what that means, and I really don't care. You know I told you months ago that we were going to my mother's for her birthday and to make sure the plans for her retirement were in place," Tricia snapped.

"Tricia, you may have mentioned it, but I swear, I didn't know you had made plans. Months ago? With everything Tank has going on, I can barely remember what time I have to be at work every day." Titus stretched his legs on the coffee table in front of him. "But I do know I can't go because I don't have no vacation days to spare."

"You have plenty of days to go to Atlanta." Tricia's voice raised an octave.

"That's important."

"And my mother's birthday isn't?"

"I ain't say that." Titus sighed.

Tricia couldn't believe Titus. The thought of arriving at her mother's house without him was something she hadn't planned on and definitely didn't want to deal with. Her sisters would have a field day if she came alone, and her mother would be disappointed. There was no way she was going to be able to tolerate being there by herself in front of her family and all of their friends. No damn way.

"I'm not going by myself, Titus. You know how I am when I fly," Tricia told him. "My nerves can't take it."

"Then drive, Tricia. It's only like five hours away. You can leave the house when I leave for work Friday morning, and you'll be at your mama's house before lunchtime."

"You want me to drive five hours by myself, Titus? Who would even want their wife to do that?" Tricia whined.

"What's wrong now?" Tank walked in and asked. The question seemed to be directed at his father rather than her.

"Your mom wants to see your grandma next weekend, but she doesn't wanna drive," Titus told him. "So, she's upset."

"Oh, well, did you check to see if maybe the train goes there, Mom? Because I know you ain't catching no bus." Tank laughed and flopped on the sofa beside Titus.

"I'm upset because I planned this trip months ago, and now your father is acting as if he didn't know. And he's saying that you can't go," Tricia explained to her son.

"It's your grandmother's birthday, and there is a dinner planned. She's expecting us to be there, especially you, Tank."

"Oh." Tank shrugged. "I didn't know."

"Tarik, don't you want to see your grandmother?" Tricia asked, hoping if she showed him how important the trip was to her, he would help persuade Titus.

"I mean, I guess. But, Mom, I got practice."

"You can miss practice for your grandmother's birthday, Tank. You haven't seen her in a while."

"We saw her last summer when we were at the family reunion that you and your sisters argued at the whole time, remember?" Titus laughed.

"That was the worst." Tank shook his head. "All that screaming about everything. And remember the fight over the T-shirts everyone was supposed to wear?"

The incident her husband and son were referring to was a weekend the summer before when they all gathered at a cabin large enough to hold the entire family in Tennessee rented by Felicia, who took pleasure in telling everyone how much she paid for it. Of course, she made it seem as if it were a deal, but Tricia knew better. Tricia offered to help with the cost, but Felicia wouldn't let her. So instead, Tricia decided to have family T-shirts printed for everyone. Unfortunately, upon arrival, they were given gift bags with shirts inside and instructions to wear them the following day for the family photo. Tricia was livid, especially when both her sisters insisted that Tricia should have told them what she was planning.

"You're really overreacting," Violet said.

"We asked for everyone's input for weeks, and you never mentioned anything about wanting to bring shirts," Felicia added. "How were we supposed to know?"

Tricia spent the entire weekend at odds with everyone and complaining to Titus and Tank. Her one moment of enjoyment was the family photo where she, Titus, and Tank wore the shirts she brought instead of the ones worn by everyone else. Needless to say, even though Violet and Felicia were smiling in the picture, they weren't happy at all.

"I don't have to stay here and listen to this. All I want to do is spend time with my mother for her birthday, and now I can't." She shook her head and brushed away the invisible tears in the corners of her eyes. "Tank is leaving for college in a few months, and she wants to see him. She's getting older, and I would hate for something to happen to her. She's older, and you know she has some health issues. I expected better from both of you."

"Mom, please don't." Tank leaned forward and touched her arm.

Tricia quickly pulled away from him and stormed out without saying anything else. She went upstairs into her bedroom and closed the door. She'd verbally expressed herself to make her point, but there was another method she planned to use as reinforcement so that Titus would know exactly how she felt.

Hours later, he climbed in bed and reached for her.

"Don't," she said, moving all the way over to the edge of their bed.

"Whatchu mean? Tricia, stop tripping. Look at the calendar. Tonight is on the schedule," Titus said, sitting up and pointing to the small calendar hanging above her nightstand where she kept her schedule for everything, including nights designated for sex.

"Going to visit my mother for her birthday next weekend is also scheduled, but that ain't happening, is it?" she responded.

"Tricia," Titus said. She ignored him, and he tried again. "Tricia."

He exhaled loudly as he stood up. Her eyes remained closed, and she didn't move as he loudly closed the door as he left the room. *Now who's mad?* she thought as she went to sleep.

The next morning, the first thing Tricia saw when she opened her eyes was a folded piece of paper attached to the calendar. She hopped up and carefully removed it. The airline logo at the top was clearly recognizable, and her eyes quickly scanned the flight itinerary for her and Tank the following weekend. There were also hotel and car reservations, all of which were paid in full. Tricia would undoubtedly still have to deal with folks questioning about where Titus was, but she was confident that Tank and the news of his state championship win and upcoming All-American Game would overshadow his father's absence.

A note on the bottom of the page in Titus's handwriting read:

> *Make sure Tank hits the gym every morning, and he has to be back by 5:00 p.m. Sunday. Enjoy your trip.*

She looked back at the calendar with a satisfied grin. The next date with a star on it was three weeks away. Not only had she gotten her point across, but she'd also bought some free days of not having to fulfill her wifely bedroom obligations in the process. Now all she had to do was find her mother the perfect birthday gift that would outshine anything her sisters would even think of giving her.

***

As she sat at her desk shopping online instead of working, she got a call from Mr. Matthews. Tricia knew he was calling to follow up with her, but other than the failed conversation she'd had with Titus, she had nothing to tell him about. She thought about ignoring the call, but then she remembered how nice and pleasant their conversation had been.

"Hello, Mr. Matthews." She spoke low into her cell phone. Although her desk wasn't near anyone else's, she didn't want to risk anyone seeing her on a personal call.

"Everett," he corrected her. "How are you, Mrs. King?"

"I'm good. I know you're calling to get an update from me, which I kind of don't have," Tricia explained.

"It's fine. I understand."

"I mean, I did bring it up to my husband. But like you said, he wasn't really receptive," Tricia told him. "But I still plan on talking to Tarik without his father."

"Oh, really?" Everett sounded surprised.

"Yes. Like I told you, I think he should really consider Burke and everything it has to offer. He and I are traveling to visit my mother next weekend, and I'm sure we'll have some one-on-one time without any distractions."

"That sounds great. If you like, I can email you some talking points that you can discuss with him. And you know you can call me if either of you has any questions or concerns about anything."

"I appreciate that. Who knows, maybe we can tag team him and get this thing done." Tricia laughed, then gave him her email address.

"Sounds like a plan. I'll be waiting on standby for your call," Everett said. "But you guys have a safe trip and enjoy the time with your mother. I'm glad Tarik is getting some family time in before he goes off to school."

"Yeah," Tricia said. "I'll speak with you soon."

She ended the call and went back to finding the perfect gift for her mother. Her phone chimed, and she looked down and saw the email that Everett sent.

Chapter 13

Janelle

"Special delivery," Holly, one of the office administrators, said as she walked into Janelle's office. In her hands was a vase that held a huge bouquet of flowers.

"Whoa," Janelle commented as Holly placed the vase on Janelle's desk. "Thank you."

"Enjoy. Don't forget the meeting in fifteen minutes, conference room west," Holly said, pausing to admire the bouquet once more before exiting.

Janelle smiled at the arrangement of red roses, pink lilies, and greenery. She loved fresh flowers and was impressed by Sherrod's thoughtfulness. Her grin was wide as she picked up her desk phone and dialed his number.

"Thank you," she said when he answered. "They are beautiful."

"Wow, you got them already?" he asked. "They said it would take a couple of hours."

"Yeah, they were just delivered to my desk," Janelle said as she leaned over and sniffed one of the roses. "I guess if I was thinking about cancelling on you tomorrow night, I definitely can't now."

"You weren't gonna be able to do that anyway." He laughed. "I would've shown up on your doorstep and made you come to dinner with me."

"Sir, I do believe that would be considered stalking, kidnapping, and false imprisonment. You trying to go to jail, huh?" Janelle giggled.

"Trust me, I believe you are definitely worth serving time," Sherrod said sexily, causing Janelle to blush.

"Well, I have to get back to work. Thank you again."

"I gotta go push these pills myself. I'm glad you like them, though," he told her. "I'll call you later."

Janelle took another sniff, grabbed her laptop off her desk, then headed off to the staff meeting down the hall, still smiling. She didn't have a clue what was discussed, because the entire time she was in the conference room, she kept thinking about Sherrod and their date.

"Who's got you cheesing like that?" Dexter purposely bumped her as he passed after the meeting was over.

"Why can't I be smiling because it's Friday?" she asked.

"Because even though they just announced that we would possibly be working mandatory OT for the next two weeks, that smile hasn't left your face."

"OT means more money in my paycheck. So that makes me happy." Janelle shrugged.

"Lying heifer," Dexter said. "And what happened to our lunch date this week?"

They arrived at Janelle's office, and both stopped and stared. Sitting right beside the bouquet of flowers that Janelle received earlier was another bouquet. The second vase held another arrangement that was equal in both size and beauty.

"Okay, now I see why you're cheesing," Dexter said, walking in before she did. "Two bouquets. You must be showing someone some special attention to deserve all of these."

"I'm not showing anyone special anything. It's probably a mistake. They brought the first one earlier than they were supposed to anyway." Janelle pushed past him as she walked behind her desk.

"Well, let's see who sent these impressive mistakes." Dexter reached into the second bouquet and took out a small card.

"Give it." Janelle tried to snatch it from him, but he quickly moved away from her reach.

"Ah, ah, gotta be quicker than that." He laughed. "'Nellie-Nelle.' Okay, that's cute."

Janelle's mouth fell open at the nickname that only one person had for her. She reached for the card again. "Dex."

"'Thank you. I'm sorry. I miss you. Ty-Boogie,'" Dexter read aloud. "Ty Boogie. That definitely isn't teacher bae's name. His name starts with a J."

"Shit," Janelle whispered as she reached for the card in the other vase, but once again, Dexter beat her to it. She folded her arms and leaned against the edge of her desk, waiting for him to read what it said.

"'Janelle.' Okay, this one is a little more formal." Dexter cleared his throat. "'Thank you for giving me another chance. I promise you won't regret it. Rod.'"

"Shit," Janelle said again.

"Well, my my my. Two admirers, both of whom are very polite and eloquent. Care to explain?" Dexter asked, putting both cards back into their original places.

"Not really."

"Well, you're not smiling anymore, so I'm thinking these flowers aren't a good thing."

"One is. The other definitely isn't. But I need to make a call, and I need some privacy," Janelle said. She hadn't spoken to Titus since she called to tell him about Tank being at church. She'd ignored his texts, phone calls, and even the email he sent. Her talk with Sherrod caused her to really think about her future and what she wanted, and the reality was that Titus couldn't be a part of it. She loved him, but she couldn't continue whatever it was they were doing. The last thing she needed right now was his sending flowers and cards, trying to get her attention. She had to nip it in the bud. Now.

"I understand. I'm outta here anyway. Enjoy your weekend, Nellie-Nelle. You still owe me lunch. Hell, we'll probably need two lunch dates to discuss all of this."

"You're right," Janelle agreed. "And please close the door. I'm probably about to be really loud."

Dexter closed the door, and Janelle quickly dialed Titus's number. He barely got the word "hello" out before she was already speaking.

"What are you doing, Titus? Why would you do this?" she groaned into the phone.

"What do you mean? Did I do something wrong?" he asked innocently.

"You know what you did. And you've gotta stop. I told you this." Janelle sat in her chair.

"Nellie, I just wanted to say thanks for finding Tank, that's all. And I know they're your favorite," Titus told her.

"You didn't have to do that. I'm serious, Titus."

"I know, and I get it. But I was thinking maybe we could do a day trip next weekend. Drive a couple of hours and hang out, get a bite to eat. What you think? Just you and me," Titus said.

There was once a point in time when Janelle would've been excited and quickly accepted his offer. Quick trips with Titus were so much fun, and they enjoyed the brief getaways when he could sneak off. Oddly enough, Janelle wasn't excited.

"No, Titus. We can't go anywhere next weekend or any other weekend. I love you, but I can't do this anymore. Take care," Janelle told him.

"Nellie." Titus sighed.

"Bye, Titus." She ended the call, then she did something she'd never done. She blocked him. It was time.

It seemed like it had been ages since Janelle had hung out with her girls at the nail spa. It felt good to laugh and joke with them. It was like old times as she sat with her feet in the warm water of the bubbling foot tub of the chair as it massaged her back, sipping champagne with Natalie sitting on one side of her and Nivea on the other. The three of them caught up on gossip, discussed reality television, and tossed out ideas for their next girls' trip.

"I'm telling you, we should go to Carnival in Brazil," Natalie suggested.

"I don't know about Brazil," Nivea said.

"Why not?" Janelle asked. "Carnival does sound like fun. I was watching Lil' Kim and her friends on that show *Girls Trip*. They had a blast."

"First of all, they chartered a damn yacht. We ain't balling like that," Nivea pointed out. "And the number of dudes in Brazil with HIV is alarming. Higher than most other countries."

"What?" Janelle gasped. "How do you know that, and more importantly, why?"

"Research." Nivea smiled.

"Who researches that?" Natalie asked. We looked at one another, then answered her question simultaneously. "Nivea."

"What?" Nivea shrugged as if her knowing the HIV rate of males in Brazil was as common as knowing the temperature outside.

"Weren't you and Jarvis talking about going to Brazil a little while ago?" Natalie asked.

Janelle cut her eyes over at her and said, "We talked about a lot of things a while ago."

"So, y'all are done?" Nivea leaned toward Janelle and asked.

"Yeah, we are." Janelle nodded. "It was fun while it lasted."

"Damn, Jarvis was fine," Natalie said for the hundredth time as she shook her head.

"He's not the only fine guy on the planet, Nat. There will be another one coming along, I'm sure. I'm sorry, friend. I know you enjoyed looking at him."

"I did. And I'm glad you understood my constant staring at him." Natalie laughed and raised her glass. "To Jarvis: you had a good run."

"Here here," Janelle said, tapping her glass against Natalie's.

Nivea held on to her glass. She looked at Janelle and asked, "So, I guess Titus is back on your radar now since you and Jarvis are done?"

Janelle frowned, slightly offended and caught off guard by her question. "What? No. Why would you think that?"

"I'm just wondering, that's all." She shrugged.

Janelle had pondered mentioning her date with Sherrod while they were all together, but decided not to. There was something off about Nivea. She was engaged in the conversations, but she seemed bothered.

"Is something going on with you, Niv? You okay?" Natalie asked, confirming that Janelle wasn't the only one sensing a hint of an attitude.

"No, why would you ask me that?" Nivea said. "I'm fine. As a matter of fact, I'm better than I've been in a long time. This pedicure is everything."

"Just checking." Natalie and Janelle exchanged a look of confusion.

"Hey, Nivea," another customer said as she walked by. Then she stopped and said, "Girl, I wanted to ask you, where did you get that jacket you had on Sunday at Brutti's? It was so cute."

Nivea looked at the woman and said, "Some online boutique. Thanks."

"Brutti's? You were at Brutti's Sunday?" Natalie sat up and asked.

"We texted you and asked you to come with us to brunch," Janelle said. "You didn't even respond."

"I went in there to pick up a to-go order for me and my cousin. I told y'all I was with her. It was before y'all went anyway," Nivea explained. "Dag, y'all act like I can't eat nowhere without y'all."

"That's not what we're saying at all," Janelle said. Her fun time with her girls had gone left real quick, and she was ready to go home and get ready for her date.

"Damn, you look amazing. Definitely worth kidnapping," Sherrod said when Janelle opened the door. She had chosen to wear a black bodysuit covered with a colorful, oversized cardigan and long black boots. Her normally curly hair was straightened and hung slightly past her shoulders. She'd had her eyebrows shaped while she was at the nail spa and even had some lashes applied. Not only did she look good, but she felt better than she had in a long time. Sherrod looked equally as nice in a pair of black slacks and a thick cable-knit sweater.

"You're looking quite dapper yourself. Would you like a glass of wine before we leave?"

"Maybe we can save it for a nightcap instead?" He hugged her. Between the depth of his voice, the warmth of his arms, and the recognizable scent of his Dior Sauvage cologne, she was instantly turned on.

"You're that confidant that I'm gonna invite you back for a nightcap?"

"I am." He nodded.

"We'll see how the night goes." She winked and followed him out the door.

"Trust me, I'm sure it's gonna go great." He took her by the hand.

"Where are we going anyway?" she asked when they got into his car.

"Somewhere I know you're going to like and I've been wanting to go for a while. Buckle up and enjoy the ride."

Chapter 14

Sylvia

The dining room of Maison Brouchets was full. The room held over sixty tables, and there wasn't an empty one. On the far wall was a small stage with a pianist, violinist, and percussionist who entertained the diners with softly played eclectic mixtures of jazz, old-school R&B, and classic rock songs. The ambiance was just as enjoyable as the food and definitely worth the price, which was not cheap.

"Would you like dessert?" the waitress asked as she cleared the dishes from the table.

Sylvia looked at Garry. He'd invited her to dinner and brought her to one of her favorite restaurants in order for them to talk, but they hadn't discussed anything important. They both seemed to be avoiding the inevitable.

"I could go for something sweet. What about you, Syl?" he said.

"How could we not indulge in some crème brûlée?" Sylvia nodded.

"Two orders of crème brûlée, please. Oh, and two coffees," Garry told her.

"Coming right up," the waitress said.

"Coffee?" Sylvia commented. Garry rarely drank coffee unless he was extremely tired, and never at night.

Garry shrugged. "I could use a pick-me-up after all those carbs I just ate."

"You have a point," Sylvia told him. "I ate more than you did."

"I think we're about even."

Sylvia looked at him. "Garry, we've been dancing around the conversation we're supposed to be having."

Garry took a deep sigh and said, "I know. I guess because I've been enjoying this so much that I didn't want the good vibes to end."

"I get that. But who knows, maybe it will be positive," Sylvia said in an effort to ease the anticipation.

"True. Well, I know you said you have something to tell me, so why don't you go first?"

"I'd actually like for you to speak first."

"Okay. I know I've apologized, but I feel like I need to say it again. I'm sorry for the situation I put you in and the damage that it's caused our family. I never wanted to hurt you or Peyton. I love you both so much. You are my world, and so is Jordan."

"Garry." The last thing Sylvia wanted to hear was the same spill he'd said to her over the past few weeks.

"Wait, I'm not done. Actually, I'm just getting started. I was wrong for expecting you to just forgive me and take in a child you never knew about, my child, and go on with life as usual as if my actions were that minuscule, which they weren't. I lied to you for years, and you didn't deserve that. I understand why you're frustrated with me, and I don't want to make things any worse. I've done enough damage. You asked me to leave, Syl, and I get it. So as much as I don't want to, I know that it's best. I've found a place to stay."

The waitress brought the dessert and coffee that Sylvia now no longer wanted. She stared at the sugar-crusted top of the pudding, not knowing how to react to what Garry said. A million things had run across her mind when he said he had something to tell her, but this wasn't one of them.

"Syl?" Garry called her name softly.

"Wow." Sylvia finally found her voice. "Okay. Wow. I mean, that's good news, I guess, huh?"

"I wouldn't call it good news. But it's news."

"Congratulations. Where will you be moving to?" Sylvia tried to sound pleasant, but it was a struggle. Granted, she'd been the one to ask him to move out, but she wasn't expecting it to happen, at least not so soon. She was bewildered at the reality of her husband actually leaving their home.

"I'm actually going to move into Randi's place," Garry said.

"Randi's? That's four hours away." Sylvia frowned. "I didn't even know that was an option."

"It's actually Jordan's place. Her mom left it to her. I was going to rent it out, but now it makes sense to just go there and take her home," he explained. "I know it's a little far, but I'm still—"

"Take her home?"

"Yeah. It's been a difficult transition for her, and you know how she's been complaining about wanting to go back to her old school and her friends. I was thinking maybe—"

"You were thinking, you decided," Sylvia murmured. "You still don't get it."

"What?"

"I didn't even know anything about Randi leaving the house to Jordan. You haven't told me about her leaving Jordan anything. I've been one of this child's main caretakers since the day her mother was buried. Don't you think this is something we need to discuss?" Sylvia told him. "You don't even have to answer it. We both know you didn't."

"Syl."

"You know what else you didn't think about? You didn't think about how this would affect our entire family. You wanted to do what was easiest instead of what's best," Sylvia said, reaching for packs of sugar to put in her coffee. She was anxious and needed something to do. Sweetening her coffee seemed like an opportunity for her to utilize her hands instead of wrapping them around her husband's neck. "It's easier for you to take Jordan and go four hours away instead of dealing with our issues and fighting for your marriage."

"I didn't know if that was even an option, Syl. You told me to leave." Garry sat back in his chair.

"Did you ask? Did you come to me to discuss any alternatives to your leaving?" Sylvia looked up at him. Garry shook his head, and she said, "Exactly. You hate having difficult conversations."

"I thought that's what we were going to talk about tonight. This hasn't been easy for me to tell you. And I am fighting for my marriage. I love you. That hasn't changed."

At that moment, the song the band started playing caught Sylvia's attention. *God truly has a sense of humor,* she thought as she listened to the music of "How Deep Is Your Love," one of her and Garry's favorite songs.

"You've gotta be kidding me," she said.

"It's a sign." Garry smiled.

"It's a coincidence." Sylvia picked up her spoon and dug it into her lukewarm dessert.

"What was it that you wanted to tell me?" Garry said, now eating his own dessert.

Sylvia wasn't sure if she even wanted to tell him, especially now that he said he was leaving. Thinking about what she'd just told him about avoiding difficult conversations and taking the easy way out, she knew she had to take her own advice.

"I've been going to therapy."

"With Dr. Brewer? Without me?" Garry put his spoon down.

"No, with Amanda, at church. And yes, without you."

She saw him purse his lips slightly and knew he wasn't too pleased with what she said. "Are you sure that's wise?"

"I do, because God knows I feel a lot better after meeting with her. And I know you're thinking that because she works for the church, she'll probably tell people our personal business, but she's a licensed professional, Garry, and is held to the same guidelines and laws as any other therapist. Personally, I think she's better because she's invested in our family and our healing."

"Okay." Garry gave her an apathetic shrug. "And what made you decide to go see her?"

Sylvia took a deep breath. "I ran into Sherrod, and after talking to him, I had somewhat of a breakdown."

Garry's stare was incredulous, and he leaned forward. "What the fuck did he say to you? When? Why didn't you tell me? I swear, I'm gonna kill him."

His voice was so loud that the people sitting beside them glanced over. Sylvia gave them an apologetic look, then whispered, "Garry, stop. You need to calm down."

"Calm down? You just told me this man disrespected you to the point where you had a breakdown and needed to seek therapy," Garry snarled.

"That's not what I said. Did you even hear me? I said I talked with him."

"And then you had a breakdown and went to see Amanda."

"But he wasn't the cause of it. I was."

"What do you mean?" Garry's eyes narrowed.

"I mean that I've been holding on to so much for so long that the burden of it all got to be too much. Talking to him and hearing everything he said, dealing with everything already and the possibility of what we might be facing, it was just too much," she confessed, her eyes filling with tears. "I was trying so hard to be the strong, supportive wife for you and our family, and I ignored the fact that I needed help."

"Damn it. You should've told me." Garry now had tears of his own. "I'm your husband. I'm always gonna be there for you. For us. You don't have to handle this by yourself."

"And neither do you. But you act like you do," she fired back at him.

"I don't mean to."

"But you do." She picked up her napkin and dabbed at the corners of her eyes. "I don't want this to turn into an argument, Garry. That's not what we're here to do."

"You're right. And I don't want that either. You said you were worried about the possibility of what we might have to face. What did you mean?"

"Sherrod."

"Sylvia, that guy is crazy. Don't listen to him."

"Garry, despite how you feel about him, I could tell that he loves Jordan like she was his own daughter. And she loves him. They have a bond. And I believe he's sincere when he says he wants what's best for her."

"Don't be fooled, Syl. He talks a good game."

"This guy has nothing to gain by fighting for custody. He's a doctor, for God's sake. He ain't hurting for no money as far as I can tell. Do you think he wants her for some kind of inappropriate reason?" she suddenly wondered, although she didn't get any kind of perverted vibe from him.

"No, Syl. I hate him, but I can honestly say I don't think he'd do anything like that, or anything to hurt her. And I really don't know what he has to gain or why he's fighting so hard. But he's full of shit. He wants a fight? I'm ready for it. Best believe I'm gonna do what's right for my daughter."

"You still don't get it, do you?" She shook her head.

"What?"

"Let me ask you something. Do you even care what's best for your daughter? Because from what I'm seeing, both of you are acting off pride and ego and not seeing that this poor girl is getting caught in the crossfire. And what I'm not going to do is allow that to happen. You wanna move into Randi's house, great. But Jordan is staying where she is. Whether you like it or not."

"Can I get you guys anything else?" the waitress came over and asked.

She shook her head and said, "No, we're finished. You can bring us the check."

"Be right back."

"Syl," Garry said.

"I'm done talking for now, Garry. We've both said what we needed to say. I'm ready to leave."

Garry paid the check, and they left the restaurant without saying anything else to each other. They were standing in the front of the restaurant waiting for the valet to bring the car when Sylvia heard a familiar laugh and turned around.

"Janelle?" she said, recognizing not only her sister but the man standing beside her. Instinctively, she grabbed Garry's arm and began praying for all of them.

Chapter 15

Janelle

"Are you sure you're okay?" Sherrod asked as he drove. It had to have been the fifth time he'd asked that question since they'd left the restaurant.

"Yeah, I'm fine." Janelle nodded. Truth was, she didn't really know how she was. Certainly, she was grateful that what could've easily taken an ugly turn didn't. She'd been excited when they arrived at the restaurant. The anticipation of having a romantic dinner at Sylvia's favorite restaurant quickly disappeared when, just as they were about to enter, she heard someone calling her name. The last person she expected to see was Sylvia, and definitely not Garry.

"Hey, Syl, Garry." Janelle smiled nervously and tried not to panic as she maneuvered her body so that she would be standing in front of Sherrod.

"Don't tell me you're out with this guy," Garry said, his eyes looking from her to Sherrod then back to her.

"What? You gonna try and keep me away from her, too?" Sherrod asked. "I know you blocked my number from Jordan's phone."

"Damn right I did. That's what a father is supposed to do: protect his child from predators like you who take them from home without permission."

Sherrod glanced over to Sylvia. "Look, I apologized for that and explained—"

"I don't give a shit about that. I've told you to stay away from my daughter," Garry barked.

"I can't do that, and you know why," Sherrod said. "You know what Randi wanted."

The valet pulled up and hopped out of Sylvia's SUV. "Here you are, sir."

"Garry, go ahead and get in the car," Sylvia told him.

"And maybe you can go in and let the hostess know we're here." Janelle nudged Sherrod. He looked down at her and nodded but didn't move until Garry did. Sylvia looked just as relieved as Janelle did when the two men went in different directions.

"So, you and Garry are good," Janelle said. "I'm glad."

"That's still to be determined. It was just dinner so we could talk. What's up with you and him? I thought you were going to take a step back until we figure this all out."

"Same here. It's just dinner to talk. Nothing serious," Janelle answered. "Why you ask me like that?"

"I mean, it just seems odd, that's all."

"Odd for who?"

"Him, you, us," Sylvia said with an attitude.

"Whoa, I told you it's not serious." Janelle gave her a cautious stare.

"Janelle, to you it's not that serious. But for once, can you stop being selfish and look at the bigger picture? You think it's not that serious, but it becomes very serious when your decisions affect this family," Sylvia said as she turned to walk away.

"Syl, it's just dinner," Janelle called out to her.

"I hope so." She opened the door to the truck and climbed in the seat beside her husband. "In the meantime, until this is sorted out, I'm asking you and him to stay away from my daughters. Both of them."

By the time she closed the door, Garry was driving off. Janelle turned and slowly walked into the restaurant where Sherrod was waiting.

"Everything good?" he asked.

"Not really, but you already knew that."

"Our table should be ready in a few minutes." He gave her a compassionate look, then said, "But we don't have to stay if you don't want to."

"Are you sure?" she asked, not wanting to disappoint him but relieved for his offer. Any kind of appetite she had was gone after the confrontation with her sister and brother-in-law.

He grabbed her hand and nodded. "I'm positive. I'll go get the car."

Unlike the drive to the restaurant, which was full of jokes and laughter, the ride back to her house was reticent and uneasy. Janelle's thoughts were focused on the conversation she and Sylvia had. She'd just reconciled with her sister, and now they were at odds again. Sylvia being surprised and a little annoyed was understandable, but there was also some slight hypocrisy. She'd said she was done with Garry, but there they were on a date, the same way Janelle and Sherrod were. And her telling Janelle to stay away from the girls added insult to injury and hurt her feelings. It didn't seem fair.

"Janelle?"

Janelle realized Sherrod had been talking, but she hadn't heard anything he'd said. "Huh?"

"I asked if you wanted to stop and grab something to eat from somewhere else."

"No, I'm not hungry. You can just take me home."

"You sure?"

"Yeah." She nodded.

Twenty minutes later, they pulled into her driveway. Sherrod turned off the engine, and they sat in silence for a little while.

"I'm sorry about all of this," she told him.

"What are you apologizing for? You didn't do anything wrong."

"I still feel bad because I know how much you were looking forward to going to dinner, and so was I."

"Oh, so you admit you were excited about me?" he teased.

"I didn't say all of that. Calm down." She smiled slightly.

"But, Janelle, I was just excited to see you. I didn't care if we went to dinner," Sherrod said. "That's all."

"That's sweet." She sighed.

"I'm a sweet guy." He shrugged and pretended to straighten the tie that he wasn't wearing. "Besides, even though we didn't have dinner, we still have our nightcap waiting for us."

Janelle glanced over at him. "Sherrod, I don't think that's a good idea."

"Why not?"

"I don't think any of this is gonna be a good idea, to be quite honest. It's just too . . ."

"Too what?"

"Too much. My sister and her family, well, my family has a lot going on right now, including Jordan. I don't want to do anything that'll make it worse," Janelle explained. "I like you. You know that. But right now, our seeing each other just doesn't make sense."

She opened the car door and got out. Sherrod hopped out at the same time, rushing toward her. "Janelle, wait."

"What is it?" Janelle asked, now wanting to hurry inside her house. All she wanted to do was get undressed, climb in bed, and cry herself to sleep.

"At least let me walk you to the door."

"Okay." Janelle let him take her by the hand as he escorted her to the front door. She reached into her purse and took out her key, then turned to face him. "Thank you."

"Janelle, we can figure this out." Sherrod's voice was as soft as the look he gave her. His finger caressed the side of her face. "I know we can."

"Sher—" Janelle's words were cut off by Sherrod's lips, which covered hers. Her head tilted, and her eyes closed as she became lost in the warmth of his mouth. He pulled her body close, and she instinctively put her arms around his neck as her handbag slid to her shoulder. The kiss ended with their foreheads pressed together and both of them smiling.

"Please don't make me kidnap you." He whispered, "Because you know I will."

"One drink."

They went inside her home, and while she changed into shorts and a T-shirt, he opened and poured the wine. She snuggled beside him on the sofa.

"Okay, so my brother-in-law hates you, and based on her reaction tonight, I'm pretty sure that my sister's level of dislike for you is fairly up there. So your approval rating from my family so far isn't that great."

"But I have your vote of approval and of course Jordan's. And let's be real, Aunt Connie loves me. So if you look at it, I have three votes to their two," Sherrod pointed out.

"The jury's still out on Peyton, and we know Nivea's going to veto this too." Janelle took a sip of wine. "And Natalie usually sides with her for some reason."

"Janelle, listing all of the people in your life who agree or disagree with our being together isn't helping," Sherrod said. "Baby, relax."

"Relax? You were the one who said we were going to figure it out. That's what I'm trying to do. And really, I'm not even concerned with the beef between you and Garry right now. The two of you are caught up in a competition to see whose dick is bigger, and neither of you realizes that it's affecting more than the two of you." Janelle sat up. "Do you know Sylvia accused me of being selfish for going out with you tonight? The two of you are the ones being selfish."

"I'm sorry she said that."

"I hate that my sister is going through all of this. She's slowly breaking. I can see it. And I don't want to add anything that's going to make her life any more chaotic than it already is." Janelle blinked back tears. "She is pissed and scared. And yeah, I know she makes me mad and gets on my nerves at times, but I love her. She's the one who always looks out for everyone else. I don't want to betray her. I want to help her."

"I don't want you to betray her. You think I want to be at war with Garry and your sister? I'm trying to do the one thing my best friend asked me to do if she died: take care of her daughter. It breaks my heart when Jordan calls me, well, used to call me and cry for me to come and get her. Let me show you something." Sherrod reached into his pocket and took out his phone. He typed on the screen then handed it to Janelle. "Read."

Janelle stared at the display of text messages, all between him and Jordan. The exchanges were daily, Jordan telling him how she missed her mom and wanted to go home. She complained over and over again about having to go to a new school and having no friends. She also told him she didn't like Peyton and felt like an intruder in their home. But for each negative complaint, Sherrod responded with encouragement and positivity. Over and over, she threatened to run away, and Sherrod begged her to stay. He promised Jordan that he would find a way to see her, but said that despite her being uncomfortable, he was sure she was in a safe place with people who cared about her. They laughed about Aunt Connie, and Jordan said she was glad that she was there for her. Sherrod even suggested that Jordan talk to Sylvia. Janelle continued reading, and then she saw her name. Jordan sent him a text telling him about the day she was about to run away and Janelle stopped and talked with her. She said Janelle was nice and pretty, and she thought she was cool. Janelle couldn't help smiling. The last text had been the one she sent him, telling him Janelle was at the house. He asked her to call Janelle. After that, the messages stopped.

"When she went back inside on Sunday after you and I talked, Garry took her phone. He thought she'd snuck out and called me, so he blocked my number. He told her if he found out it was unblocked or that she talked to me again, he would file a restraining order and have me arrested for stalking," Sherrod said as he took the phone from Janelle.

"Have you talked to her?" Janelle asked.

"I can't confirm or deny in an effort not to incriminate anyone." He pulled Janelle to him. "I hate this just as much as you do. I hate that you feel like you have to choose sides."

"Maybe I don't have to." Janelle looked up at him.

"What do you mean?"

"What if we all were on the same side?" Janelle said.

"Who's side would that be?" Sherrod gave her a suspicious look.

"Would you be willing to have another meeting with Sylvia?"

"I don't have a problem with it." He shrugged. "If you think it'll help."

"I believe it will." Janelle nodded.

"Set it up," Sherrod said, staring into Janelle's eyes. "And just so you know, the only thing I'm selfish about is wanting to be with you."

Janelle smiled and kissed him. She'd come up with a surefire plan to help her sister and Sherrod and, most of all, Jordan. In the end, they all would be happy. That was, if Sylvia agreed.

Chapter 16

Tricia

"You guys have a safe flight," Titus said as he took the suitcases out of the trunk of his car. "Tank, FaceTime me when you're in the gym. Today, tomorrow, and Sunday, no excuses."

"I'm on it, Dad," Tank said as they shared their secret handshake. Then he hugged his father.

"Tell your mother I said happy birthday. Oh, I almost forgot this." Titus reached into the car then handed her a small plastic bag from Pandora.

Tricia opened it and looked. "What's this?"

"The gift wrapped one is for her," Titus told her.

"And the other one?" she asked.

"Guess you'll have to open it and see." He shrugged and waved as he got into his car.

"You ready, Mom?" Tank called to her.

"Yep, let's go," Tricia said, grinning at the unexpected gesture from her husband.

After they boarded the plane, she took the unwrapped box out and opened it. Lying on top of the soft, white cotton insert were three of the newest charms to add to the already-full bracelet she wore. For a second, Tricia felt a little bad for still not having sex with him. But she told herself that despite the surprise gift he'd just given her, it didn't change the fact that he wasn't on the trip with her, so the punishment was deserved.

She put the top back on the box, and after sending Titus a quick thank-you text, she settled into her seat and tried to relax. Not only was she nervous about the two-hour flight, but the anticipation of being around her family for the next two days had her on edge. She was looking forward to seeing her mother and could even deal with her brother. But when it came to Felicia and Violet, she didn't know what to expect. She distracted herself from thinking about her sisters by talking to Tank about his opportunity to attend Burke.

"I don't wanna go there. I already told that alumni guy, Mr. Masters."

"Matthews," Tricia corrected him. "Don't you realize how huge this could be for you?"

"Not interested. Besides, I'd rather go to an HBCU," Tank explained.

"What's that?" Tricia frowned. "I've never heard of that school."

Tank shook his head at her. "It stands for historically black colleges and universities."

"You'd rather go to a black school instead of an Ivy League one? Do you know how ridiculous that sounds?" Tricia asked.

"No, it's not. There are some HBCUs that are just as competitive as Burke."

"I'd rather you attend a university that's diverse like the real world," Tricia told him.

"I have my entire life to deal with diversity and racism and bias, oh, and white privilege. Going to an HBCU will give me the opportunity to celebrate my history and being with other like-minded students in an environment where we can thrive and embrace our culture instead of being critiqued and criticized for it," Tank said. "I've been in diverse schools my entire life. Now I wanna go to a black one."

"So, you've chosen a school?" Tricia asked. "You've made a decision."

"No, not yet. But I'm just saying, I'm leaning toward the offers I got from HBCUs: Hampton, Xavier, Prairie View, North Carolina A&T . . . I got several choices, all full rides, same as Burke. Not interested, not going," Tank said, putting his earphones on and leaning back in his seat. He may have been done talking for now, but if Tricia had her way, the conversation was far from over.

"Come on, Tank. We're going to your grandmother's house," Tricia said a couple of hours later as she checked her reflection in the mirror of the hotel bathroom.

"I thought the party was tomorrow. I gotta go work out. You heard Dad," Tank said.

Tricia walked into the room where Tank's long and lanky body was sprawled across one of the two queen-size beds, texting on his phone. "The party is tomorrow. But we're going over for a little while to spend a little time."

"I can spend time with her tomorrow. I'm tired. We just got off a flight," Tank said without looking at her.

"I was on that same flight, and I'm tired too," Tricia told him. "Get up."

"Mom, please. This is the first time I've gotten to relax in weeks. And I'm hungry. Can't you just cut me some slack?"

"No. I'm not cutting you anything. Funny how you're too tired to go see your grandmother, but not too tired to work out. Get your ass up and let's go," Tricia snapped. "We can eat at her house."

Tank sat up and glared at her. "Fine."

"Change into something nicer, please."

He looked down at his T-shirt, joggers, and sneakers and asked, "What's wrong with what I'm wearing? You said the party is tomorrow. Why am I changing?"

"Just do what I asked," Tricia said. "I'll meet you downstairs in ten minutes, and don't make me come back up here."

Ten minutes later, she was still sitting in the rental car in front of the hotel where the valet had parked it, waiting for Tank, who hadn't come out yet. She called his phone, but he didn't answer. The only reason she didn't leave him was that she refused to go to her mother's home by herself, especially knowing that her younger sister was still living there.

"Tank, if you don't hurry up and bring your ass . . ." She began leaving a voicemail when he came sauntering out the front doors, dressed in an outfit that was almost identical to the one she'd asked him to change out of. The only difference was that the T-shirt and sneakers were a different color, and he now wore a large pair of headphones over his ears. He started to walk around to the passenger side of the car when she honked the horn and pointed. "You're driving."

"Not only are you forcing me to go, but you're making me be your personal chauffer? Bet." Tank shook his head as he adjusted the seat of the car so he could fit comfortably.

"I figured it'd been a while since you've driven since you've been grounded, and based on your attitude, it'll probably be a while before you drive again, so I suggest you enjoy it while you can," Tricia warned.

"Trust me, I'll be driving off to school soon," Tank grumbled.

"What did you say?"

"What's the address we're driving to?" Tank had enough sense to correct himself.

"You don't know where your grandmother lives, Tarik?" Tricia shook her head.

"I know where Grandma Regina and GrandTee live," Tank said, referring to Titus's parents, who lived even farther away than her mother, yet Titus managed to take Tank to visit at least three to four times a year.

"Here." Tricia gave him the address.

"Tricia, you're here," her mother said as she opened the door and gave her a big hug. "It's so good to see you."

"It's good to see you too, Mama." Tricia enjoyed the warmth of her mother's arms and held on for what was probably a little longer than expected.

"Tank, look at you." Her mother looked up and noticed her grandson standing behind his mother. "So tall and handsome."

"Hello, Grandmother," Tank said, hugging her.

"Come on in here." Her mother led them in the door. The sound of music and the aroma of food welcomed them inside. Tricia saw a few of her mother's neighbors sitting in the living room, and a couple of cousins. She politely spoke as she followed her mother into the kitchen, where her mother's two sisters were chopping ingredients as they sat at the table and drank liquor.

"Mama, I thought the party wasn't until tomorrow," Tricia said.

"It is. But we started celebrating a little last night. And Bertha and Shelia just came over to help me cook a few things." Her mother stirred a large pot that was on the stove.

"Hey, Tricia." Her aunts waved.

"Why are you cooking? I thought Felicia was having the food catered. You shouldn't have to cook for your own party. If I had known this, I would've hired a caterer," I said, shocked that my sister had dropped the ball but now seeing an opportunity to make it right. "As a matter of fact, let me call Kroger and see if we can order some platters and maybe some chicken. We probably still have time."

"Girl, stop it. You know Felicia got the food taken care of. I just wanted to have a little of my own special dishes like potato salad and macaroni and cheese. I didn't want anybody else making that."

"Well, at least let me help," Tricia offered.

Her mother, along with Bertha and Shelia, all turned to look at Tank, who stood in the doorway laughing uncontrollably.

"What's funny?" Tricia asked.

"You offering to help cook. Wait 'til I tell Dad." Tank doubled over.

"We know your mama don't cook," her mother said. "But at least she offered. Come on over here and let us see how handsome you are. I heard all about that winning basketball game."

Tank walked over and stood beside her mother. "Yeah, it was pretty cool."

"So, you pick a college yet?" Aunt Shelia asked.

"He has several opportunities. Burke University is really after him," Tricia bragged.

"What? Burke? That's awesome. We're so proud of you," the three older women said to Tank at the same time.

"I have a few offers I'm still considering." Tank shook his head at Tricia.

"Well, the family is proud of you," Aunt Bertha told him.

"We sure are, nephew," Violet announced as she walked in and hugged Tank. "You something like a big deal, huh? Looking like your daddy, you probably got plenty of chicks."

"Nah, I don't." Tank grinned sheepishly.

"Just one? What's her name?" Violet nudged him with her elbow.

"Tank has more important things to worry about right now than some fast-tail girl," Tricia said. "He's been selected to play in the All-American Game in Atlanta next month. That's his priority right now."

"All right now, Tank." Aunt Shelia clapped.

"Congrats on the game, nephew." Violet then whispered loud enough for everyone to hear, "And the girlfriend. You can tell me all about her later."

"Did you bring the pans?" her mother asked Violet.

"Yes, ma'am. I did." Violet held up the bag of foil pans she was carrying. "Felicia's on her way to the venue to make sure it's set up."

"Hello to you too, Violet," Tricia said.

"Hey, Tricia," Violet said politely. "I wasn't sure if you were speaking to me. The last time you saw me, you told me to never say anything to you ever again."

Again, Tank giggled. Tricia gave him an evil glare, then turned to her sister and said, "Where's Bethany?"

"Her father is picking her up from day care. She'll be here in a little while," Violet said.

"Oh, I thought the two of you weren't together," Tricia said.

The smile on Violet's face disappeared and was replaced by a look of embarrassment. "We're not. But we are cordial, and we still coparent our child."

"That's right, baby. And despite everything, he's still a good daddy to Bethany," her mother said.

Tricia still didn't know what had caused the breakup of her sister's marriage. Her mother always referred to it as "internal issues." Tricia was hoping to find out exactly what the cause was this weekend.

"And where is your husband, Tricia? Tank, where's your daddy? Is he here?" Violet asked with a smug look.

"No." Tank shook his head.

"Oh, is he back at the hotel?" Violet continued.

"Tricia, y'all ain't staying here with your mama?" Aunt Bertha asked, saving Tricia from having to answer the question.

"Now you know she ain't staying here," Violet said. "Only five-star accommodations for her."

"No, we're staying downtown. Tank needs to be somewhere that has a fitness center for him to work out in while we're here. As a matter of fact, we need to be going so he can get his training done for the night," Tricia said.

Tank's eyes widened, and he opened his mouth to say something, but the daring look Tricia gave him caused him to stay quiet.

"You're not going to stay and see your sister and brother, the rest of the family?" her mother asked. "Everyone is coming over. Tank can see some of his distant cousins."

"We will see them tomorrow," Tricia told her. "Let's go, Tank."

"You made me change and drive all the way over here for fifteen minutes?" Tank complained when they got into the car. "And we didn't even eat."

"We can get something to eat on the way back to the hotel. Or we can order room service and relax. You said you were tired anyway," Tricia said. "I wasn't expecting all of those people at the house. I didn't think Violet would be there, and I didn't feel like dealing with Felicia."

"Mom, why the hell did we even come on this trip?" Tank asked.

"You know why we came, Tank. We're here to celebrate my mother's birthday with the family," Tricia said.

"But you don't even like your family," Tank said.

"That's not true. I love my mother. And do you know how they would talk about me if I didn't show up?" Tricia looked at her son as if he were crazy.

"Who cares? You talk about them all the time anyway. What's the difference?" Tank asked her. "You know as well as I do that tomorrow is going to be a total shit show, excuse my language."

"That's not going to happen," Tricia told him, hoping that she would be the one who was right, and not him.

Her mother's party was a celebration fit for a queen and resembled one. The venue was perfectly decorated like a palace with her mother seated at the front on a throne, wearing a crown and even carrying a scepter. There were a band and a deejay, food, liquor, and more food, and a huge cake, and more liquor. Everyone was in attendance: all of her mother's friends, coworkers, family, and church members, enough people for Tricia to not only slip out undetected when she needed, but also to avoid her siblings, who were too busy entertaining guests and enjoying themselves. Tank seemed to be having fun with a few of the other teenagers in attendance.

"From Titus," Tricia said after they all sang "Happy Birthday." She presented her mother with the gift-wrapped box her husband sent.

"It's beautiful." Her mother gasped as she opened it and took out the silver bangle bracelet holding the same three charms he'd given Tricia. Other onlookers oohed and aahed at the gift.

"And this is from me." Tricia handed her another box.

"Mama, we agreed we would open your gifts at home, not here, remember?" Felicia stated.

"This gift is special." Tricia rolled her eyes.

"All of the gifts are special," Felicia said in a tone that was as stiff as the fake smile on her face. "We don't want to take away from the party by opening gifts."

"She can just open this one," Tricia said.

"Yes, she can, at home." Felicia took the box from their mother and handed it to Violet's soon-to-be ex-husband. "Can you put this over there with the other gifts?"

"No problem." He shrugged.

"Okay, Mama. Let's go cut this cake." Felicia brushed past Tricia and took their mother by the hand.

Although she wanted to, Tricia refrained from cussing her sister out. The last thing she needed was for Felicia to have an opportunity to say Tricia embarrassed the family. Instead, she went and found her son and told him it was time to leave.

"Man, you can go. I'm staying," Tank told her.

"No, we're leaving now. Let's go. I'm not coming back to get you."

"I can Uber back to the hotel. Or get Aunt Violet or someone else to bring me," Tank said. "Plus, I want some cake."

The teens Tank was sitting with were all staring at her. Tricia felt herself become flushed. "Fine."

Tricia returned to the hotel alone. After getting undressed, she called Titus to tell him what happened.

"I already know," he said. "Tank told me."

"Told you what?" Tricia asked.

"That you threw a temper tantrum over your gift and left during the cake cutting," Titus told her. "He said the party was off the chain though and the cake was the bomb. I told him to bring me a piece."

"Titus, I didn't throw a temper tantrum." Tricia sighed. "I was just ready to go. You know how my sisters are. "

"And I know how you are. But listen, I'm about to go hit this gym. Tell Tank he'd better run that cake off on the treadmill in the morning."

"I'm going to tell him something all right," Tricia said. But she forgot all about the choice words for her traitorous son, because by the time he got back to the hotel room, she was fast asleep. When she woke up the following morning, he was already down in the hotel fitness center. By the time he got back to the room, he barely had time to take a shower, get dressed, and pack for their return flight home. They were stopping at her mother's house on the way to the airport to discuss the plans for the retirement party that Tricia had volunteered to pay for.

"You know you don't have to do this," her mother said as they sat in the kitchen. "Your sister just threw me that big old birthday party. Don't you think a retirement party would be overkill?"

"Don't be ridiculous, Mama," Tricia insisted. "You worked for that post office for over forty years. You deserve to celebrate, and I'm gonna make sure it happens."

"Okay, if you wanna do it, then who am I to object?" Her mother laughed.

Tricia took out a pen and the notepad she'd bought specifically for this purpose and flipped it open. "Now, what date are we looking at?"

"Well, I believe my last day of work is in July."

"Okay, July." Tricia's cell phone rang, and she took it out of her purse. "Hello. Hey, yeah, he's right here. Tank, phone." She walked into her mother's living room, where Tank was sitting and watching *SportsCenter*.

"Who is it?" He frowned.

"Take the phone." She held it out, and he took it from her hand.

"Hello?"

"I want cereal!" Bethany toddled into the living room and yelled.

"Bethany, come back here and put your shoes on." Violet chased after her.

"I'm sorry, I can't hear you," Tank said, putting a finger into his ear that didn't have Tricia's phone pressed to it.

"Go outside on the porch so you can hear better. There's too much going on in here to have a decent phone conversation." Tricia rolled her eyes at Violet, who was now tossing a still-whining Bethany onto the sofa with one hand and trying to hold a pair of tiny sneakers with the other.

"Bethany, stop," Violet pleaded.

Tank opened the door and slipped outside, and Tricia went back into the kitchen.

"Was that Titus? You should've let me talk to him to thank him for my gift," her mother said.

"No, Ma, it wasn't him. It was someone else," Tricia said. "Now back to these party plans. How many guests do you think will be there?"

"I don't really know." Her mother shrugged.

"Well, how many do you wanna invite?" Tricia asked.

"I'm not sure."

"Mama, you've gotta give me something to work with." Tricia sighed.

"Work with for what?" Felicia asked as she walked into the kitchen. After hugging their mother, she handed her a small handbag. "Hey, Mama, Aunt Bertha left her purse last night. She told me to drop it off here, and she'll come pick it up after church."

"Thank you, baby. And thank you again for everything you did yesterday. I just can't stop smiling. That wasn't just a party. It was something else." Her mother smiled and shook her head.

"I'm glad you enjoyed it, Mama." Felicia poured herself a cup of coffee and sat at the table. "I thought you were leaving today, Tricia."

"I am. Our flight leaves in a couple of hours," Tricia said, closing the notebook and putting it into the Chanel bag on the table in front of her.

"Tricia, your sister can probably give you the information you were asking me about."

Tricia shook her head. "No, Mama. I'll figure it out. We have a date. That's all I need for now."

"What information? Date for what?" Felicia asked.

Tricia stood. "I need to be getting to the airport."

"Tricia, sit down," her mother said. "You don't need to be getting nowhere. Come on and let's get this thing planned."

"What thing? What y'all doing?" Felicia asked again.

"Tricia's getting the ball rolling on my retirement party in July."

"Oh, okay. You did mention Tricia volunteering to be in charge of that."

Tricia could hear the sarcasm in Felicia's voice, and she knew her comment wasn't sincere. "I'm thinking a reception at one of the hotels would be nice, Mama. And we can reserve a block of rooms for out-of-town guests."

"I don't really have a lot of out-of-town people, Tricia. But a hotel party would be nice. That would probably cost a lot of money, though," her mother said.

"What about a nice brunch? They're a little less expensive, and that would be really different," Felicia suggested.

"I'm not worried about how expensive it is. My husband and I have plenty of money, and we can afford to pay for whatever we need to."

"Sorry," Felicia said. "Well, you and your husband go right ahead."

"Cereal! Cereal!"

Violet came in, carrying Bethany on her hip. "I'm making you cereal right now."

"Violet, let Deon know I appreciate all of his help last night and thank him for bringing the gifts over to the house for me," Felicia said.

"You know he only did all that to get in my good graces," Violet said. "If I say thank you, he's gonna expect me to show him my gratitude, and that ain't happening."

"Who knows, that gratitude might be just the thing y'all need to work on y'all issues." Felicia laughed.

"Gratitude and a good meal work wonders for reconciliation." Her mother gave Violet a suggestive look. "I saw y'all dancing last night all lovey-dovey."

"You peeped that too, Mama?" Felicia gave their mother a high five, and they giggled.

"Y'all need to stop it." Violet shook her head.

"You better listen to me, baby sis. If you want, I can give you some great recipes for the kitchen and the bedroom." Felicia elbowed Violet, then took Bethany from her and whispered loudly, "I'm gonna get your mama and daddy back right."

Tricia shook her head and murmured, "I'd be careful taking advice from someone with that track record."

"What did you say?" Felicia's head whipped around, and she glared at Tricia.

"Tricia, stop. That's wrong," Violet said.

"Why is it wrong? Her track record for marriage isn't the best. She's zero for two: two marriages, two divorces. That's damaging. If you really wanted some sound advice, I would think you would ask someone in a solid marriage for over a decade. I'm just saying."

Felicia looked at Violet, then back to Tricia. "Are you calling me damaged because I had the strength and sense enough to leave situations that are toxic, rather than staying in them? Because that ain't the case. I'm educated, successful, accomplished, financially stable, beautiful, and I'm very capable of keeping a man."

"And yet you don't have one, correct?" Tricia responded.

"Tricia," her mother said.

"By choice, honey, not by force," Felicia snapped. "And I support Violet whether she stays married or chooses to walk away."

"And I appreciate that, sis." Violet gave her a nod of approval.

"All I'm saying is it don't even take all of that," Tricia said.

"All of what?" Violet frowned.

"You don't have to cook, clean, work fifty hours a week, or even do tricks in the bedroom. I do none of that, and I have managed to keep a man, a good man," Tricia said matter-of-factly. "Face it, the reason you don't have a man and yours has one foot out the door is because you don't know what you're doing."

"And you do?" Violet yelled.

"Obviously." Tricia nodded. She'd been waiting years for this conversation to happen, and the time had finally arrived, and she was ready. "When I had Tank, y'all talked about me and swore that I was gonna end up a welfare mother. But I didn't. When I got married, y'all swore it wasn't gonna last, but it did. You walk around here with your degrees and job titles, thinking you're better than I am, but guess what? You ain't. The jealousy the two of you have for me is sickening."

"Jealous? Did she say jealous?" Felicia asked Violet.

"You girls need to stop. This is going too far now," her mother warned.

"She can't be talking about us. Jealous of what?" Violet squinted at Tricia as she waited for her to answer.

"Of me, of my husband, my son, my life." Tricia looked her younger, much smaller sister up and down. "The two of you were the pretty ones, and I was the fat one who everyone thought would end up alone. But look at me."

Felicia stood up, placing Bethany into their mother's arms. Tricia thought she was going to approach her, but instead, she stepped closer to Violet. "So, because you somehow lucked up and got knocked up by a man who stepped up and did the right thing by you, that makes you superior?"

"In some ways it does," Tricia said smugly.

"You really are pitiful." Felicia turned and smiled at Violet. "Did you know she was this pathetic?"

"It's sad, huh?" Violet shook her head.

"What's pathetic about me? How am I pitiful?" Tricia demanded.

Felicia looked her in the eye and said, "I almost feel sorry for her."

"Me too." Violet nodded.

"Let it go," their mother pleaded.

"You don't even realize," Felicia continued as she took slow, deliberate steps toward Tricia.

"Realize what?" Tricia's voice stammered. She was curious as to what her sister was talking about.

"Your husband, the one you're bragging and boasting about, ain't in love with you." Felicia continued walking until she was standing directly in front of Tricia. "And what's even sadder is that he's never been in love with you. And that's sadder than all of my failed relationships combined."

"Felicia, that's enough!" her mother screamed, startling Bethany, who began to cry.

Tricia stared at Felicia, looking for some sign of evil that would have prompted her to say such a thing, but the only thing she saw was pity. Her sister wasn't angry or disgusted when she stated what she said. She meant each and every word, and that was what infuriated Tricia.

"You bitch." Tricia's voice was stoic, as was her face. She grabbed her purse and rushed out of the house, damn near bumping into Tank, who was about to walk in.

"Here." He shoved her phone into her hand. "He wants to talk to you."

"We're leaving," Tricia told Tank. "Get in the car."

"I need to say goodbye to everyone."

"Get in the car."

"Hello, hello?" A voice came through the phone. "Tricia, you there?"

Tricia put the phone to her ear. "Hello."

"Thanks for letting me talk to him. I'm hoping I got through to him," Everett said.

"He's not in love with me? He's never been in love with me? How?" Tricia mumbled.

"Huh? Tricia, are you okay?" Everett asked.

"Why would she even say that to me?" Tricia whispered, still trying to process what Felicia said.

"Tricia." Her mother stepped onto the front porch and called out to her.

"I have to go," Tricia said, ending the call. She looked over to her mother. "I'll call you when we get home."

"Tricia, baby, wait. Talk to me for a minute. Felicia was just having a moment, that's all."

"It's fine. We have to go," Tricia yelled at Tank, who was leaning against the rental car. "Come hug your grandmother and say bye."

Tank sauntered over and hugged her mother. "Goodbye, Grandmother. I'll be sure to send you my graduation invitation."

"And make sure you send me some pictures, too."

"I will. Dad is taking me to take my cap and gown pictures this week."

Tricia unlocked the doors and got behind the wheel of the car. When Tank climbed in, she started the engine.

"You're driving?" He sounded surprised. "I can't believe you made me talk to that guy. I told you I'm not going to that school. It's my choice, not yours. Dad is gonna be pissed when he finds out."

Tricia glanced over at him and said, "Fasten your seat belt."

She backed out of her mother's driveway and drove to the airport without saying another word.

Chapter 17

Sylvia

"I have a surprise for you," Kenny said. "Come outside."

"Kenny, we have a meeting at Councilman Rogers's office in thirty minutes. I don't have time for surprises, and neither do you," Sylvia told her business partner. Here they were about to have one of the biggest meetings they'd had since starting their company three years ago, and he was playing games. She loved Kenny, and he was the ideal person to work with, the yang to her yin, but he could be a little too laidback at times.

"I know we have a meeting, Syl. I was the one who scheduled it, remember?" Kenny told her. "Grab your purse and come on. We can ride together."

"I have an appointment this afternoon. I need to—"

"Syl, just come on and bring your ass," Kenny groaned. "Damn, can't even surprise you."

"I'm coming." Sylvia grabbed her purse and laptop bag and headed downstairs. "Aunt Connie, I'm gone. I'll be back after I pick up Peyton."

"I'll be here," Aunt Connie yelled from another part of the house. "The pot roast and potatoes will be ready when you get home. And I'm making homemade rolls."

Jesus, I told her no heavy meals during the week, Sylvia thought as she walked out the front door. She loved her cooking and the convenience of meals being prepared daily. But if her aunt didn't start making some healthier meals, she was gonna have to actually utilize the gym membership she paid for every month.

"What do you think?" Kenny yelled as soon as she stepped out the door.

Sylvia stopped in her tracks and held her breath as she stared not at him, but the vehicle he was standing beside. There, parked in her driveway, was her dream vehicle: a candy-apple red Range Rover Sport. It was as if God were shining directly on it and she heard angels singing in the background.

"Oh my God," Sylvia said as she approached Kenny. "Where did you get this?"

"You know my boy Gene, the wholesale buyer? He called and told me to come pick it up." Kenny beamed.

Sylvia ran her fingers along the beautiful exterior. "You lucky bastard."

"It ain't for me. It's for you," Kenny said.

"What?" Sylvia looked at him as if he were crazy. "Me?"

"Yeah. Everyone knows how long you've talked about this damn truck. He immediately told me to bring it so you can check it out. Now, let's go. Here." He tossed her the key fob and jumped in the passenger seat.

Sylvia was too stunned to move at first. She stood, mouth gaped, eyes glued to the fob she was holding, and wondering if someone was playing some kind of prank. Her eyes blinked, and she decided that if he was, she was going to take full advantage of it while she could until whoever was punking her jumped out and said, "Gotcha." As she got behind the wheel and submerged herself in the luxury that now encompassed her, she inhaled and grinned. The Range Rover was just as beautiful on the inside as it was on the outside.

"I take it you like it?" Kenny laughed.

"Like is an understatement. Oh, wait." Her body turned, and she reached for her purse that was in the back seat, rummaging inside until she found what she was looking for. She pulled out the Gucci sunglasses, which she splurged and bought over a year ago and rarely wore, and placed them on her face. "Okay, I'm ready."

"Really, Syl?" Kenny shook his head at her.

"Look, I may never get the chance to drive anything like this again. I at least need to look good driving it. Let me have my moment."

Sylvia took the longest, most scenic route ever to the office building where their meeting was being held. What normally should have been a fifteen-minute drive took over twenty, and though she was usually anal about punctuality, Sylvia wasn't bothered that they had no time to spare when she pulled into the parking lot. She was on cloud nine as she floated into the conference room where Councilman Derrick Rogers was waiting for them. The anxiety and nervousness that Sylvia had felt all week preparing for their consultation had somehow disappeared, and by the time she finished with her presentation, they had signed a contract: one of the biggest since starting their company.

"We did it." Kenny clapped as they walked out of the building and into the parking lot.

"That was incredible. All of our work and preparation paid off. I can't believe this." Sylvia gave him a high five. "That video you created was perfect."

"Nah, your delivery was what did it. Man, Syl, I ain't seen you this confident in a long time. You blew them away," Kenny told her. "I admit, I was a little worried with everything you got going on right now, but you handled it."

"You were doubting me?" Sylvia gasped and placed her hand on her chest.

"No, I would never doubt you. I just hoped your head would be in the game when it was time. And it was."

They arrived at the Range Rover, and Sylvia touched the hood. "It was the truck. It brought me good luck."

"Well, that's a sign that you definitely need to buy it," he said.

"Syl, wait!"

Sylvia turned around to see Hampton Davis, Lynne's ex-husband, waving as he approached them. Any other time, she would've just waved back and kept it moving, but considering that he had been the one to set up the meeting with the city councilman, who also happened to be his cousin, she waited to speak with him. She at least owed him that much.

"Hey, Hamp."

"I heard the meeting went well and congratulations are in order." Hampton smiled.

"Indeed they did," Kenny told him.

"That's great. I told Derrick he would be impressed with your work, and he was. He's already making a call to the tourism office about hiring you to work on a project in their department," Hampton informed them.

"Are you serious?" Sylvia looked over at Kenny, who seemed just as pleased to hear this information as she was.

"Very serious. I just wanted to say congrats and tell you this is just the beginning for you guys," Hamp told her.

"Well, Hamp, we appreciate you looking out and putting the word in for us," Sylvia said.

"It was no big deal. I mean, despite what went down with me and my situation, I still consider you a friend, Syl. And that's what friends do. They look out for one another." Hamp smiled.

"You're right about that," Kenny told him.

"Undoubtedly, it was what you all presented in there that impressed them and sealed the deal, but who knows, maybe one day you can return the favor."

"You know we will." Kenny shook Hampton's hand.

"I'll catch y'all later, and congratulations again," Hampton said, then walked back to the building.

"Why would you tell him that?" Sylvia asked Kenny as she unlocked the doors and they climbed inside.

"What?" Kenny asked innocently.

"I'm not promising to return nothing. My loyalty is to my best friend, not him," Sylvia reminded him. "The same best friend whose life he almost ruined."

"The same best friend who told you to reach out to him about this opportunity. I mean, he's legit. And because of him looking out, now you can really buy this thing."

"I wish I could. Garry would have a damn cow. You know how many times I've said I wanted this truck. It's not really practical, and I know he's gonna say no now that Peyton is going off to school and Jordan is with us. I mean, I wish I could, but not this time. One day though."

"I hear you, Syl, but at least see what Gene is talking about. You saying all this without even knowing how much it costs. Which, by the way, I do, and I'm telling you right now, it's one helluva deal," Kenny said as he typed an address into the truck's GPS system. "But it's up to you. Now take me back over there to get my car."

"Wait, I need to go to my house to get my own car first," Sylvia said, adjusting her Gucci frames. "I have another appointment I can't be late to."

"Sounds like we need to hurry and get over to Gene's place then. Drive."

Instead of arguing, Sylvia followed the instructions the GPS gave her, and they arrived at Gene's small lot. Sylvia took her time getting out of the SUV, not wanting to relinquish the key just yet. Gene walked out of the building and to them.

"Whatcha think?" he asked.

"I think it's pure perfection," Sylvia told him.

"The moment I saw it, I thought about you, so I went ahead and got it even before I called Kenny to tell him," Gene said. Sylvia handed the key fob out to him, but he didn't take it. "Why you giving that to me?"

"Kenny said he was picking his car up. I'll ride with him," Sylvia said.

"You don't like the Range?"

"I love the Range. But I can't get it right now." Sylvia sighed. "My child is headed to college, and I have some other major stuff going on, Gene. I appreciate you trying to look out for me, though."

"Sylvia, just take it for a couple of days and check it out. We are family, and I know how long you been wanting this thing. I got it for a helluva deal, so you know I'm gonna look out. Just keep it 'til the weekend, and then let me know." Gene shrugged.

"I'll just be torturing myself." Sylvia tried to hand him the key again, but he refused.

"Sylvia, didn't you say you had somewhere to be?" Kenny walked over and opened the door for her. "I'll hit you up later about the York web design I came up with."

Sylvia looked at her watch and saw that she was now pressed for time and needed to get to her appointment. "I don't know why I'm doing this. I'll see you guys later."

"I like them shades, too, Syl." Gene laughed. "They look as good on you as this truck does."

Sylvia enjoyed her luxury ride and smiled all the way to the church. There were a few empty spots available near the front door, but she didn't want to chance anyone parking too close and dinging the Range Rover with their carelessness, so she parked in a space where the entire row was empty. She stepped out and admired the truck once more before walking away.

"Syl?"

She turned to see Garry a few feet away from her. "Garry, what are you doing here?"

"I came to, uh . . . Well, you said you were meeting with Amanda, and I was gonna see if we could meet with her together."

"I thought you were in Phoenix this week," Sylvia said, not only surprised to see her husband, who was supposed to be out of town until the weekend, but also because he'd shown up for the counseling appointment she'd mentioned the weekend before.

"I was, well, I am. I fly back out on the red-eye tonight and go back."

"You flew in today just for this? And you're flying right back out?"

"Yeah, I did."

"Wow," Sylvia said, impressed by his effort but still cautious.

"It's not as if I don't have plenty of frequent flyer miles to use," he said with a faint smile.

"You do have a point."

Garry's eyes went past her. "Syl, whose truck is that?"

She'd been so shocked to see Garry that she nearly forgot about the Range Rover. She turned around and said, "It's a loaner. Well, not exactly a loaner, but more like a test drive. Kenny's cousin Gene, he told me to check it out for a couple of days."

"Check it out for what?" Garry asked.

"Check it out to see if I wanna buy it. I need to get in there. I'm almost late."

They went inside the doors of the church that led to the administrative wing, where Amanda's office was located. Even though the door was open and Amanda was sitting at her desk, Sylvia still knocked.

"Right on time." Amanda looked up and smiled. "Come on in."

"Um, Amanda, I'm not alone." Sylvia moved to the side so that Garry, who was standing behind her, could be seen. "I didn't know he was coming. He didn't tell me anything."

"Well, what a welcome surprise. Come on in, you two." Amanda waved them inside her office and then rose from behind the desk and hugged the two of them. Sylvia took her usual seat on the end of the sofa, and Garry sat beside her. After closing the office door, Amanda said, "It's so good to see you, Garry."

"Good to be here, Amanda." Garry nodded.

"Let's start with prayer." Amanda reached out for their hands. Garry and Sylvia stood up, and they formed a mini circle and bowed their heads.

"Amen," they all said when she finished and took their seats.

"Well, since you're here, Garry, for the first time, why don't you start by sharing a little bit of what made you attend this session. And please know this is a safe space," Amanda said.

Garry shifted uncomfortably, then cleared his throat. "Oh, uh, I ain't think I'd be going first."

"It's okay." Amanda gave him a nod of encouragement.

"I wanted to come to show my wife that I'm willing to work on our marriage and our family. It was my actions that got us to this point of brokenness, and now I have to take action and fix us," Garry said. "I love her, and I'll do whatever I need to do, even if that means flying home every Wednesday and coming here with her."

Sylvia stared at the carpeted floor, listening to what Garry said. She knew that he meant well, and she was appreciative of his effort.

"Sylvia," Amanda said.

"I'm surprised to see him, and glad." Sylvia nodded. "It's a step in the right direction?"

Amanda titled her head to the side. "Is that a question or a statement?"

"Both, I think. Does that sound crazy?" Sylvia asked.

"There's no such thing when it comes to your feelings. So to answer your question, no, it doesn't sound crazy," Amanda said, which made Sylvia feel a little better about her statement.

"I believe our biggest problem is communication," Garry volunteered. "We've always worked great as a team, and we talk our way through the tough moments. But we've hit a wall that we can't seem to get past. And it's frustrating both of us."

"Okay." Amanda looked over at Sylvia, but before she could say anything, Garry continued.

"Prime example, she says that I make decisions without discussing them, but today, she pulls up in a new Range Rover that she hasn't mentioned. That's a major decision, isn't it? So I'm just trying to figure this all out and get us back on track." Garry sat back and crossed his leg at the knee. "She said she wanted me out of the house. I find another place to move, and she's upset. We have a breakdown in communication that's tearing us apart."

"Sylvia, how do you feel about what he's saying?" Amanda quickly asked.

Sylvia took a slow, deep breath before she responded and took a moment to reflect on everything she'd discovered about their marriage over the past few months. Her first instinct was to agree with everything Garry was saying, because in some ways, he was right. Then she thought about the journey of self-discovery that she'd recently started and was glad that they were in what she'd come to feel was a safe space to release and talk about her feelings. It wasn't the time to back down and accept what he said. It was time to speak up.

"We most definitely have a communication issue. Right now, we're both juggling a lot both in our separate lives and as a family, and it's just a lot to discuss most of the time. So as much as we talk, we usually end up arguing," Sylvia said. "So, to avoid arguing, we just don't talk."

"And that's where the problem comes in—" Garry started.

"But that's not our biggest issue or what's tearing us apart. It's not," Sylvia interrupted him, and he turned with a look of surprise.

"Continue, Sylvia," Amanda said softly. "What do you think is the cause of the marital breakdown?"

Sylvia looked up at Amanda. "Trust issues."

"Syl, I've told you over and over again that what happened with Randi only happened once. It was a mistake, and I regret that it took place. And God knows I'm sorry, but I've never been with anyone else. You are my everything, and I promise I'll do anything to make it up to you and protect you and our family. You can trust me," Garry pleaded. "I've apologized, and I'll say sorry however many times I need to. You said you forgave me."

"I do forgive you, Garry. But you still don't get it. You still can't see it," Sylvia told him.

"See what? What don't I see? That no matter what I do these days, it's wrong? That even though I've been trying to fix it, you're not satisfied? You said you were fine with Jordan coming to live with us. But—"

"Stop it, Garry. Please stop." Sylvia shook her head. "This has nothing to do with Jordan or Randi or even the one-night stand you had. It's not about me trusting you."

"Then what do you mean?" Garry asked.

"Sylvia, explain it," Amanda told her.

Sylvia turned and looked at Garry. "You don't trust me."

"That's ridiculous. I know you would never cheat on me, Syl." Garry reached for her hand that was lying on the sofa, but she pulled away.

"I'm not talking about infidelity, Garry. I'm talking about that you don't have enough faith in who I am or what I am to trust me." The words came tumbling out all at once. She kept talking for fear that if she stopped, she wouldn't have the courage to start again. "Whenever there's a problem, an issue, or a concern, you expect us to bring it to you, and you step in and fix it. You handle it. You make the decision."

"I'm your husband, Syl. That's what I'm supposed to do." Garry frowned.

"But when it comes to your problems, hurts, and traumas, you don't bring them to me, but I'm your wife." Tears welled in Sylvia's eyes. "I'm wondering when I became some weak woman you can't even confide in when you're hurting, or angry, or afraid. You've protected me since the day we fell in love, and I let you because I thought it was because you loved me. But it's not. It's a control mechanism that you do not out of love, but out of fear. And that's what I've come to realize and what is tearing us apart: you are married to a woman who you don't trust."

Sylvia looked over at Garry. He sat, staring at the floor in front of him, not saying a word.

"Garry?" Amanda said.

"I'm okay," he answered. "I'm just listening and processing right now."

"Garry, do you feel like it's your sole responsibility to handle all of the problems and challenges you guys face?" Amanda asked.

"I thought that was my role as a husband and a father. I make sure everyone and everything is good. I work hard. I am a great provider. I am supportive and loving." Garry nodded. "I guess I didn't realize it was a problem, so forgive me if I'm a little confused."

"You are all of those and more," Sylvia agreed. "But you're not perfect. You've never come to me with anything you're dealing with. We've been together almost twenty years, and I can't recall a time when you've ever come to me because you've been worried, or sad, or stressed out. You never complain about anything. The only time I've heard you admit to being afraid of anything was the other day when you admitted being scared that Sherrod would fight for custody of Jordan. And that was only because of what happened at the game. You are the king of hiding things, and then you wonder why your children don't share anything with us. It's learned behavior. It's a trust factor."

"But, Garry, why don't you feel comfortable sharing your fears or concerns with Sylvia?" Amanda offered.

"Because he believes I'm weak," Sylvia answered for him.

"Sylvia." Amanda warned, "Allow him to speak."

Sylvia relaxed in her seat, wondering how she'd allowed them to get to this point. If Randi's death hadn't happened and Garry's biggest secret revealed, would this be happening? Until that point, their marriage was fine? Would she have even realized that Garry considered her somewhat of a trophy wife: a pretty woman he had at home to raise their daughter and have sex with?

"Because I love my wife, and she has enough on her plate, raising our daughter and taking care of the home while I'm gone most of the time working. I don't know where this whole trust thing is coming from, because I've trusted her enough for years, long enough to handle our household while I'm not there," Garry said. "I trusted and believed in her enough to tell her to quit a job she hated and start her own business."

Sylvia flinched, pinched by his words. "No, you told me to quit my job to, yet again, fix a problem. I wanted to report the issues I was having with my boss to HR, and you said, 'No, just quit. I make enough to support our family anyway. You don't have to even deal with those people. Quit.' And so I did. In the end, it worked out and ended up being the right decision, but it was your way of fixing it so you wouldn't have to hear me complaining. You fixed it. Quit, end of discussion. Same way you're sitting here fuming about that Range Rover in the parking lot."

"Because number one, buying a new car, especially an expensive one, makes no sense right now. Peyton is going off to school, and that's gonna have additional expenses for me to take care of. The budget can't handle it right now. I might have to hire a lawyer for this custody thing with Sherrod." Garry tossed his hands up in frustration.

Sylvia looked up. Amanda's eyes met hers, and they exchanged a look of understanding.

"What?" Garry asked, seeing the exchange.

"Garry, I want you to just take a moment and think about what you just said," Amanda told him.

Garry looked down and then closed his eyes. "Oh, I was speaking so fast, I said *I*, but I meant *we*."

"But that's not what you said," Amanda told him. "Although you may not realize it, your need to be the 'fixer' in your household has somehow overshadowed that you do have a partner to help you handle problems. You don't have to do it alone."

"I just want to do what's best for my—I mean, our—family. I want Syl to be happy."

"You're her husband, Garry, not her father. And you're not responsible for her happiness, she is. And right now, she's not happy because she's your helpmate, but she feels like you don't trust her enough to ask for or depend on her for help. That's not right, and that's not Biblical. Sylvia's right. You all have a trust issue."

Sylvia felt as if a load that she didn't even realize she'd been carrying had been lifted. Time and time again, she'd second-guessed her thoughts and feelings. Now they were finally out in the open, and they could begin working on them together. "Garry, listen, I don't want you to think this is a 'point out all of Gary's faults' session, because that's not what this is. I definitely have some deficits of my own."

Garry seemed surprised by her statement.

"You're not the only one who bears some fault in all of this. I've been so caught up in the freedom of not having to make decisions or avoiding difficult conversations when I didn't agree with one that you made, that I ignored a lot of stuff that bothered me. I was so glad that I didn't have the big problems in our marriage that other people had, like money issues, out-of-control kids, abusive situations, that I didn't want to bother you with the small issues. I should be able to recognize when something is bothering you. We should've both been more aware."

"You're right," Garry said.

"Well, I think this has been good, really good. How about the two of you?" Amanda asked.

"I agree." Sylvia nodded.

"Definitely," Garry said.

Amanda closed the session out in prayer and hugged them. Sylvia reassured her that she would be back for her appointment next week, while Garry just thanked Amanda for her time. They walked out of the building in silence.

"Thank you for coming, Garry," Sylvia told him.

"It was very, uh, enlightening."

"You coming back to the house? Aunt Connie cooked pot roast," Sylvia said. "I have to pick Peyton up from track practice."

"How about I pick her up instead?" Garry asked. "I mean, if it's okay with you."

Sylvia squinted at him. "Are you trying to be funny?"

"No, not at all."

"I think your picking her up would be a great idea. Thank you. I'll see you back at the house." Sylvia stepped closer and gave him a hug.

"Yeah."

Later, Sylvia was in the den, watching television with Aunt Connie when she heard the front door open.

"Mom, I'm home," Peyton yelled.

"Awesome. You and your dad can go ahead and get washed up for dinner so we can go ahead and eat," Sylvia yelled back.

"Uh, Dad's not here," Peyton appeared in the doorway and said. "He left."

"What do you mean, he left?" Sylvia stood.

"He said he had a flight to catch and he would see us this weekend. Is everything okay? Because he was acting kind of weird."

"Weird how?"

"I'm not sure, but it kinda looked like he'd been crying."

Chapter 18

Janelle

"Wow, that's deep. This whole situation is deep." Dexter sat back and stared at Janelle. They were finally on their sushi lunch date that she'd been postponing, and she caught him up on everything that had transpired in her life, including the basketball game drama and Tricia showing up at Sylvia's. She also explained who Sherrod was and the dilemma of dating him.

"Very deep." Janelle nodded.

"So, you're sure you wanna get involved with this guy, Janelle, especially considering the circumstances?" Dex asked, using his chopsticks to pick up a roll. "It sounds like it can get kinda complicated and messy."

"I know. Right now it is. But I have a plan."

"And what's that?"

"Well, I'm going to utilize my job skills and training, and I'm going to mediate. I mean, I am certified," she said, taking a sip of her sake. The blank look on Dex's face was not the reaction she was expecting or hoping for. "What?"

"That's your plan?" He sighed.

"What's wrong with that? I've already convinced Sherrod to have a sit-down meeting with Sylvia. Now all I have to do is get her on board and agree."

"And what about Garry?"

"See, that's the beauty of this plan. I'm going to get Sylvia and Sherrod on the same page, and they can combine forces and win." Janelle nodded. "Brilliant, huh?"

"Let me get this straight. Your plan is to convince Sylvia to partner with her husband's archnemesis, who is trying to snatch his daughter from him? And that's gonna uncomplicate things?"

Janelle exhaled loudly, "Well, when you say it like that, it makes me sound evil and sinister, which I'm not. The thing is right now, Sylvia is looking at Sherrod through this tainted lens, and I want her to see that he truly does have Jordan's best interest at heart. Once she understands that and sees the side of him that I do, things will be better."

"And you can't just explain that to her?" Dex asked. "Like, 'Syl, I know you're not really feeling Sherrod right now, but I would like for you to sit down and get a better understanding about who he is and his relationship with Jordan and Randi.'"

"That's what I said I was gonna do." Janelle tossed her hands up dramatically.

"Uh, no, you said you wanted them to combine forces against Garry and win," Dex pointed out.

"Well, they do have that option, and it would give her more incentive to sit down and meet with him. I'm not saying she has to."

"I would definitely leave that part out if I were you. Now, what about the other thorn on the rose that is Sherrod?" Dex asked.

"Nivea." Janelle stated the name Dex was referring to. "Can't I just wait and tell her?"

"Janelle, you just sat here and told me that Sherrod encompasses everything you want in a guy and more. You enjoy being with him, you're attracted to him, and you're actually ready to pursue a real future with him, something you haven't considered doing with anyone in a long time. She's one of your best friends, and she deserves to be told. And I'm thinking she's probably gonna be just as happy for you as I am." Dex reached across the table and touched her hand.

Janelle smiled. "You're happy for me, Dex?"

"I am. I've always told you that you're amazing and deserve to be with someone as awesome as I am." Dex nodded. "And Sherrod sounds like he may just be it."

Janelle screamed with laughter as she snatched away from him. "I can't stand you, Dex."

"You can. But I am rooting for you, and if you believe Sherrod is worth all of this, then I'm rooting for him too. But you owe Sylvia and Nivea a conversation. Today."

"Today?" Janelle's eyes widened. "But it's Friday. Fridays are supposed to be for fun."

"Yep, today," Dex said. "Both of them."

"Cheers to the freakin' weekend." Janelle gulped down her remaining sake.

Janelle decided that of both the difficult conversations she was tasked to have, the one with her sister would probably be the more difficult one. They hadn't talked since their exchange of words outside the restaurant almost a week ago. Every time she went to reach out, she stopped.

As she sat at her desk, she closed her eyes and sent the quick text, asking if she could stop by after work before giving it a second thought. If she had, she probably would've changed her mind. She was relieved when Sylvia messaged her back, saying that she wasn't home but on her way to Peyton's school to watch the track team. Janelle was overjoyed because this gave her the opportunity to talk to Syl in public. She hurried out of the office and over to the school.

Her eyes scanned the back parking lot of the school, but she didn't see Sylvia's car. Fighting the urge to leave, she decided to go over to the bleachers and wait for her there. To her surprise, when she walked through the gate, she heard Sylvia yelling.

"Come on, ladies! Let's go!"

Janelle climbed the steps and made her way beside her. "Hey."

Sylvia looked surprised. "Hey, what are you doing here?"

"I came to check on you." Janelle gave her a quick hug.

"Oh, really?" Sylvia smirked. "Why?"

"Because you're my sister, Syl. That's why."

"Let's go, Peyton!" Sylvia yelled again as Peyton came running full speed ahead past them.

"Run, P, run!" Janelle screamed, then said, "How are you?"

"I'm fine."

"That's good. And the girls, they're okay?"

"They are."

"I already know Aunt Connie is fine. I heard about the surprise visitor."

Sylvia shook her head. "God, that was so funny."

Janelle could see a faint smile, even though she still wasn't looking at her. "I bet it was. I don't know why she's playing so hard to get. That man likes her."

"You know she's a hard nut to crack and loves playing hard to get."

"I love that woman. Sometimes I wonder how it would be if Mama were still here and they were hanging out together at this age. The Golden Girls wouldn't have nothing on them, that's for sure." Janelle sighed with a soft laugh.

Sylvia closed her eyes for a second, then finally turned to Janelle. "Janelle, what is it that you want? You did not drive all the way the hell over here on a Friday evening to reminisce about Mama."

Janelle leaned forward a little and said, "I really did wanna check on you, Syl. But I wanna talk to you too."

"About what?" Sylvia asked.

"About the other night at the restaurant."

"There's nothing to talk about, Janelle." Sylvia stood up. "Didn't you say it was just dinner and no big deal?"

"I did. And it was. But Syl, I like Sherrod, and I want to date him," Janelle admitted.

Sylvia's eyes flashed with anger for a second. Then she said, "You're a grown-ass woman. Date who you want: Sherrod, Titus, and whoever else. I don't give a damn."

"Sylvia, wait," Janelle said as Sylvia stepped down then began to walk off. "Don't leave."

"Janelle, I don't have the time or energy to deal with this right now. I told you I don't care." Sylvia continued down the bleachers.

"But you're my sister. I want you to care."

"There are a lot of things in life I want, Janelle, but sometimes we don't always get what we want."

"Syl, please just stop and talk to me. I get it. I know it's real complicated right now. But if you just talk to me and let me explain . . ." Janelle damn near had to run to keep up with Sylvia, who was taking long strides across the parking lot.

"Explain what?" Sylvia finally stopped and turned around.

"Sherrod is a great guy."

"So I've heard," Sylvia said sarcastically.

"He is, Syl. But I think you met him under unusual circumstances, and your view of him is a little tainted. And right now, you both have one thing in common," Janelle said.

"And what's that?"

Her sister was a little more hostile than she anticipated, and having her agree to another meeting with Sherrod was going to be a long shot. So Janelle decided to ignore Dex's advice and go with her original idea.

"You both want Jordan. But the thing is, more than he wants custody of Jordan, Sherrod wants what's best for Jordan, and we all know right now that's with you," Janelle said matter-of-factly.

"What the hell are you saying, Nellie?" Sylvia folded her arms.

"I'm saying that the two of you sit down and talk for starters. You can understand Sherrod's relationship with Jordan and see that he doesn't have any kind of underlying motive or malicious intent. Then he can help you win physical custody of Jordan and you allow him visitation," Janelle explained. Sylvia stood and stared at her without saying anything. Janelle gave her a few seconds to process before she said, "Let's just sit down and talk, the three of us."

"You are amazing." Sylvia's words were slow and deliberate. "A-freakin'-mazing."

"I'm so glad to hear you say that." Janelle's excitement at her sister's words was short-lived when she looked over to see Sylvia storming off again. She chased her. "Syl, wait."

Sylvia kept repeating the word "amazing" over and over. Janelle was about to ask her where she parked when Sylvia stopped beside a gorgeous red Range Rover and opened the door.

"Just so we're clear, not only have you decided to pursue a relationship with this man, but he asked you to come and tell me he wants to sit down and talk to me?" Sylvia said.

"Syl, whose truck?"

"That's not important right now. Answer the question."

"Yes, he wants to talk." Janelle nodded.

"Man, that dick must be amazing." Sylvia shook her head in disbelief.

"What?" Janelle gasped. "Why would you say something like that?"

"Because it's gotta be. Why else would you have the audacity to try to convince me to not only have a sit-down with this man but form an alliance to go behind my husband's back and underhandedly scheme to take his daughter away from him? Obviously, you're dickmatized." Sylvia climbed into the shiny SUV.

Janelle was too stunned to speak.

"Aunt Nelle!" Peyton yelled from across the parking lot.

Janelle waved at her niece, then turned back to her sister. "Syl, I haven't even slept with him. And I swear, he didn't have me—"

"Janelle, that's what you said. Did you not say it was an invite for the three of us? I'm assuming that means you, me, and him, right?" Sylvia said. "I have to go. Tell your new boo Sherrod thanks, but no thanks."

"Syl, please wait," Janelle pleaded. "That's not what I meant."

"That's what you said," Sylvia said as she closed the door.

"Aunt Nelle, what are you doing here? I've missed you." Peyton ran up and hugged Janelle.

"I came by to see your mom and to check you out, speed demon." Janelle fluffed Peyton's long ponytail.

"Awww, thanks. That's why you're my favorite auntie," Peyton told her. "Aunt Nelle, guess what? Tank's dad knows a guy with a yacht, and he's gonna see if we can take prom pics on it. Wouldn't that be so cool?"

"A yacht? That would be the bomb. And for the record, I'm your only auntie." Janelle smiled.

Sylvia rolled the window down. "Peyton, is practice over?"

"No, we just got a five-minute break. Aunt Nelle, isn't this truck fire? I told Mom she looks amazing in it." Peyton smiled.

Janelle looked over at Sylvia and said, "Yeah, amazing."

"Get back out there, Peyton," Sylvia said. "I have an errand to run. I'll be back in a few."

"It was good seeing you, Aunt Nelle. I'll make sure to text you the schedule of our meets. Love you." Peyton hugged her again.

"Love you too, sweetie," Janelle said, then watched Peyton run back toward the school. By the time she turned back to talk to Sylvia, she was pulling off.

Janelle sighed and walked across the parking lot to her car. She truly should've listened to Dex. Not only had she failed to get Sylvia to agree to meet with Sherrod, she had somehow made things worse. As she headed over to Natalie's apartment, which was her next destination, she wondered if the conversation with Nivea was even going to be necessary, because her potential romance might be ending before it even began.

"You're hella early," Natalie said when she opened the door.

"I know. I brought tequila and limes," Janelle said as she walked in and flopped down on the sofa. Natalie's apartment was always warm and cozy, much like Sylvia's.

"Oh, damn, so are we happy or sad?" Natalie picked up the plastic bag of items Janelle brought in.

"All fucked up and confused," Janelle whined.

"Well, what is going on, friend?"

"There's too much to even tell right now. And I don't wanna say it twice. I just need a shot or two before Nivea gets here."

"Uh, well, you only have to tell whatever it is once, because unfortunately, she's not coming," Natalie called from the kitchen.

Janelle sat up. "What? She's flaking on us again? You lying!"

"Nope. She sent me a text and said something came up last minute and she would catch up with us later this weekend."

God, Janelle thought, *it's a sign*. A feeling of slight relief came over her since she no longer was faced with having to tell Nivea about Sherrod. She was still curious as to why her best friend was so unavailable these days.

"She definitely got somebody new," Janelle said.

Natalie walked in carrying a tray with the bottle of tequila, two shot glasses, a salt shaker, and the limes that were now sliced and in a tiny bowl, and placed it on the coffee table. She plopped down beside Janelle and said, "Now, why are we getting wasted tonight?"

Janelle stared at Natalie as she poured them each a shot. She really needed to talk but was hesitant. If she told Natalie before telling Nivea, there was a slight chance that Natalie would tell. Then again, even though she and Nivea had been friends longer, she still trusted Natalie. So she picked up the salt, poured it on the back of her hand, downed the shot in one gulp, then sucked the lime like a pro. A warm sensation came over her, and her nerves relaxed. She followed the same routine twice more, then proceeded to tell Natalie all about her dilemma.

Chapter 19

Tricia

"Well, your blood pressure is fine, and everything else looks good," Dr. McPherson said as Tricia sat on the examination table. "How long did you say you've been feeling ill?"

"A couple of days now," Tricia told him. "I went out of town last weekend, and it started when I got back."

It wasn't a lie. It had been one hell of a week, and she didn't feel like talking to anyone. Not only was there a blowup with her sisters at her mother's house, but Tank also gave her the silent treatment on the plane. Then there was Titus, who seemed to have an attitude when he picked them up from the airport. The ride home was quiet, and as soon as they got to the house, Titus unloaded the car, and then he and Tank went to basketball practice. Tricia couldn't get what Felicia and Violet said about Titus. She told herself they'd just said it to hurt her because they were jealous, and she wouldn't allow that to happen. She unpacked her bags and tried to push it out of her mind by settling into the den and watching her shows that she'd recorded.

A few hours later, she was in the kitchen, pouring herself a glass of wine when Titus and Tank came through the front door.

"That's why I had you work out while you were gone. See there." Titus laughed.

"I did work out, Dad. That ain't mean I was gonna be able to run suicide drills for fifteen minutes. Y'all tried to kill a brother." Tank chuckled.

Tricia stood in the doorway of the kitchen, watching father and son interact. Tank looked over at her, his smile left his face, and then he shook his head and ran up the stairs. She knew he was still upset with her about the phone call with Everett.

"What were you thinking when you made Tank talk to that dude? We already discussed that he wasn't going to Burke," Titus asked her.

"I was thinking that I want my son to hear everything they were offering him. And we didn't discuss anything. I didn't even know Burke was trying to recruit him until Ev . . . Mr. Matthews called me. I thought Tank should have an in-depth conversation with him one-on-one without any interruptions."

"You thought wrong."

"Don't tell me what to think, Titus. You forget sometimes that Tank is just as much my son as he is yours."

"Well, your actions over the past few years has demonstrated that you seem to have forgotten that too," he said, walking past her and into the kitchen.

She was right behind him. "What did you say?'

"Tricia, forget it, okay? I don't even feel like arguing about this." Titus opened the refrigerator and took out a beer.

"I don't care what you feel like doing, Titus." He went to walk past her, but she stood in front of him. "We're not done here."

"You may not be done, but I'm about to go watch the basketball game."

His dismissive tone made her even madder than she already was. He hadn't asked how the party went or about the trip. He hadn't called once while they were gone, although he did send a good morning text each day with a reminder for Tank to work out. Here she was, trying to talk to him about something that she felt was important about their son, and he was unbothered.

The words of her sisters echoed once again in her head as they'd done over and over again. She stared at Titus and asked, "Are you in love with me?"

Titus looked at her as if she were crazy, almost as if he was amused. "What? Oh God, here we go with the bullshit."

"It's not bullshit. It's a simple question. Answer yes or no."

"I'm not answering it at all." He tried to go around her once again, but she blocked him with her body.

"Answer the damn question."

"I don't know what's got you tripping, but I'm pretty sure it's got something to do with your sisters." He shook his head. "You need to go upstairs, lie down, and sleep it off, or online shop it off, or whatever it is you need to do to get your mind right. Now move."

"Are you in love with me, Titus? That's all I want to know."

Titus's eyes held mine for a moment. I searched them for some sort of affirmation, but there wasn't one. He took a swig of his beer. "Tricia, I just wanna watch the game, that's all."

"Have you ever been in love with me, Titus?" She sucked in her breath after the words left her mouth.

Again, he just looked at her for a second. "Why are you doing this?"

"Doing what? Asking you simple questions that you refuse to answer?"

"Letting whatever dispute, disagreement, dialogue you and your family had mess with your head. I know that's what this is. It happens every time you're around *them. Now they got you asking dumb-ass questions." He took another swig.*

"You haven't. Answered. The questions, Titus." She took breaths between her words.

"Tricia, I have taken care of you and Tank since the day he was born. I work hard, I go above and beyond to make sure both of you have everything you need and most of what you want. I'm a damn good father. I don't ask you for a dime to pay one bill in this house, which, by the way, is the house you picked out and wanted. I don't complain, I've never put my hands on you, I don't run the streets, and I bring my ass home every single night. About the only thing I do ask you for is ass every now and then, and at this point, I'm so used to getting turned down, I hardly ask for that either. It is what it is." Titus stared at her. "You and Tank have been my life for the past seventeen years, and from what I can see, you've lived a damn good life because I love both of you. Now you wanna stand here and question whether I'm in love with you? You're tripping. Now move so I can go watch the basketball game."

When he went to go around her that time, Tricia didn't stop him. She was too stunned not only by what he said, but also by what he didn't say. All this time, all these years, had they all been a lie? She'd thought her sisters were lying, but now she wasn't sure.

Tricia was an emotional wreck, to the point where she was physically ill and hadn't gone to work all week. Titus had tried to make nice, but she'd iced him out. Luckily, he had sense enough to leave her alone. Not that he had a lot of time to be concerned. Once again, he and Tank spent most of their time at practice. Titus would come home from work with dinner, shower, change clothes, then head over to the school. Tricia spent most of the week either in bed or in the den watching television. On

Saturday, her mother encouraged her to go to the doctor to make sure it wasn't anything more serious. So now, here she was at the urgent care clinic not too far from the house.

"I don't think it's any type of bug or virus you may have contracted either. I see in your chart that you've taken meds for anxiety and mild depression. Are you still taking them?" The doctor looked at her.

"When I need them." Tricia shrugged. It had been a while since she'd even filled her prescription, mainly because until Titus forced her to go to Tank's game, followed by his disappearing act, she hadn't really been stressed or anxious.

"Well, has anything major happened where you may have needed them and not had them?" he asked. "Everything okay at work and at home?"

Other than the fact that I just found out my husband has been lying to me for the past seventeen years? "Work is fine." Tricia sighed.

"Sounds like it may be something going on at home then." He said it as if he were talking to himself and not her. "I'm going to recommend you make a follow-up appointment with whatever doctor you're seeing for the antianxiety and antidepressant meds. Who's your therapist?"

"Therapist?" Tricia frowned. "I don't see a therapist."

"Who prescribed the meds for you?"

"My PCP," she said with an attitude. "I don't need no therapist. I'm not crazy."

"I didn't say that you were. But I'm sure when your PCP diagnosed you and gave you your prescription, he advised you to seek additional treatment."

Her doctor had suggested that she see a counselor, but he hadn't mandated it. And since the medicine he prescribed made her feel better, she didn't.

"Can't you just write me out the same prescription?" She frowned.

"Unfortunately, I can't. Listen, there's nothing wrong with seeing a therapist. Drugs do help temporarily, but you need to get to the root of whatever it is that's really making you sick."

"My family," Tricia murmured, not knowing if she was referring to her husband, son, or sisters, or maybe even all of them.

"Could be." Dr. McPherson stood. "And if that's truly the case, then I would advise seeing a family therapist."

"But I feel sick now. My stomach is in knots, and I feel nauseated all the time. Aren't you going to do something to help me?"

"I just did." He smiled and walked out of the room.

Titus called as she was pulling out of the parking lot. "What did the doctor say?"

"He said you're making me sick and we need to go to therapy," she said, twisting the doctor's words.

"I doubt that's what he said."

"I'm serious. And I think he may be right. So I'm going to find a therapist for us to go to counseling as a family."

"Nope, that ain't happening. You may go to see a therapist, but I'm not. I'm fine and so is Tank. I'm not gonna even disrupt his life with that all because you're tripping over some bullshit-ass question as a result of an argument with your sisters," Titus responded.

"It's not about you and Tank all the damn time, Titus. It's about us," Tricia said.

"What about us? Was something wrong with us before this weekend?"

Tricia remained quiet. Until her sisters made the statement, she really didn't have a problem with anything, well, not anything major. But the fact that he couldn't or wouldn't answer the question was still disturbing her. Certainly, a therapist would put him in a position where he would have to at least give her an answer and, if need be, show him his obvious neglect and disrespect by not only refusing to answer but causing her undue stress.

"We're going to therapy."

"Yeah, we'll see. Anyway, I'm glad it's nothing serious. I'll pick up pizza and bring it for dinner. You on your way back home?"

"No, I'm not," she told him, suddenly feeling the need to release the tension she now felt in her chest. "I'm going to the mall."

"You're going to the mall on a Saturday? Damn, see? You're feeling better already. No therapy needed. You got your favorite kind of therapy: retail." He hung up.

"That'll be $222.11," the woman who'd rung up her purchases in Lane Bryant told her.

Tricia handed her the store credit card, which was also paid for by Titus. After paying, Tricia put the card back in her wallet, gathered her bags, and walked out of the store, almost bumping into someone. Tricia opened her mouth to cuss out whoever it was, but the woman apologized before she could say anything.

"Oh, I'm sorry. Oh, Tricia."

Tricia realized it was Sylvia Blackwell, Peyton's mother. "Hello. Sylvia, right?"

"Yes. How are you? How is Tank? I heard about his being selected as a McDonald's All-American. That's incredible. I'm sure you're excited about that." Sylvia smiled. She was a pretty woman, average height and build, thick hair pulled off her face. She was wearing a red sweatshirt with sorority symbols on the front. Another woman who was with her wore a jacket with the same symbols. They both wore black leggings and tall black leather boots and carried just as many bags as Tricia, from various stores.

"He's good. And yes, we're quite excited." Tricia nodded. "This is my best friend, Lynne. Lynne, this is Tank's mom, Tricia."

"Nice to meet you. I've heard so much about your son and the fabulous prom plans." Lynne smiled.

"Prom plans?" Tricia frowned.

"Don't worry, I've told Peyton that those upscale ideas that she and Tank have will be scaled back. Pictures on a yacht? I don't think so." Sylvia laughed.

"Aw, come on, I think the photo session on the yacht was a fabulous idea." Lynne giggled, then asked Tricia, "Don't you think that's cute?"

Tricia had no idea what they were talking about. She felt the heat climbing the back of her neck, and she was uncomfortable. She considered laughing as if she were in on the joke, but she didn't have the energy or desire to be fake, so she simply said, "I don't know what you're referring to."

The two women glanced at one another, and their laughter subsided. Sylvia gave her an apologetic look. "Oh, Tank asked Peyton to be his prom date the other week. And he agreed to attend hers. I thought you knew."

"No, I didn't," Tricia told them.

"Well, with the upcoming All-American Game and decision day coming up, Tank probably hasn't had time to tell you. But I will definitely reach out and get with you to discuss logistics and details. I still have your number," Sylvia said.

"It was nice meeting you, Tricia. Congratulations to Tank again," Lynne said.

"Thank you."

The two ladies walked away, laughing and mumbling. Tricia imagined they were probably talking about her for some reason or another. She looked down at her own outfit: a Disney sweatshirt, ill-fitting jeans, and sneakers. Her braids were tucked into a bun at the back of her neck. She pushed her glasses up on her nose and headed to the food court. There seemed to be a line at each and every restaurant, and she stood in the center of the madness, trying to decide whether to endure the shrieks of the crying toddler throwing a tantrum in front of the hibachi spot, or just leave. Her cell phone rang, and she answered.

"Hello."

"Hey, Tricia. How are you?"

"Hi, Everett. I'm okay." She'd considered calling him to apologize for everything that had happened during their last phone call, Tank's rudeness, and her confused mumbling, but she was too embarrassed.

"That's good to hear. I was just calling to check on you. You seemed kind of upset last week."

"I'm sorry about that. I was in the middle of a moment when Tarik gave me the phone. And I'm sorry about his attitude, as well." Tricia walked over to a nearby empty table, set her bags in one chair, and sat in the other.

"Hey, no apologies needed for either one of you. And Tarik didn't have an attitude at all. He's a great young man who knows exactly what he wants, and that's a good thing. Not something to apologize for."

"I appreciate that. I tried talking some sense into him, but, I mean, I don't want you to feel as if you wasted your time."

"I don't think that at all. As a matter of fact, I have something for you."

"You do?" Tricia said.

"I do. I'll be in town early next week. If you'd like, we can meet up somewhere, or I can drop it off at your house."

Tricia thought about the reaction Titus would have if he saw or found out Everett was at their house, and she quickly said, "We can meet up. It's cool. Just let me know when and where."

"Great. I'll call you later in the week. Enjoy the rest of your weekend, Tricia. And again, thanks for at least allowing me to talk to Tank about his opportunities at Burke. You're a great mom."

"I appreciate that." Tricia smiled. By the time she got off the phone, her entire demeanor had changed, and she felt better than she had all week for some reason. Her phone rang again, and this time it was her mother.

"Hey, Ma," Tricia said, deciding to leave the crowded mall.

"Hey, baby. Are you okay? I've been calling and calling you."

"Yeah, I was under the weather a little this week, but I'm better. I'm leaving the mall."

"Shopping always makes you feel better," she said. "Are you sure you're okay?"

"I don't know, Ma. I went to the doctor, and he suggested that we go to family therapy, but Titus doesn't wanna go."

"Why do you need to go to therapy? Y'all having problems?"

"No, well, I don't know."

"Tricia, now you listen to me and you listen good. Ain't no point in trying to fix nothing that ain't broke. You said yourself you got a fine husband, a good son, and a nice family. You ain't have no complaints all this time, so why you complaining now?"

"Mama, I asked him if he was in love with me, and he ain't answer. He had the nerve to act offended."

"I don't blame him. I knew when them girls said that to you, it was gonna be a problem. Now look at you, being sick, trying to make him go to therapy." Her mother sighed. "You can't make a grown man do nothing he don't wanna do. Especially one who ain't got a reason to do it. Not answer no questions, not go to therapy, nothing."

Tricia didn't say anything. The light mood she felt moments before answering the phone was now gone, replaced by thoughts of Titus and his refusal to go to therapy, and now her mother telling her what she should or shouldn't be doing. Even more so, what she couldn't do.

"Tricia, you there?"

"Yeah, I'm here, Mama."

"You hear what I'm saying?"

"Yes, Mama." Tricia sighed, walking out of the mall, now feeling sick all over again. She looked across the parking lot and saw Sylvia and her friend laughing as they got into a black Volvo SUV. She thought about the plans her son had for prom and suddenly smiled. "Mama, I gotta go. I'll call you back tomorrow."

Chapter 20

Sylvia

"Syl, what's wrong?" Lynne asked.

Sylvia sat staring at the message on her phone that she'd just received that left her stunned and confused. She held the phone out so Lynne could see what she saw. "What the hell?"

"Girl, what?" Lynne sounded just as confused. "What happened? I'm so lost."

"Me too," Sylvia said as she tried calling the number that the message came from, but it went straight to voicemail. She hung up and tried dialing it again. Same thing. This time, she left a message. "Hey, Tricia, this is Sylvia. I just got your text about Tank not being able to attend prom. I'm sorry you and your husband have decided that he can't attend, and I was hoping we could maybe talk about it. The kids have been looking forward to this, and I don't want them to be disappointed. Please give me a call back."

"Did I miss something?" Lynne looked at her.

"If you did, I did too. I mean, you were standing right there and were part of the same conversation that I was. Maybe she's feeling some kinda way since Tank didn't tell her, but that's no reason for her to say he can't go." Sylvia said as she drove.

"I think she's on some bullshit. You know Titus wouldn't do this. He ain't like that."

Sylvia nodded in agreement. "I don't think it's him either. It makes no sense."

"Lord, Peyton is going to be so hurt. She probably doesn't even know about this," Lynne said.

Sylvia knew this was going to devastate her daughter. Despite being under punishment, Peyton was still excited about both upcoming proms and all she talked about. Sylvia was even beginning to enjoy the endless dresses Peyton sent pictures of.

"Probably not. I mean, we just talked to the woman, what, an hour ago? This is ridiculous. Nothing could've happened that fast." Sylvia instructed Siri to call her daughter via Bluetooth.

"Hey, Ma." Peyton's joyful voice came through the speakers of the truck, a sign that she had no idea she no longer had a prom date.

"Hey, baby. What're you doing?"

"Trying to convince Dad to take me to the hair store," Peyton said a little too loudly, as if she was wanted to make sure her father heard her.

"Your father's home, I mean, there?" Sylvia frowned. She hadn't seen nor verbally spoken to Garry since he abruptly left before she got home from their therapy session. They'd texted, but it had been very stiff. And he hadn't mentioned coming back, nor did she ask.

"Yeah. He got here about an hour ago," Peyton said.

"Oh, okay. Well, where's Aunt Connie and Jordan?" Sylvia asked.

"In the kitchen making something. You know how bud-dy-buddy they are," Peyton said with noticeable sarcasm.

"Peyton Janelle, that was uncalled for. You're already skating on thin ice. You should be in there with them, getting some lessons from Aunt Connie yourself."

"You ready?" Garry's voice was in the distance.

"I can't. I'm going to the hair store," Peyton said, "Did you want something, Mom? Why did you call?"

Sylvia had almost forgotten why she'd called her daughter in the first place. "Oh, nothing. Peyton, have you talked to Tank?"

"No. He's training really hard for the game next weekend, so he hasn't really been available. But I did let him know he was invited over for dinner once this All-American stuff is over."

Sylvia looked over at Lynne. "Okay, honey. I'll see you when I get home."

"Okay. Bye, Mom. Love you."

"Love you too."

"See? She has no idea, and I can bet you that boy doesn't know either," Lynne told her. "Are you gonna tell her?"

"I don't know what I'm going to do." Sylvia sighed as she took a screenshot of the text and forwarded it to another contact in her phone.

"About Peyton or about Garry or something else?" Lynne asked. Her best friend knew her very well, and Sylvia appreciated that she picked up on the fact that the answer she'd given applied to multiple situations she was facing right now.

"Pick one," Sylvia replied.

"Hey, you know I get it. Hampton showed up at my house last night, Garry shows up at yours today—"

"Wait, what? Hampton showed up? Why? Better yet, why are you just now telling me this? We've been out shopping all day, and you're just now saying something?" Sylvia almost stopped in the middle of the highway they were traveling on.

"I was gonna mention it when we went to eat, but I got a feeling we're not going, so now is just as good a time as any, I guess." Lynne shrugged.

"Why the hell did he come over? What did he want? Did you screw him, Lynne, and don't lie to me." Sylvia tried to keep one eye on the traffic while looking over at Lynne to see if she was going to tell the truth.

"Hell no, I didn't screw him, Syl. You know better than that. And he said he came over to check on me because I'd been on his mind. Some bullshit. He only stayed for about thirty minutes. He was on his way to a date with some thot."

"How do you know? Why would he stop at your house on his way to a date, Lynne? Did he tell you that?"

"No, but I could tell. He had on 'date' attire. You know, nice shirt, designer jeans, blazer, and, Syl, he had on this damn cologne. This sexy-ass cologne. And of course, his hair was all edged up and his beard, which is a nice salt and pepper now. He looked amazing." Lynne closed her eyes and touched her chest dramatically.

"Shit, Lynne, you say you ain't screw him, but sounds like you wanted to." Sylvia laughed.

"Nah, that ship has sailed."

"But it can always return to port," Sylvia suggested. "I think you should give him another chance. You said yourself that he seems to finally have his shit together."

"Nope. Hamp has someone new in his life. I think that's what he wanted to tell me, but he didn't. He's in a relationship, and she's young, or at least she's younger. But I'm happy for him."

"I think you're wrong. I think he came over to see where your head is at and where you guys stand."

"Kinda like why Garry probably came home today, huh?" Lynne pointed out.

"Deflection is not your strong suit." Sylvia rolled her eyes.

"Maybe not, but I made my point. It may not seem like it right now, but I believe you and Garry are gonna work through all of this. It's gonna take some time and work, but I just think y'all are gonna be good."

"And what makes you so confident? Because right now, I'm not even sure about that," Sylvia confessed.

"Because one, he showed up for your appointment with Amanda, which shows he's willing to do whatever it takes. And two, when Janelle mentioned teaming up with Sherrod, you had Garry's back, and despite your being angry, you put his needs before yours. Both of you still have love for one another, unconditional love," Lynne said.

Sylvia turned into the driveway and parked behind Lynne's BMW truck. She pointed to the 4,000-square-foot home that her best friend lived in, and said, "Thanks, Lynne. I love you, and I'm so proud of you."

"For what?" Lynne frowned.

"For being you, and for not giving up when you lost everything. Look at what you have now. You are strong and resilient and so deserving of love, but sometimes I think you're so busy looking back that you can't look forward sometimes. The same way you believe Garry and I aren't hopeless, you aren't either."

Sylvia leaned over and gave her a hug. Both women wiped the tears that they now had. Lynne grabbed all of her bags out of the back seat, and Sylvia waited until she was safely in the house before backing out and going home.

When Sylvia walked in the house, Aunt Connie and Jordan were in the kitchen putting the finishing touches on a cake they'd just baked, Peyton was in her room watching some hair tutorial on YouTube, and Garry was in the den watching college basketball. It didn't even feel like Saturday night. There was a time when Saturday nights were family nights for her, Garry, and Peyton. They'd go to dinner, the movies, miniature golf, the arcade, get ice cream, all kinds of adventures. They would share nonstop laughter, and she and Garry would hold hands and sneak kisses to avoid the loud, "Ewwwww," Peyton would yell when she sometimes caught their PDAs. She missed those times and wondered if she'd ever get to experience them again.

She took her bags upstairs, then came back down and went into the den. "Hi."

Garry looked over at her and smiled faintly. "Hi."

"I didn't expect you here this weekend." He went to say something, but she stopped him when she said, "But I'm glad to see you."

He looked relieved. "I'm glad to see you too, Syl."

"Did you eat?"

"No, not yet. Aunt Connie and I are gonna order Chinese after they finish the cake."

"Chinese, huh?" She thought for a second. "How about we do something else?"

"We can do something else if you like. Would you rather have pizza? Or maybe I can run and get something else. It doesn't matter. I'm good with whatever you want." Garry shrugged. Usually, he made the decision when it came to dinner selections. Seeing him so willing to appease her was nice.

"Peyton!" Sylvia walked into the foyer and yelled up the steps.

"Yeah?"

"Get dressed and come on. We're going out," she announced, then walked into the kitchen. "Ladies, finish it up. We're leaving in five minutes."

"Where we going?" Aunt Connie asked.

"Out. Now hurry up." Sylvia grabbed her plastic cake cover out of the food closet and placed it over the cake they'd just finished icing. "Let's go, ladies! Jordan, put Gypsy in her cage."

Aunt Connie and Jordan looked at her like she was crazy, then finally rushed up the stairs.

"Mom, I'm in the middle of doing my hair," Peyton wailed from her room.

"Put a hat on and finish it when you get back."

"Syl, what are we doing?" Garry asked.

"It's Saturday night. We're going to dinner, all of us, as a family, like we're supposed to, something we haven't done in months. As a matter of fact, I don't think we've done it since Jordan moved in."

"Why are we doing this?" Peyton plopped down the steps one by one. "I thought we were ordering Chinese. I look a mess."

Sylvia patted the baseball cap on her daughter's head. "You look adorable."

Aunt Connie and Jordan came down a few moments after Peyton, and then they all piled into Sylvia's SUV.

"I can't believe you took the Range back," Peyton commented as she climbed into the back seat.

Sylvia glanced over at Garry, who looked just as surprised, and shrugged. "Believe it."

Shanghai Hibachi was one of their favorite Saturday night spots. It had been months since they'd been there, but the host greeted them as if they'd just been there the day before. The family was seated around the grill and enjoyed an entertaining and delicious meal. Sylvia looked around and saw that each and every one of them, including Jordan, was smiling. After dinner, Garry suggested they stop for ice cream sundaes, but Jordan suggested they go home and make their own sundaes to go with the cake she and Aunt Connie made. To her surprise, Peyton nodded and agreed with the idea. They stopped at the store, and Garry ran inside and grabbed everything they needed for a home sundae bar: ice cream, chocolate syrup, nuts, whipped cream, and cherries.

"Thanks, Syl," Garry told her as he wiped the kitchen table. They'd agreed to clean up after the dessert party everyone enjoyed.

"For what?" Sylvia rinsed the bowls and spoons before putting them into the dishwasher.

"For this, for tonight. This was . . ."

"Needed," Sylvia said. "We needed to get away from this house and go out somewhere to enjoy."

"We did. And I didn't realize it, but you did. I appreciate it, and I appreciate you," he told her. "Come, sit. I'd like to talk."

Sylvia went and sat across from him. "I'm glad we all enjoyed it, though. I can't lie, I was a little nervous, but I'm glad I just went with my gut and didn't have time to even think about what could've gone wrong."

"I'm glad you did too. But I want you to know that I heard everything you said at Amanda's office. And you were right, and I'm sorry. I have a trust issue, but I don't want you to think I don't value you or your opinion. I think I became so caught up in being the head of our household that I neglected being in a relationship, if that makes sense," Garry explained.

"Makes a lot of sense, Garry. And you're right. Remember the 2-2-2 rule?"

Garry laughed. "Boy, do I. Those were the days."

When they'd first married, they'd adhered to the rule that they would have planned date nights every two weeks, take a weekend trip every two months, and go on a one-week vacation each year for just the two of them. It worked for years, until his work schedule became hectic, Peyton had gotten older and had more activities, and now, she realized, he had another child he was trying to make time for. The 2-2-2 rule became nonexistent.

"I messed up in a lot of ways, Syl, and I have a lot I need to work on within myself. I have a lot I've been dealing with the past few years. The death of my dad, even though I never really knew him, which is weird to me. Why do I even care about the death of a man who abandoned my mom and me?"

"He was still your father, Garry," Sylvia said softly.

"My mother's death, Miranda's." Garry looked at her. "We weren't together, but she was—"

"I know, Garry."

"Now there's this Sherrod situation. And my job."

"What about your job?" Sylvia frowned.

"Sylvia, I've never told you this, but I hate my damn job." He put his hands on his temples.

Sylvia stared at him. "What?"

"I hate it, Syl. I hate traveling, I hate the corporate games I have to play, I hate sales."

Her husband had worked as a district manager for Xerox for decades. He'd been promoted, won awards and accolades and more honors than she could count. The shelf in the living room held plaques, certificates, and trophies from the company. His bosses loved him, and his coworkers loved him. Hearing him say he hated his job was a total shock to her.

"Garry, why are you just now telling me this?"

"Because I know I can trust you with anything, including my burdens and fears." He whispered, "I have to trust that you won't be disappointed in me for telling you."

"You've been going to a job you hate for years, Garry? Why?"

"Because the job I hate allows me to provide for my family. And that's all I thought that mattered, until now."

Sylvia walked over and hugged him and allowed Garry to cry into her chest. They weren't tears of sadness as they'd been before. They were tears of relief, and she was happy to wipe them. "It's okay, Garry. You're going to be fine. We're going to be fine."

"Don't worry, Syl. I'm not going to quit. I hate it, but I only have a few more years until I retire, and with Peyton going off to school, and Jordan—"

"I thought you said you learned." Sylvia put her finger against his lips to silence him. "You don't have to fix everything by yourself, Garry. You say you're learning to trust me, right?"

"I am." He nodded.

"Good. We got this, and God's got us." She smiled and hugged him again. For the first time since they'd been married, it suddenly felt as if the roles had reversed. She was the one comforting and supporting her husband, being the strong one, when he was usually the one holding her and everyone else up. Sylvia knew what they needed to do. She just hoped Garry was truly willing to trust her decision.

Chapter 21

Janelle

It was after nine o'clock on Saturday night when Janelle woke up. She'd been nursing a hangover all day. After having several too many tequila shots with Natalie the night before, she'd taken an Uber home, drunk a Gatorade, taken three Tylenol PM, then climbed into bed and slept the day and her headache away. Groggy and hungry, yet well rested, she took a hot shower, after which she sat on the side of her bed and got herself together, or at least tried to.

"Damn, six missed calls." She picked up her phone. Two were from Natalie, two from Sherrod, one was from Nivea, and the other was a "scam likely" number, which she immediately blocked. There was also a text from Sylvia with a screenshot of a message from Titus's wife. "What the hell?"

"Hello," Sylvia answered.

"Syl, I've been asleep all day. I just got your text. What the hell is going on?" Janelle asked.

"I have no idea. I sent it to you so you can find out," Sylvia replied. "I've tried calling and texting her, but I think she's got me blocked for some reason now, which is even crazier."

"OMG, is Peyton devastated?"

"She hasn't even said anything, so I don't think Tank's told her yet. If she doesn't mention it, then I'm not going to. I'm pretty sure Tank has no idea his mom sent me this message. And I'm wondering if his dad knows she sent it."

"I get it, and no worries. I'll look out and let you know. And you're probably right, Tank is probably thinking his parents are going to change their minds, and all of this will blow over, which may be why he hasn't said anything to Peyton about not going to prom," Janelle suggested.

"True. Well, let me know if you find out anything."

"I will, Syl. Don't worry, my niece will be going to prom with Tank, I guarantee it. I'm glad you called me," she told her, grateful that despite their strained relationship, she still knew she could depend on her when she needed to. "Everything else okay?"

"Yeah, it is. I'll talk to you later. Oh, and Janelle, one more thing."

"Yeah, what's up?"

"Let Sherrod know I'm willing to have that sit-down he invited me to."

Janelle stood up so quickly that she became dizzy and had to sit back down. She couldn't believe Sylvia was agreeing to meet with him. Her excitement was hard to contain, but she forced herself to remain calm. "Cool, I'll let him know."

"Bye," Sylvia said, and the call ended.

Janelle decided to call Sherrod before reaching out to Titus. "Hey, sorry I missed your call. I've been knocked out."

"I see. I guess that means you enjoyed girls' night?" He laughed.

"Probably enjoyed a little too much." Her night with Natalie, albeit infused with liquor and Nivea-free, had been enjoyable. Janelle told Natalie all about her decision to date Sherrod and her concern about how Nivea would react. Natalie agreed with Sherrod in that he and Nivea dealt with one another in high school and were never serious, and she felt that there shouldn't be an issue. She also said that she supported Janelle's decision and was happy she'd finally found someone worth being with. When Janelle then told her about making the complicated situation with Garry and Sylvia even worse, Natalie told her to just take a step back and allow things to settle between her sister and husband before approaching her again. By the time both of them passed out on the sofa, the stress and nervousness she'd felt earlier was gone.

"Well, I'm glad you're feeling better. I was gonna ask you if you wanted to go grab something to eat, but when I didn't reach you, I stopped on my way home from work, and now I'm full."

"I'm glad you thought about me."

"Of course. Do you need anything?" he offered. "You got water and electrolytes?"

"What makes you think I need those?"

"Oh, I've been around you and your girls, remember? A few times, actually. I doubt that y'all were sitting around discussing books and drinking tea last night," Sherrod joked.

"First of all, my girls and I love to read, and we discuss books all the time. And we drink tea." Janelle laughed.

"Y'all may spill tea, and I'm thinking if you do drink it, it's probably Long Island Iced."

"I'm not going to sit here and let you paint me and my besties as a bunch of ratchet, gossiping drunks who don't read, sir." Janelle pretended to be insulted. "I have water and electrolytes to go drink."

"You're hilarious, you know that?"

"So I've been told. On another note, I talked to my sister, and she's agreed to talk with you." She sighed.

"Seriously? Oh, damn, that's what's up. When?" Sherrod asked.

"She didn't say, but I think we need to just give her a little space and don't press the issue right now. Just know that she's willing. That's the good thing and the most important," Janelle said, remembering what Natalie suggested.

"I understand. Thanks again for helping me deal with this, Janelle. I'm grateful."

"You're welcome. I'll give you a call tomorrow."

"Have a good night."

As soon as she hung up, she sent a text to Titus and told him they needed to talk ASAP. It didn't take five minutes for him to call her back.

"Hey, Nellie."

"I need to discuss something with you. It's important. I'm headed to the gym."

"I'll be there," Titus said.

Janelle threw on a pair of leggings and slipped her favorite oversized sweatshirt over her sports bra, and put on her running shoes. When she arrived at the twenty-four-hour fitness center near her house, she waited in the car. Titus pulled up beside her a few minutes later and rolled his window down.

"We going in or staying out?" he asked.

Although she was dressed in her workout clothes, Janelle hadn't even planned to work out. She was still feeling the effects of her hangover a little. "We can chat out here."

Titus got out of his truck and got into her car and grinned. "Nice shirt."

She looked down and saw that they were both wearing the same Mission College sweatshirt: the place where they'd met years ago. "I guess you have great taste."

"I do. I picked you, didn't I?" he said.

"Uh, you picked someone else too," she reminded him. The smile quickly left his face, and she took out her phone. "Speaking of which, what the hell is this about?"

Titus stared at the screen, frowning. "Wait, she sent this to you too?"

"Hell no, it was sent to Sylvia earlier today," Janelle told him. "You knew about this and ain't say nothing? Titus, what the hell?"

"I knew, but I didn't know," he stammered.

"So, it's true? Tank isn't going to prom?"

"Yes."

"Yes, what? Yes, he's going, or yes, it's true?" Janelle folded her arms and waited for his answer.

"I can't believe she sent this shit to Sylvia." He shook his head. "She sent me a screenshot, but I half read it. I thought it was a message to Tank. And I kinda ignored it."

"Well, as you can see, it wasn't a message to Tank. It went to my sister. And now Tricia, your wife, the woman you married, has Syl blocked for some dumb-ass reason. Do you know how upsetting this shit is?"

"You act like I had something to do with this."

"Well, it says that you and she decided that. You are her husband, right? Or does she have another one we don't know about?" Janelle asked.

"Yo, I ain't decide shit. Hell, I'm the one who's been listening to my son make all these damn prom plans that's gonna stretch my pockets. Do you know how much I gotta shell out for two custom tuxedo jackets he wants? I definitely ain't say he couldn't go. I wouldn't do that to those kids, Nellie, you know that. Don't even worry about it. Tell Syl to ignore it." Titus sounded just as angry and confused as she'd been when she saw the text. "She's just tripping right now, has been for the past couple of days, really. I'm sorry she—"

"Listen, Titus, my family is dealing with enough bullshit right now and don't need any more. I don't know what the fuck you and your wife have going on or what kind of games y'all—"

"Hold the fuck up, Janelle. Don't say 'y'all' or include me in this, because I told you I ain't have nothing to do with it," Titus snapped.

"Well, I'm just going by what the text says. Instead of going to her about this bullshit, I'm coming to you as a courtesy. The same way you say I know you, you know me very well, and one thing I don't play about is my family, especially my niece. Now if you can't get to the bottom of why she felt the need to send this bullshit-ass, cryptic shit, and I need to personally check her ass, I have no problem doing it, because the same way she rolled up on my sister's house, I'll roll up on her." Janelle's voice was just as intense as the stare she gave him. In all the years they'd dealt with one another, she'd never threatened him about his wife. Then again, until now, she'd never had a reason to.

"Damn it, Nellie, I said ignore it, and I apologized," Titus barked.

Janelle's head snapped back. Not only was this the first time they'd had a heated argument, but this was also the first time he'd raised his voice at her. She'd never seen him so angry, and she hadn't intended to upset him. But hearing that the text her sister received was some kind of sick joke had pissed her off. "Titus, just fix it. And whatever it is she's tripping about, as you said, keep my family out of it, and more importantly, these kids."

"I will," he promised. The two sat in silence for a while until finally, he asked, "We good, Nellie?"

Janelle took a deep sigh, then said, "Yes, Titus, we're good."

"You wanna go in and hit the treadmill for a few? I'm thinking we both need to release some tension. Unless, of course, you wanna do something else." He raised an eyebrow at her.

"Get out of my car, Titus." She reached past him and opened his door.

"Damn, it's like that? Can I at least get a hug?"

"Fine," she told him, opening her own door and stepping out of the car. He walked around, and she hugged him. He tried to kiss her, but she pushed him away. "See, this is why."

"Okay, okay. I forgot you're seeing someone. How's that going?"

"It's going great." Janelle gave him a suspicious look.

He pouted and said, "Can't say I'm glad to hear that, but I'm happy for you."

"Thanks, Titus."

"Guess I'll see you at prom night?"

"Maybe." She turned to get back into her car, and he popped her on her behind. She shook her head at him, and he laughed as she pulled out of the parking lot.

When she got home, she sent her sister a text, letting her know that Titus said to ignore the message and prom was a go.

Thank you, Nellie, Sylvia texted back.

Nellie. Janelle grinned. Syl calling her by her nickname was a sure sign that things were moving in the right direction. Hopefully, all would be well.

Chapter 22

Tricia

The inside of Dr. Adam Guyser's office was small and tight with bare walls, a small sofa, a desk, and a filing cabinet. Tricia sat on one end of the sofa, and her husband sat on the other. Neither one said anything as they waited for Dr. Guyser, who happened to be the first name to pop up when she Googled "family therapist." When she called for an appointment, the receptionist told her that the next available appointment was in two weeks, but Tricia told the woman that it was an emergency situation that needed to be handled immediately, per the physician who had treated her days before. The receptionist put her on hold, then came back with an appointment time for the following evening. As she'd expected, getting Titus to agree to therapy wasn't hard. She'd been a little worried when he didn't immediately respond to the screenshot of the message she'd sent to Sylvia. But later that night, he'd come home pissed and angrier than she'd ever seen him before.

"What the fuck is wrong with you?" he screamed so loudly when he walked into the bedroom that Tricia sat up.

"What? Why the hell are you screaming?" she gasped.

"I'm screaming because you sent that bullshit-ass message to Peyton's mom saying Tank isn't going to prom. And you had the nerve to act like I agreed to that

bullshit. What the fuck is wrong with you, Tricia?" He glared at her. Beads of sweat were on his temples and forehead, and he looked like a madman.

"It's not bullshit, Titus." Tricia's voice was calm and serene. She knew that if she reacted by yelling, her plan wouldn't work. "You told me to select another punishment, and I did. Furthermore, I wouldn't have had to send the message had I known anything about his going to prom in the first place. Her mother was standing there, telling me all about these elaborate plans. I sent that message as a favor so the poor girl would have plenty of time to find another date."

"Why the fuck wouldn't he go to prom, Tricia? It's his senior year, and he has a girlfriend." Titus shook his head in disbelief. "You stay on some damn bullshit, I swear. I don't know what the hell is wrong with you these days."

Tricia swung her legs from under the comforter and sat on the side of the bed, facing him. "Maybe we should go to therapy and find out what's wrong with me."

Titus inhaled so deeply that the entire top of his body leaned back. "Therapy? You pulled this bullshit stunt because of some fucking therapy? Are you fuckin' crazy?"

"Dad, what's wrong?" Tank rushed into the bedroom, looking panicked. Tricia was sure he'd never seen his father so upset. He'd certainly never heard them argue like they were now.

"Everything's fine, Tank. Your father and I were just trying to figure out how to tell you that you're not going to prom, that's all."

"What? Why?" Tank said, his face in shock.

"Because you were supposed to be punished for not coming home, remember? I agreed that you could prepare for and attend your All-American Game and would pick another punishment later. That was the

agreement, correct?" She looked from her son over to Titus, who was breathing so hard that his chest was rising and falling.

"But prom, Mom? That's not fair." Tank shook his head.

"Tank, leave the room," Titus told him.

"But what about prom?" Tank asked. "Can I go?"

Tricia looked over at Titus and said, "Your father will let you know. Close the door behind you."

Tank sulked as he walked out, puling the door behind him. When he was gone, Titus looked over at her. "You've pulled some bullshit moves before, Tricia. But this . . . this one right here is borderline evil."

"How is wanting to seek help for me and my family evil, Titus? You need therapy just as much as I do. Have you thought about that?" she asked. "You can't even answer a simple-ass question. You want me to agree to Tank going to prom? Then you need to agree to go to this."

Titus closed his eyes for a second, then said, "Fine, I'll go. I got some things I need to get off my chest anyway. But I'm not making my son go."

"I can accept that. I'll make the appointment," she said, climbing back under the covers.

Titus didn't sleep in the bed that night, and he hadn't since. He also hadn't spoken to her outside of a simple "okay" response when she sent him the date, time, and address for the appointment. Tricia hated that he was angry at her, but had he just cooperated when she asked him the first time, none of this would have happened. It was his fault.

"Mr. and Mrs. King, I'm Dr. Guyser. Nice to meet you." The doctor finally entered and shook their hands. Short, balding, dressed in a pair of khakis, button-down shirt, and sensible shoes, he looked like he'd just finished a round of golf before arriving. In his hand were a file folder and a pair of glasses that he slipped on after sitting at the desk.

"Nice to meet you, Doctor." She nodded while Titus remained silent.

"So, what brings you two in today? I see noted here that there's some sort of crisis you all are dealing with. What's going on?" he said, looking at the folder.

Again, Titus said nothing. He just stared at the floor in front of him.

"Well, um, we, uh, are having communication issues," Tricia stammered, then cleared her throat. "As you can see."

The doctor looked over at Titus and said, "Do you agree, Mr. King?"

Titus's demeanor remained casual as he shrugged and shook his head. She cut her eyes at him and shifted uncomfortably. One thing about Titus, he was a people person and was always friendly. Folks enjoyed being around him, no matter who they were: neighbors, co-workers, coaches, players, other parents. When she was with him and they were around others, he did all the talking. That's what he was: a talker. Now he was sitting there acting like he was a mute.

"Okay, you've been married seventeen years. That's quite some time," Dr. Guyser stated. "Tell me about the beginning of your relationship. How about you start, Mrs. King?"

"Oh, well, we met when I was eighteen and got married when I was nineteen, right after our son was born. Titus was in the military, and I was a stay-at-home mom for a while. We have a beautiful home, and our son is headed to college. He plays basketball, and he's also smart. He was actually being recruited by Burke University," Sylvia said.

"Okay, you both were kind of young. Was he your first love?" Dr. Guyser asked.

"I believe so." She nodded. "Yes, we were each other's first loves."

"Mr. King?"

"She was a virgin, and I was her first," Titus mumbled.

Tricia shifted slightly and looked away. Titus always believed he'd been her first, mainly because that's what she'd told him when they first met. But he wasn't. Hell, he wasn't her first or her second. He wasn't even her third. Truth be told, had Tarik been born a month earlier, she and Titus probably would've never seen each other again because Tank would have a different father.

"And despite the current communication issue, has your marriage been successful?" Dr. Guyser asked.

"Yes." Tricia nodded. "I can honestly say we really haven't had any major issues. Until a few days ago, that is."

"And what happened a few days ago?" Dr. Guyser asked.

"Ask him." She looked over at Titus, hoping to get him to talk.

"Mr. King? Would you consider your marriage to be good until a few days ago?" Dr. Guyser looked at Titus.

"Whatever she said." Titus sighed.

"See?" Tricia emphasized with her hand. Titus was being an ass, and this wasn't going the way she expected. Her frustration was increasing by the minute, and their session was only an hour long.

"Mr. King, I'm going to need for you to contribute just a little more in order for me to help you and your wife," Dr. Guyser said.

Titus didn't say anything at first. Then he sat up and said, "Fine. For the past seventeen years, I've done everything a husband is supposed to. I was at junior college when she had our son and had just signed the paperwork for my engineering internship I was supposed to work that summer. But my mom calls me and tells me her mom called and she's in labor, so I go in time to see my son being born. It was love at first sight. I promised her that she didn't have to worry about raising him alone. She tells me unless I plan on marrying her, I'd better get used to some other man raising my son because she had no intention of being a single mom. I dropped out of school and married her. I've always gone above and beyond for my son because his mom checked out on being what I consider a suitable parent from jump. I gave her a pass in the beginning because she was young and inexperienced, and for the first few years, I was deployed. But when I saw that he needed me, I changed career paths and chose one that would allow me to be a more hands-on parent, which I am. Ask anyone we know. There isn't a better father out here than I am.

"For the most part, we stay out of her way because she bitches and complains about everything. We go on vacation, she complains about crowds, the weather, the noise, everything. She hates being around other people, and she's mean. Which is why she has no friends. Everyone we know, including my family and friends, handles her with kid gloves and walks on eggshells around her. Hell, nobody ever comes to our house to visit because they don't want to be around her. She works when she wants to, not because she has to. Whatever she wants, she gets, and when she doesn't get it, watch out because she's going to make sure you're punished. I do the cooking, the cleaning, the grocery shopping, and laundry, so she doesn't have to do that either. Our once-a-month sex life, if that's what you want to call it, is built around a damn calendar that she creates. I don't even try to ask for ass anymore because, most of the time, I'm just tired of her saying no and the excuses she gives. She's manipulative, miserable and controlling.

"But she's my wife, and despite all of her bullshit, I still have love for her because not only is she the mother of my son, I'm really the only one she has in her life, other than her mother. I've never once left, and the word 'divorce' has never come out of my mouth. And after all these years, everything I've sacrificed and all that I've done and continue to do for her to show how much I care, turns out it's still not good enough. Last week, she started tripping more than ever. You wanna know why I'm here, Doc? I'm here because if I didn't agree to coming today, my son wouldn't be able to go to prom. And I would do anything for my son. Is that enough of a contribution?"

Tricia slowly drew in air, suddenly feeling constricted and hot. Her leg began shaking nervously, and she wasn't sure what she felt more: anger or embarrassment.

"Are you okay, Mrs. King?" Dr. Guyser asked softly as he wrote in the folder. Not only had Titus given him plenty to note, but he'd also given her plenty to process.

She blinked several times and said, "Yeah, I'm good. Obviously, my husband and I should've come in to see you a long time ago. Our marital issues are bigger than we thought."

"Correction, your issues are bigger than you thought. I don't have any issues with my marriage. I do everything expected of me and then some." Titus cut his eyes at her.

"Not everything," she snapped. "You can't even answer the damn question, Titus. That's why we're here in the first place."

"You still don't get it."

"Get what?" Dr. Guyser sat forward, clearly engaged by the conversation the couple was not having.

"That this bullshit is a waste of time that I'm not participating in, and it's not going to get her what she wants this time," Titus said as he stood up.

"Now, Mr. King, that's not an accurate statement. Marriage counseling can be very beneficial to both parties," Dr. Guyser volunteered.

"Let me ask you a question, Doc," Titus said.

"Ask away."

"Can any amount of therapy make someone fall in love with someone? Someone they've known for years and never been in love with?" Titus asked.

Dr. Guyser sat back in his chair and seemed to be deep in thought before answering. "Well, there are a lot of benefits to therapy in regards to emotions, but—"

"You're not answering the question," Titus told him.

"No, it can't," he relented.

"Thank you. What my wife fails to realize it that marriage is a contract between two people who agree to live their lives together. That's all it is. People fall in and out of love every day, and as a result, they leave their marriage. The thing that makes them stay is their commitment to their responsibilities, not because they're 'in love.' Now I have a basketball practice to get to. Dr. Guyser, thank you for your time." Titus shook his hand and walked out of the office.

Tricia picked up her purse and said, "Well, I guess our time is up. I'm sure my husband won't be back again. This was very eye-opening for me, though. Thank you."

"Same time next week then?" Dr. Guyser asked.

"What? He's not going to come back here. You heard him." She shook her head.

"I did hear him. That's his decision. But it doesn't have to be yours, Mrs. King. I'm actually more concerned about you and your reaction to what he said than I am about your husband."

"What do you mean?" Tricia was confused. Her entire reason for being here was to prove a point to Titus. She didn't and wasn't going to.

"Mrs. King, can you tell me the last time you were happy?" he asked. "Truly, undoubtedly happy?"

Tricia frowned. She tried to think of an answer and mentally went through her life: childhood, teen years, marriage, motherhood. Birthdays, holidays, anniversaries, big moments, little moments, she tried and tried to think. Her eyes met Dr. Guyser's, and she whispered, "I can't."

Chapter 23

Sylvia

"Maaaaaaaa!" Peyton's voice sounding like a fire engine caused Sylvia to cringe in the bathroom mirror that she was staring into as she applied her mascara. Her fingers were already trembling with nervousness, and her daughter's distress call, which she was sure wasn't even necessary, wasn't making things any better.

"Peyton, what have I told you about screaming for me?" Sylvia yelled back to her.

"Ma!" Peyton's voice was now in her bedroom.

"What is it, Peyton?" Sylvia put her makeup down and walked into the room.

"Can you take me to the beauty supply?"

The blank stare on Sylvia's face should've been enough of an answer, but in case it wasn't, Sylvia replied, "What? No. I told you I had a meeting this evening."

"Can you take me before you go?" Peyton pleaded. "I only have to get two things, that's it."

"I won't have time," Sylvia stated. "Didn't your dad just take you to the beauty supply this weekend? And you have a hair appointment next week."

"He did. But I just saw something on the internet that I wanna try myself. Can you take me after your meeting?"

"Peyton, no, I can't. We can stop while we're out tomorrow."

"Fine," Peyton said before turning and going back to her room.

Sylvia checked her watch. She was scheduled to be downtown in an hour. She didn't know why she was so nervous. *Maybe because of him,* she thought as she looked at her ringing cell phone.

"Are you sure about this, Syl? Maybe this is a bad idea," Garry said after she answered.

"I'm positive, Garry. You're worried for no reason. We just need to clear the air and get in accord like adults," Sylvia told him for what seemed like the umpteenth time. "Are you almost home?"

"Yeah, I should be there by six." He sighed.

"Great, we can ride together. I'll be ready when you get here."

As soon as she hung up, her phone rang again, and this time it was Janelle. "Syl, change of plans."

"What kind of change of plans?" Sylvia asked.

"We can't meet at my office. They're doing some electrical work in the building and maintenance says we have to be out by five. So Sherrod and I are just going to come there. Is that cool?"

"What? Janelle, I don't think that'll work. You know the girls are here and Aunt Connie," Sylvia groaned.

"Can't you send them out somewhere? Like, to the mall or the movies?" Janelle suggested. "I already told Sherrod, and that works better for him since it's closer for him to get to and me too."

Sylvia sighed. "Let me try to think of something. I'll call you right back."

She sat on the side of her bed and tried to think of somewhere to go other than their house. Going to a restaurant or another public place would be too much of a risk, especially considering the last time the four of them had come face-to-face. The possibility of the conversation getting loud was strong. Cancelling wasn't an option either. Sylvia needed to think of a plan and think of it quick. Aunt Connie being there wasn't much of a concern, but Jordan and Peyton were another story. Sylvia dialed Lynne's number.

"Hey, are you busy?" she asked her best friend.

"Just got to the nail salon. What's up?" Lynne asked.

"Never mind," Sylvia groaned. "I was gonna see if you could come and get Jordan and Peyton and get them out of the house for me."

"Why? Wait, isn't the big meeting at Janelle's office this evening?"

"Is it, but there's been a venue change. Go ahead and get your nails done."

"Call me later."

Sylvia had only one other option. She went downstairs into the den where Aunt Connie was sitting and watching *Judge Judy,* one of her favorite shows. "Aunt Connie, I need a favor."

"What kind of favor would that be?" Aunt Connie barely looked up from the TV.

"I need you to take Peyton to the store for me and take Jordan with you. And I need y'all to go to dinner, too." Sylvia hadn't mentioned anything to her about the meeting with her sister and Sherrod, and now wasn't the time to tell her. If she had, it would have turned into an entire discussion, and there was not time for it.

"Say what now?" Aunt Connie turned her head.

"I need y'all out of the house for a little while, please." Sylvia gave her a nervous smile.

"Syl, you ready? Let's go!" Garry yelled as he came through the front door.

Aunt Connie's lips formed a smug smile, and her eyes gave her an insinuating look. "Oh, you do, huh? Y'all need some privacy? I guess therapy's working out better than you thought, huh?"

"Really, Aunt Connie?" Sylvia shook her head at her aunt, winking at her.

"Syl!" Garry yelled again.

"Dad? You're home?" Peyton called out.

"Why does everyone find it necessary to yell in this house?" Sylvia groaned, then walked over to the doorway of the den. "Garry, gimme a minute."

"We gotta go. Traffic is heavy out there." Garry pointed to his watch.

"There's been a slight change of plans."

"What kind of change of plans?" He frowned.

"Hey, Garry, welcome home." Aunt Connie now stood behind her, still smiling.

"I'll explain in a few minutes. Go upstairs," Sylvia told him.

"Yes, Garry, you go on upstairs. She'll be there soon." Aunt Connie winked.

After giving Aunt Connie an odd look, he shrugged and went up the steps. "Yes, P, Daddy's home."

"It's not what you think." Sylvia turned to face her aunt.

"Hey, you don't know what I'm thinking. Trust me, if my husband had just come home after being gone for over two weeks, I guarantee my thoughts would be way freakier than yours. But I do have a question," Aunt Connie said.

"Yes?" Sylvia was afraid to even ask.

"How are we supposed to get there?"

"You can take my truck, Aunt Connie." Sylvia reached for her keys hanging on the holder near the door and handed them to her.

"Your truck is too fancy. It's got all those knobs and computer gadgets."

"Aunt Connie, it's the same as any other car. Arrange the mirrors, put it in gear, and press the gas. Don't even worry about all the other stuff. You've been driving since you were sixteen. I'm not worried."

"Fourteen. My daddy taught us early on," Aunt Connie pointed out. "But I don't know."

"Peyton, come down here!" It was Sylvia's turn to yell over her aunt. "Jordan, come out of your room!"

A few moments later, both girls appeared.

"Yeah?" Jordan asked.

"Aunt Connie is gonna take y'all out," Sylvia announced.

"Out where?" Peyton frowned.

"To the beauty supply and to get food," Sylvia told her, hoping her daughter wasn't going to object and have an attitude. She didn't have time to deal with it. Time was ticking.

"Oh." To Sylvia's surprise, Peyton let out a sigh of relief and even seemed happy to hear this. "For a second, I thought she was about to make us go do something down at the church."

"And what if I was? Then what?" Aunt Connie's tone was threatening as she tilted her head and waited for Peyton's answer.

"Uh, nothing, Aunt Connie," Peyton quickly responded. "We can go wherever you wanna go. I'm happy to go with you."

"Good, now go get your jackets and let's go," Aunt Connie told them.

As entertained as she was by the family moment, Sylvia needed for them to hurry and leave. She still had to go upstairs and update Garry that her sister and Sherrod were both on their way.

"Thanks, Aunt Connie," Sylvia said.

"Young lady, isn't there something else we need to discuss?" Aunt Connie asked.

Sylvia paused, knowing that somehow Aunt Connie must've sensed that there was something else going on. "I . . . we—"

"How am I supposed to pay for this little outing you're sending me on?"

"Oh, yes. No worries, Aunt Connie. You know I got you. One sec." Sylvia rushed into the kitchen to grab her purse, taking all the cash out of her wallet and her check card. By the time she was putting it all into her aunt's hand, the girls had returned and were ready. "Y'all have fun."

"Oh, we will." Aunt Connie grinned as she stared at the money and card.

Finally, they were gone. Sylvia raced up the stairs where Garry was waiting in their bedroom.

"Now what's going on?" he asked.

"Janelle and Sherrod are coming here instead. They'll be here in a little while."

"Here? They're coming to our house instead? Syl, I told you I had a feeling—"

"Garry, stop it. Listen to me, this is happening whether you like it or not. You don't wanna be here, then fine, you need to leave now because in the next ten minutes, they're gonna be here. The choice is yours," she told him. "But if you stay, understand that you have to trust whatever I say during this process, Garry. This ain't gonna be your way or no way. Those days are over."

Garry's slight frown was noticeable as he inhaled deeply. "I'm staying."

"I'm glad." Sylvia nodded. For a brief moment, she thought about giving him a hug, but now wasn't the time, and she didn't want him to think that his agreeing to be a part of this conversation with her sister and Sherrod meant that their marriage was resolved. It wasn't. They'd made progress, but she wasn't ready to just kiss and make up. Not yet, anyway. Besides, there was no telling how this was going to play out, but she hoped the odds were in her favor for all of their sakes.

"It's just that Sherrod is so damn—"

The sound of the doorbell interrupted him. Sylvia whispered, "Saved by the bell. And Garry, again, you're going to have to let some of that stuff go. It's not about you."

"I get it."

"Look, let me go down first, and you wait a little while, then join us."

"You don't think we should go together, like a united front?"

"Not initially. You said you trust me, Garry. And of course, we're united. You are still my husband, despite our issues."

"Okay, I'll wait."

Sylvia went downstairs and opened the door, expecting to see Janelle, but only Sherrod was there. "Oh, uh, hi."

"Hi, Sylvia." He looked just as nervous as she felt.

"Come on in. Where's my sister?" She led him into the living room.

He sat on the sofa. "She should be here any moment. I think I got like a five-minute head start on her. I guess I should've waited in the car for her, huh?"

"No, you didn't have to do that, Sherrod. Can I get you something to drink?" Sylvia offered.

"No, I'm good. Where's Jordan?" he asked, then added, "And Peyton?"

"They're out with Aunt Connie," Sylvia told him, sitting in one of the chairs.

"Oh, goodness, how is Aunt Connie?" Sherrod laughed.

Sylvia had almost forgotten that Sherrod was her aunt's pharmacist. "She's still Aunt Connie. I'm sure the girls will be quite entertained while on this outing."

"No doubt they will," Sherrod said. "Listen, Sylvia, I want to just thank you for agreeing to sit down and have this discussion with me. Like I told you before, I couldn't love Jordan any more if she were my biological daughter, and her mother knew that, too. And in all honesty, Garry did. And because of that, for some reason, he felt like I was a threat to him, which I never wanted to be."

"Uh, maybe we should kinda wait for Janelle, Sherrod," Sylvia told him.

"Yeah, you're right. She should be here, because we're gonna need her legal advice on our strategy on how we're going to team up and fight Garry and win custody." Sherrod nodded.

"And do what?" Garry walked into the living room, taking both of them by surprise.

"What the hell? Why is he here?" Sherrod asked.

"What the hell do you mean, why is he here? I live here. You're sitting in my house!" Garry told him, then turned to Sylvia. "What is he talking about, teaming up against me? You said he wanted to sit down and talk about a resolution, Syl."

"He is, Garry. Calm down and sit down." Sylvia stood and reached to touch him, but he snatched away.

"Calm down? Nah, ain't no calming down." Garry shook his head.

"Man, I ain't even know you were gonna be here," Sherrod told him. "I thought this was going to be a sit-down with Sylvia."

"A sit-down to do what? Take my daughter? You really thought that shit was gonna happen? That my wife would actually agree to something like that?" Garry asked him.

"I'm here, ain't I? I ain't just pop up over here uninvited," Sherrod told him.

"Is that what he thought he was coming here to do?" Garry directed the question to Sylvia, who stood beside him.

Her heart pounded in her chest. All she wanted was for Garry to sit his ass down for one second so she could explain to both of them what was about to happen, or what she thought was going to happen, because at this point, it wasn't looking very hopeful. "Garry, I did agree to sitting down with—"

"Wow, ain't this some shit?" Garry threw his hands up in disgust.

"Like I said, I ain't come here uninvited, man," Sherrod said.

"Man, shut the hell up," Garry told him.

Sherrod stood. "Who you talking to?"

"I'm talking to you."

The two men squared off, and Sylvia jumped between them, a hand on each of their chests, in an effort to separate them. "Both of you, stop it now!"

"What the hell is going on?" Janelle came running into the living room just in time and pulled Sherrod toward her. "Garry, what are you doing here?"

"This was probably your idea, wasn't it? You want this dude so bad that you're willing to do anything to help him, huh? Even try to take my daughter? Well, you know what? All of y'all can go to hell." Garry said to Sylvia, "But you want me to trust you, right?"

"Don't talk to my sister like that," Janelle snapped.

"Janelle, just chill," Sylvia said.

"I'll talk however I wanna talk," Garry screamed. "Y'all think I'm gonna just sit back and let y'all take my daughter from me?"

"So, you just gonna act like you ain't the one who called this meeting, Syl?" Janelle frowned.

Before she knew it, things were out of control, and they all were yelling at one another. It was hard to even determine who was siding with whom. It was total chaos, and Sylvia didn't know how to regain control of the situation.

The sound of glass shattering caused all of them to stop and turn just in time to see Aunt Connie standing in the foyer holding another plate over her head, about to smash it to the floor and add to the broken glass by her feet.

"Aunt Connie," Sylvia gasped.

Aunt Connie walked into the living room and slowly looked at all of them. "What is wrong with all of you? Have you lost your minds?"

"No, Aunt Connie." Janelle was the first to speak. "Our conversation just got a little heated."

"It was more than heated. Y'all been going at it for the past five minutes. I know because that's how long I stood in the doorway before deciding to get your attention," Aunt Connie told them. "Now, I don't know how this meeting came about, and I don't even care. But I know it's about the well-being and welfare of a young lady we all care about. Or so you all claim to care about."

"She's my daughter. Of course I care about her," Garry said.

"And what's that supposed to mean? That we don't?" Janelle glared at him.

"Now he wants to brag and tell everyone that she's his daughter. Seems funny he ain't mention her a couple of months ago, isn't it?" Sherrod shook his head.

Garry pulled his fist back and aimed it. Before he could release the punch, Aunt Connie touched his shoulder. "No, you will not."

Sylvia slowly released the breath she hadn't realized she was holding as she saw her husband's arm drop to his side. This was all her fault, and she knew she had to accept responsibility for the madness that she'd caused. "This is on me, Aunt Connie."

"I don't give a damn who it's on. I'm sick of this nonsense between all of y'all. Now listen to me and listen to me good. Y'all figure this shit out and figure it out quick.

Because if y'all don't, you better believe I'll be the one with full physical and sole custody of Jordan and dare any of y'all to fight me on it. Quiet as it's kept, that might be the best decision any way. All of y'all are claiming to love her so much, then damn it, put the bullshit to the side and act like it." Aunt Connie's words resonated in the room, and they all stared at her. "We all love her, and whether y'all like it or not, that makes us all family."

As Aunt Connie stormed out, Sylvia rushed behind her and stayed on her heels all the way up the stairs into the room over the garage that was now her bedroom.

"I'm sorry, Aunt Connie," Sylvia said as she watched Aunt Connie snatch her purse that was lying on the edge of the bed and toss it on her shoulder. "I didn't mean for this to happen at all. Janelle told me Sherrod wanted to talk to me about Jordan, and I agreed. I knew if I told her Garry would be there, he might've changed his mind. So they came over here without knowing Garry was gonna be home. I messed up."

"Yep, you shole did. Sounds like those people downstairs are the ones you need to be apologizing and explaining to, not me. I've said what I had to say to all of y'all about the situation. We'll be back in a little while," Aunt Connie told her.

They went back downstairs, and her aunt slipped out the door without saying another word. She peeped out the window and almost did a double take as she saw her aunt climb into the passenger side of her SUV. Sitting on the driver's side was Peyton. Her daughter checked the mirrors, then backed out of the driveway like a pro. Instead of opening the door and protesting, Sylvia found herself smiling. *Leave it to Aunt Connie to always somehow lead by example and always be right.* Now it was time to follow the advice she'd been given and make sure the rest of their family did too.

Chapter 24

Janelle

The fact that Garry didn't take off behind his wife came as a surprise to Janelle. She at least expected him to leave the room. But he didn't. Oddly enough, he and Sherrod both paced back and forth for a while before they each took their seats. No one said a word. It was as if they were all deep in thought, contemplating what their next move would be. The quiet did nothing to ease the thick tension, but Janelle figured it was better than the yelling and fighting that had taken place moments before.

She was pissed that Sylvia hadn't mentioned that Garry would be at the house. It was a setup, and she certainly didn't appreciate it. *I should've known something was up. Syl calling and agreeing to meet up after initially being so negative should've been a red flag. Sherrod walked right into the lion's den without even knowing it. God, I hope he doesn't think I had anything to do with this shit.* Janelle tried making eye contact with him, but he didn't even look in her direction. She heard the sound of the front door opening and closing, and then Sylvia finally returned.

"First, I want to apologize to all of you. I should've been honest and up front with all of you, but I wasn't, but you've gotta believe my intentions were, and well, they still are good. Aunt Connie is right, though. We all love and care for Jordan, and all of us are her family, whether we like it or not," Sylvia told them with tears in her eyes.

246La Jill Hunt

Despite her anger, Janelle felt inclined to issue her own apology. "I'm sorry too. I was the one who even suggested that Sylvia and Sherrod sit down and form an alliance. I had my own selfish motives and didn't consider anyone's feelings. I had no ill intent, though, please understand. Sherrod didn't do this, Garry. I did."

Garry's eyes remained on the floor in front of him. He didn't respond, which made Janelle feel even worse.

"I know you're not a bad person, Sherrod." Sylvia went and sat in the chair closest to her husband. "Jordan stresses that to me all the time. And that you're willing to fight for her lets me know how much you love her."

"I do." Sherrod's voice was barely above a whisper. "She's gone through a lot these past couple of months. We all have. But I promised her mom and I promised her that I would take care of her if anything happened."

"You don't have to take care of her. She has a father to take care of her." Garry lifted his head.

"Why do you keep saying that? Don't you think I know that you're her father?" Sherrod asked.

"Then act like it. I don't need another man taking care of my family. I'm a man," Garry shot at him. "I don't need you taking care of my responsibilities."

"Garry, no one is trying to take over or take your place. That's not what Sherrod is trying to do at all," Janelle explained. "If anything, he's been there for Jordan, and he's trying to help."

"Help her what? Sneak out of town without permission? Isn't that what he helped her do?" Garry said. "I don't need his help. He's part of the damn problem."

"Yes, Garry, you do," Janelle told him. "You just don't realize it. He sure did help her sneak out of town the same way I helped Peyton. I guess that makes me a problem too, huh?"

"That's not what we're saying at all," Sylvia interjected. "But both of you were wrong in that instance and have acknowledged that fact. Let's be real, these girls are teenagers, and they're going to do teenage things and get in trouble from time to time. They ain't perfect, and we don't expect them to be."

"I'm not trying to be her daddy, Garry. She's already got one. But she's also got me and has always had me from day one. I know you don't like to hear that, but that's what it is. Unfortunately, circumstances prevented you from being present full time, and I was there when you weren't. That never meant I was trying to take your place. I loved Randi, and I love Jordan, simple as that. But you always looked at me as a threat, and that's not what I am," Sherrod said. "I don't even think you realize that even though you and Randi didn't have a romantic relationship, you were so adamant with your rules and regulations regarding Jordan that Randi hardly even dated."

Garry frowned. "She was free to date whomever she wanted as long as she didn't have them around my child."

"I was her best friend, and you didn't even want me around your child," Sherrod said. "Everything had to be your way. And it was to a fault."

"What do you mean?"

"Do you know how upset I would be when I saw Jordan's report cards and her school absences? I could've tutored her or gone to parent-teacher conferences while her mom was working, or even taken her to school. But you wouldn't hear it. So instead of insisting on you allowing me to help, she fell back to keep the peace, and my hands were tied. I could only do so much, just like right now," Sherrod said. "It's frustrating and it . . . it hurts."

Janelle slid closer to Sherrod and grabbed his hand, now fighting to hold back her own tears. She glanced over at her sister and brother-in-law and saw there was something unusual about the exchange they were giving one another. It was as if Sherrod had confirmed something and Sylvia was pointing it out.

"We appreciate the support that you've given Jordan," Janelle said.

"We do," Sylvia agreed. "And we know that Randi's death has been hard on all of you. But we have to come up with what's going to be best for Jordan. That's what's most important. And I'm just gonna be honest, Sherrod, as much as you love her, I can't sit here and say you can just take her and she can go live with you. That's just not possible."

"I'm not gonna just walk away and give her up," Sherrod told her.

"Wait, I think it's safe to say that no one is expecting you to just walk away at this point, right?" Janelle asked, looking from Sylvia to Garry. Neither one answered, so she continued. "Would you at least, for the time being, allow some kind of visitation? The reality is Jordan needs as much support as she can get. This isn't an ideal situation for any of us, but we're gonna have to come up with the best solution for her. It's gonna take some give and take."

Whether it was the internal prayers she'd been thinking or the hours of required mediation training for her job, Janelle didn't know, but Garry looked up at her and said, "What kind of visitation are we talking about?"

Sherrod's fingers squeezed hers tightly. Janelle simply replied, "Maybe let them hang out once a week? I think that's a fair place to start. We don't have to come up with anything structured right now. It can be as simple as he can pick her up one afternoon a week for four hours, and we go from there. Is that something we can all agree on?"

"I don't have a problem with that if Garry is okay with it." Sylvia nodded.

They all stared at Garry and waited for his response.

"I don't want you picking her up and taking her anywhere without permission."

"Understood," Sherrod told him. "I would also like to be able to call and text her again. Can you unblock me from her phone?"

"I guess I could arrange that too," Garry said with a half-smile. "Well, I could use a damn drink. What about y'all?"

"Definitely," Janelle said, grateful that the mood had lightened.

"Everybody good with Jack?" Garry stood and asked.

"I'm good with whatever," Sherrod told him.

"Be right back," Garry said.

"I'll help." Sylvia followed him out.

They were finally alone. Janelle leaned her head on Sherrod's shoulder. "You okay?"

"I'm fine." He kissed the top of her head.

"I know it's not what you were hoping for, but I mean—"

"Like you said, it's give and take, and it's a start," Sherrod told her. "I'm just glad we were able to kind of talk stuff out. It was long overdue and had been a long time coming. I'd been wanting to have that come-to-Jesus meeting for a while, but Randi wouldn't let me."

"Come-to-Jesus meeting?" Janelle giggled. "You know who you sound like, right?"

"Good ol' Aunt Connie," they said in unison and laughed.

"Here you go," Garry said, handing Sherrod one of the crystal tumblers of whiskey he was holding.

"And for you." Sylvia passed Janelle a glass of wine.

"This ain't Jack." Janelle frowned, looking at the glass.

"I know. I didn't want to be the odd man out. Besides, ladies sip, they don't swallow." Sylvia shrugged.

Janelle relented and took the glass from her sister. "Salute, I guess."

***

"I guess we'll speak soon," Sherrod said to Sylvia and Garry an hour later as he and Janelle stood in the foyer before heading out the front door.

"We will," Sylvia said.

"Sherrod," Garry said, "uh, man, about that incident at the game the other week . . ."

"What incident? I don't recall." Sherrod shrugged. "We cool."

The door opened, and Peyton walked in, followed by Aunt Connie and Jordan. All three looked a bit confused for a second.

"Aunt Nelle!" Peyton hugged her.

"Uncle Rod?" Jordan's eyes widened, and she seemed as if she didn't know how to react.

"What's up, Jordan?" Sherrod went to put his arms around her, but she quickly looked to her father as if she wanted to make sure it was okay before she allowed it. Garry gave her a slight nod. Jordan and Sherrod held one another tightly for an extended moment.

"What's going on?" Peyton whispered.

Janelle sighed. "I'll tell you later."

"Well, looks like y'all decided to act like grownups and come to an understanding." Aunt Connie smiled.

"We did," Garry told her.

"We've gotta get out of here. I'm starving," Janelle said.

"Don't forget about prom dress shopping with us," Peyton reminded her.

Janelle had forgotten about Peyton's request for her to go shopping for a prom dress. The text had come while Janelle and Sylvia were in the middle of their little rift, which had yet to be resolved. And she still wasn't sure where she and her sister stood at this point. Though they'd both apologized for the part they played in the debacle earlier, she still needed to have a chat with Sylvia.

"She ain't gonna forget. We're gonna make a whole day of it. Shopping, lunch, right, Syl and Nelle? A real girls' day with all of us." Aunt Connie put her arms around both Peyton and Jordan. "We gonna have as much fun as we did tonight."

Jordan and Peyton looked as if it were taking everything within to produce the awkward smiles that were damn near identical. Janelle could only imagine what the two of them experienced while hanging out with their aunt. No doubt, it had been quite the experience.

"Sounds like a plan," Sylvia said, her eyebrows raised.

"We'll see you guys later," Janelle said, taking Sherrod by the hand and leading him out the door.

"Wow." He exhaled as they walked toward both of their cars. "That was intense, but I'm glad it was productive."

"Me too," Janelle told him. He put his arms around her waist and pulled her close. A warm sensation went through her despite the night chill.

"So, you want to go grab something to eat?" He looked into her eyes. "You said you were hungry."

"I am. But I think I'd like to eat in, rather than going somewhere. How about you grab something and bring it to my place?"

"Dinner at your place?" He rubbed his chin and gave her a mischievous grin. "Well, I was thinking we were gonna go somewhere special and celebrate my small victory."

"Trust me, it'll be special." Janelle winked before pulling his head to hers and giving him a hot, wet kiss to let him know exactly what she meant, in case the other hints she'd given him weren't enough. She wasn't sure if it was the progress they'd made with Sylvia and Garry, the two glasses of wine she'd had, or the fact that Sherrod was looking fine as hell in the shirt he wore that fit well enough to show off his broad shoulders and chest, but she was feeling some type of way.

"Damn," he said when the kiss was over. "Eating in it is. Anything in particular you want me to pick up?"

"Actually, I've changed my mind."

"What?" Sherrod's happiness quickly turned to confusion.

"You don't have to pick anything up. We can decide later and get it delivered. Let's go."

He opened her car door, and they kissed once more before she got in. It had been a minute since she'd had sex: not since she met Sherrod, which was indicative of how much she was feeling him. They'd waited long enough, and tonight the wait would be over.

Chapter 25

Tricia

"So, this is the big weekend, huh?" Mr. Dolbert asked.

It was quitting time on a Friday, and the last thing Tricia felt like doing was making small talk, boss or not. All she wanted to do was leave the building, stop for her curbside pickup that she'd schedule to be waiting, and go to her empty house. Her husband and son were in Atlanta, preparing for the All-American Game scheduled for the following day. Although she'd talked to Tank a couple of times, she had only communicated with Titus via text. Not that his being out of town even made a difference, because after the debacle at therapy, they really hadn't said much to one another. Of course, what happened at Dr. Guyser's office was probably the last thing on Titus's mind. He was too busy being consumed with Tank, practice, and speaking to the media to be concerned with the cold war that was now their marriage.

"Oh, yeah." Tricia nodded as she turned off her computer.

"I saw the interview your son and husband did on channel eleven. Great stuff. Are you having a watch party somewhere?" Mr. Dolbert smiled. "I see the school is having one over at Dave & Buster's."

"I'm gonna watch, but no party," Tricia told him. "You have a good weekend."

"Well, let him know we're rooting for him. Good luck."

Instead of prolonging the conversation that she didn't even want to be having with a verbal response, Tricia gave him a wave and a weak smile as she hurried past. Her head remained down in an effort to avoid any further small talk about her son and his upcoming basketball game with anyone else as she rushed down the corridor and onto the elevator. Miraculously, she made it out of the building, across the parking lot, and to her truck without any interruptions. It seemed that, unlike her boss, her coworkers were in just as much of a hurry as she was to leave. Twenty minutes later, she had just pulled into the parking space designated CAR TO GO when she looked up and saw someone waving at her.

"Everett?" She frowned as she rolled down her window.

"Hey, lady, I thought that was you." He walked over to the car. "I was gonna knock on the window, but that probably would've been kinda stalkerish. I remember how you almost killed me the first time I approached you."

"I did not almost kill you." Tricia smiled. "I threatened to kill you."

"Semantics." Everett shrugged.

Tricia had no idea what that even meant, so she just nodded.

"How have you been?" he asked. She hadn't spoken to him since the time he called to check on her after she got back from her mother's, but he had texted her twice to say hello. His gesture, albeit nice, was kind of odd. She'd meant to respond, but the second one had come the day that she'd gone to therapy with Titus, and of course, she'd forgotten until now.

"I'm okay."

"Wait, why are you here? Shouldn't you be in Atlanta? The game is tomorrow."

"It is. But I couldn't get any time off. It's a busy season at my job." Tricia didn't know why she felt the need to lie, but she did. For some reason, it sounded better than, "I didn't want to go."

"Man, that kinda sucks. But I get it." He snapped his finger. "Oh, wait, I'm glad I ran into you. I have something for you."

Tricia squinted through her glasses as she watched him stroll across the parking lot to his car and open the trunk. She wondered what it possibly could be. Whatever it was, he'd mentioned it before when they talked, and now he seemed adamant to give it to her.

"Hi, the name on your order?"

Tricia blinked, startled by the appearance of the waitress standing beside her car. She'd been so busy looking at Everett that she'd forgotten about her food order. "What?"

"The name for your order. You did place a Carside To Go order, right?" the girl, whose name tag read LYRIC, asked with a forced smile.

"Would I be sitting here if I didn't?" Tricia glowered at her. "Last name is King."

"My apologies. Most customers call and alert us that they've arrived, which you didn't do. That's the only reason I came out and asked," Lyric responded, then walked off. Tricia didn't have time to regret having an attitude because Everett reappeared, holding a nice-sized gift bag with the Burke University name and shield displayed on the outside.

"Here you go." He held the bag toward her as if he were presenting her with the Key to the City.

"Everett, what in the world?" Tricia was shocked as she took it from him.

"Look inside and see."

Tricia peeked into the bag. Just as she was about to reach inside, she told him, "You don't have to stand there. Get in."

"Are you sure?" He paused, then said, "Hey, they haven't brought your food out. How about we go inside instead and you can open it? I was going to get takeout myself."

"Well, okay." Tricia opened the door, grabbing her purse and the gift bag before stepping out. She hit the lock button of her key fob, then walked with Everett toward the entrance of the restaurant. They stepped inside, and the first person she saw was Lyric, who was posted up, talking with another hostess. She looked a little shocked when she turned and saw Tricia walk up.

"They're bagging your food up now. I'm just waiting for them to bring it out," she explained quickly.

"Oh, no worries, it's fine," Everett told her. "She actually decided to come in to keep me company while I order my food."

"So, you're dining in instead?' The hostess grabbed two menus from the pile in front of her.

"Well, no . . ." Tricia started.

"We can if you'd like," Everett turned and said. "I mean, we are already inside, and your food is ready. You can eat it now instead of taking it home."

"I don't know." Tricia was caught off guard by his suggestion.

"I'm sorry. I mean, you probably have somewhere to be, and here I am, intruding and holding you up."

Everett's embarrassment was somewhat amusing, and Tricia found herself relaxing a bit. His awkwardness put her at ease, and she realized she wanted to stay and eat. Not only because she was starving and her stomach had been talking to her for the past hour, but also because she really didn't have anywhere else to be or anything else to do. Her bed, numerous bottles of wine, and Lifetime movies weren't going anywhere, and the only person she anticipated talking to the entire weekend was her mother.

"No, I don't. It's fine, we can eat here," Tricia told him. She turned to the waitress and said, "Have the kitchen plate my food rather than box it up."

"I'll let them know you told me to do that," Lyric said with her former fake smile.

"You two can follow me. Would you like a booth or a table?" the hostess interjected.

"A table is fine," Tricia answered. As a size twenty-two, she knew better than to chance the embarrassment of not fitting comfortably into a booth.

The hostess led them to a table, and Everett waited for her to be seated before he sat across from her. He looked at Tricia and said, "You good?"

"Yes." Tricia nodded.

"Great."

Before the server came over to take their drink orders, Tricia's food was delivered to the table. It took two people, Lyric and another waitress, to carry everything she ordered, which included spinach and artichoke dip, a chicken quesadilla, cheese sticks, a half rack of ribs, broccoli, and fries. As they placed the items in front of her, Tricia felt her face become hot. It hadn't seemed like that much food when she placed her order online, but now she knew she must've looked pure gluttonous.

"Did you want your dessert now or later?" Lyric asked, causing her to be even more embarrassed than she already was.

"No, I think this'll be all for now," she said without even looking over at her.

"Wait," Everett said, looking at Tricia. "You want to order a drink from the bar? I could use something a little stronger than a soda. What about you? Strawberry margarita?"

Tricia's normal intensity level of anxiety had returned, and she really wanted to just get up and leave, but that would've been even more uncomfortable, so she forced herself to remain and said, "I could use a drink."

"I'm actually not your server. I was just helping bring food out. But I'd be happy to put your order in with the bar and let them know," Lyric said.

"That'd be great. Thanks for telling us that too. We certainly wouldn't want to give the amazing tip I planned on leaving to the wrong person," Everett told her. "Especially someone as unpleasant as you."

The fake smile fading from Lyric's face was just the thing Tricia needed to see. Had it been Titus across the table, he would've been apologizing for Tricia's tone, eye rolls, et cetera. Very rarely had anyone ever taken up for her. It was kinda refreshing.

"I know this looks like a lot. I forgot I ordered food for dinner and lunch tomorrow," Tricia said, coming up with an explanation she thought was believable so she wouldn't look as greedy.

"Hey, you don't have to explain. Believe me, I'm about to order just as much as you have. Heck, we're probably gonna need a bigger table." Everett laughed.

Tricia shook her head. "I know you're just saying that to make me feel better. As slim as you are, I doubt that you eat a lot."

"I love food. I just have a really high metabolism, I guess. Been like that my whole life. My mom says it'll catch up with me when I get older, but I'm forty-one, and it hasn't slowed down yet, so I think I'm good."

"Wow, you look good as hell for forty-one. I thought you were way younger than that," Tricia said before she could stop herself. She hadn't meant to say the words aloud, but she damn sure thought them. She'd for sure figured he was in his early thirties, if that.

"Thanks, I think." He laughed. "Go ahead and eat up before your food gets cold."

Tricia cautiously picked up one of the chips and said. "I hope you don't think I'm going to let you sit here and not eat some of this."

"If you insist," Everett said, reaching and helping himself to one of the mozzarella sticks.

By the time they'd finished eating, Tricia felt as if they were old friends. Everett was funny in a nerdy kind of way. He told her about growing up as an only child in the Midwest and how being labeled "gifted" when he was in junior high had been both a blessing and a curse. Tricia listened, then gave her own account of being the oldest of two "gifted" siblings, one academically and one athletically, and how she'd always felt like the "unspecial" child of the family.

"Come on, everyone is special."

"Not me. But I'm fine with that," she told him as she nursed the bottom of her margarita.

"Nope, I believe God has purposed each and every one of us to do something that no one else can do. We just have to figure out exactly what that thing is. Some people just figure it out sooner than others. For those who've discovered it, every day you wake up is another day to pursue it. For those who haven't, it's another opportunity to figure out what it is. Either way, you win," Everett explained. "Everyone has a purpose. Every life has meaning. It's why we were put on earth. Your sisters are unique in their own way, but so are you."

Tricia sat and thought about what he said. She'd never considered that her life may actually have a meaning, or that she was purposed to do anything. "Well, I'm the only one of my mother's daughters who is still married."

"Well, I'm sure there's a deeper plan for you than just that, but I definitely feel that being a wife and mother is purposeful. No doubt, that's not easy. Balancing marriage, motherhood, and working. I commend you on that." He held his glass up to toast. They both looked at her empty glass and laughed, and then he said, "You want another?"

"No, two was enough. I still have to drive home. But I do see your point," Tricia told him. "Are you married?"

"No." Everett shook his head. "I mean, I would love to meet the right woman and settle down, but it just hasn't happened."

"Well, I'm sure you will. You seem like a really nice guy," Tricia told him. She was surprised to hear that he was single. Although he wasn't overwhelmingly attractive and a bit of an oddball, he was decent looking, smart, and genuine.

"Thanks." He said, "You still haven't opened your bag."

Tricia had all but forgotten about the gift bag in the chair beside her. She shifted the now-empty plates on the table to make room before sliding her chair back and putting it in her lap. She reached inside past the crumpled tissue paper, and the first thing her hand touched was a mug. She pulled it out and saw that it was navy blue with the same Burke University crest as the bag it was in.

"Aw, this is nice. Thank you so much," Tricia told him.

"Keep digging."

She reached back into the bag, this time taking out a mousepad. There was also a nice set of pens, a keychain, and other Burke items, all navy blue. "I love all of this, Everett. Thank you so much."

"I'm glad. I mean, even though Tarik decided against my esteemed alma mater, I still wanted you to have some school swag as a token of appreciation."

"See? Look at how thoughtful you are. I don't know why you aren't purposed to be somebody's husband yet," Tricia told him as she placed her items back in the bag. "I do have a question, though."

"What's that?" He leaned forward.

"Burke's school colors are maroon and gold. All of this stuff is blue."

"True, but we get stuff in all colors. Blue's your favorite, so I went with it," he said matter-of-factly.

Tricia peered at him, shocked by his response. "Wait, how did you know my favorite color was blue?"

"Isn't it?" He frowned. "Wait, did I get it wrong?"

"No, but how did you know?"

"Well, your truck is dark blue, the first time we met you had on a blue dress and a blue coat, and your purse was blue. It was kinda obvious." He shrugged.

Tricia looked over at her blue MK bag beside her, then thought back to the night Everett showed up at her house. She had been wearing a blue dress and her blue overcoat. *I can't believe he remembered that. That's crazy.*

It was after ten at night when they decided it was time to go. Everett insisted on paying for their meal, despite her already paying when she ordered online. He even went so far as to speak with the manager and get him to refund the check card she'd used. He walked her to her truck, still parked in the same space, and thanked her for her company.

Tricia was so glad that she'd stayed and joined him. She'd had a great time, so much so that she didn't realize until she got home and took her phone out of her purse that she hadn't taken her phone off silent when she left work. She'd missed three calls from Titus. Had someone seen her and called and told him? Her son had become quite the local celebrity, and maybe someone recognized her. Did he somehow sense that she was out with another man? Dinner with Everett was innocent. She tried not to panic as she called him back.

"What's up?" She tried to sound unbothered and normal.

"Nothing," Titus said. "What's up with you?"

"What do you mean?" Tricia's heart began pounding. *He knows.* "What are you talking about? You're the one who called me three times like it was an emergency."

"I called because your mother called me. I guess she tried to reach you and couldn't."

Tricia looked through her missed call log and saw that, in addition to the missed calls from Titus, she also missed five calls from her mother and several texts. "Shit, let me call her."

"Okay, well, I was just making sure nothing happened."

"Oh, you were concerned?" Tricia couldn't resist asking.

"Of course I was concerned. Why wouldn't I be?"

Her original thought was to remind him that he wasn't in love with her, but instead, she told him, "It's not like you've been acting very concerned for the past few days before you left."

"Because you were still tripping off that therapy bull-shit. I'm fine. You were the one walking around mad at the world."

"I am mad, Titus. I can't believe you said all of that," Tricia snapped. "Do you know how hurtful that was?"

"Look, I wasn't trying to hurt your feelings. I was just, I don't know, venting, I guess. You know I didn't want to be there in the first place. But I went because you acted like it was a big deal. Now it's over. I'm sorry, a'ight?"

"Where's Tank?" Tricia asked without accepting the apology she was glad he gave. She knew if she did, he would think he was off the hook, and she would lose her leverage. He wasn't getting off that easy.

"He's with some of his teammates. He should be back in the room in a little while. They have a curfew."

"Okay, well, let me go call Mama before she sends the police over here," Tricia told him. "I'll call Tank in the morning and talk to him before his game to wish him luck."

"Cool."

"Titus?" Tricia called to stop him from hanging up.

"Yeah?"

"What's my favorite color?"

"What?" The confusion in his tone was obvious.

"What's my favorite color?"

There was a long pause, and then he finally said, "Yellow? Wait, green. Hell, I don't know."

Tricia shook her head. "Good night, Titus."

Chapter 26

Sylvia

"You like this one, Mom?"

Sylvia looked at the price tag of the dress Peyton was holding. "This is over your budget, ma'am."

"I told you," Jordan said with a shrug.

"Yes, it's a little pricy, but I think I should try it on just to see how the style looks on me," Peyton said. "Please?"

"If you want to try on a dress that you can't afford, feel free. But there's no way I'm paying that much money for a dress you're only gonna wear one time, and then buy another one," Sylvia told her.

"I know. I just wanna see how it looks, that's all." Peyton grinned, then took off toward the dressing room with Jordan by her side.

Shopping with her daughter for prom was something Sylvia had been looking forward to for years. It never occurred to her that it would be such a daunting task, and the fact that they were looking for two dresses made it even more so. For hours, they'd trekked in one store after the other on their quest to find the perfect gowns. But as exhausting as the experience was, it was also enjoyable. Probably due to the fact that Aunt Connie, Janelle, and Lynne tagged along. It had turned into a total girls' day full of laughable moments and interesting conversations, including an ongoing one about Lynne and her situation with her ex-husband, Hampton, who'd recently asked her out on a date.

"I say go for it. You said it yourself that he's gotten his gambling addiction and spending habits under control. Wasn't that the reason for your divorce, or was there something else?" Janelle asked as she skimmed through the rack of taffeta gowns while they waited for Peyton, who'd gone into the dressing room to try on yet another possible choice, assisted by Jordan.

"No, there wasn't anything else. Until his gambling got out of control, we were pretty happy. Well, at least I was happy," Lynne said.

"Obviously, he was happy too. If he hadn't been, he wouldn't be trying to get you back," Sylvia pointed out.

"Who said that's what he's trying to do? He says he wants to have dinner and talk," Lynne told them.

"Talk as in discussion or talk in some other kind of way?" Aunt Connie asked, causing Lynne to blush.

Sylvia quickly looked around to make sure Peyton, Jordan, and anyone else wasn't nearby. "Aunt Connie, can you please?"

"Please, what? I'm just trying to ask some clarifying questions. The same questions she needs to be asking before she starts daydreaming about being reunited with his ass and planning a wedding," Aunt Connie told them.

"I don't think that's what she's doing, Aunt Connie." Janelle snickered. "Jeez, that's a stretch."

"The way she was looking at the bridal gowns hanging in the front when we walked in," Aunt Connie said, "I could see you making wedding plans in your head, child."

From the look on Lynne's face, her aunt was right.

"That doesn't mean I was thinking about remarrying Hampton, Aunt Connie. I can marry someone else," Lynne said.

"But you ain't thinking about talking to no one else, are you?" Aunt Connie gave her a knowing smile.

"Aunt Connie," Sylvia hissed again.

"Hey, I'm all for talking if that's what she wanna do. Just make sure you clarify with him if the conversation is going to be a simple chat between two old friends, or a long conversation that y'all both plan to continue for a little while. Just make sure you're speaking the same language. Leads to less confusion and no heartbreak. Let me tell you what a dear friend of mine used to say: 'All the things that we been through, you should understand me like I understand you.'"

"Aunt Connie, that was a line from a Harold Melvin & the Blue Notes song," Janelle told her.

Aunt Connie winked and said, "Who do you think was my dear old friend I was talking about?"

Sylvia, Janelle, and Lynne all laughed so loud that other people in the store looked at them.

"Well, let me ask you a question, Aunt Connie." Sylvia couldn't resist taking advantage of the moment.

"Ask away, niece," Aunt Connie said.

"What kind of talking are you doing with Deacon Barnett?"

Aunt Connie grasped at her neck at the set of invisible pearls that weren't there. "Excuse me?"

"Come on now, Aunt Connie, we all know about your little secret rendezvous you've been sneaking off to when you walk Gypsy," Janelle added.

"First of all, I am a grown woman, and I don't have to sneak nowhere. And yes, I do go out at night to walk the dog before I go to bed," Aunt Connie snapped. "It ain't my fault that that fool keeps driving by at the same time and insists that he give me and Gypsy a ride home. Hell, if someone did try to do something to me, Gypsy would probably be more helpful than his slow ass anyway."

"Awwww, that's so sweet. I like him," Janelle said.

"Me too!" Sylvia nodded.

"I ain't ask you if y'all liked him, did I?" Aunt Connie rolled her eyes and walked away.

"Ohhhhhh, I think she likes him too," Janelle whispered.

"She does," Sylvia told her. "He picks her up almost every night in his Caddy while she's walking the dog. He brings her home, and they park across the street from the house, and they sit in the car for a little while. It's adorable."

"She's right, though, Lynne. You need to figure out what you and Hamp got going on before it gets too complicated," Janelle said. "I mean, before you get used to him blowing your back out on the regular."

"Jeez, Janelle, you're about as bad as Aunt Connie," Sylvia said to her sister.

"I'm just saying, see where his head is at and make sure whatever it is, is what you want. Don't compromise," Janelle said.

"They both want the same thing: each other. Hampton has been trying to get her back for years. And now she's finally willing to give him a chance, end of discussion." Sylvia went back to searching through the dresses.

"I'm just open to hearing what he's gotta say, but I gotta admit, getting my back blown out on the regular would be nice, too." Lynne sighed and smiled as if she remembered something.

"See, that's the look of love," Sylvia pointed out.

"I'm thinking that's more like the look of lust," Janelle said and walked away.

Lynne looked at Sylvia and winked. "Both of you are right."

"Lord, Lynne, don't be influenced by her," Sylvia said. "It will take more than Hamp breaking you off in order for y'all to restart your relationship. He's gonna have to come better than that, and you know it."

"First of all, I didn't say that's all it would take, but please don't act like vitamin D isn't important. Let me ask you this: if the sex between you and Garry weren't good, would you still be holding on?" Janelle said.

"What kind of question is that? Garry and I have nearly twenty years invested in our marriage. There's also the fact that I love him, he's the father of my child, my best friend . . ." Sylvia began pointing out reasons she'd told herself over and over while contemplating divorce.

"You know what they say: good sex is the glue that sometimes holds the relationship together." Janelle shrugged. "People have stayed in relationships well past the expiration date because they didn't want to lose good dick."

"Good dick? I'm not sure about that." Lynne rubbed her hand on her chin as if she was deep in thought. "Now, great dick, that may be a little different."

"What do you think, Mom?" Peyton walked up and asked.

For a second, Sylvia thought she was referring to the inappropriate conversation they were having. Her heart began racing until she realized the gorgeous gown Peyton was wearing. It was a perfect fit, and without a doubt, they weren't going to find a better dress. This one was it.

"I think it's perfect." Sylvia smiled.

"One down, one to go." Peyton squealed and rushed back to the dressing room.

When she was gone, Sylvia turned around and hissed, "And for the record, it takes much more than great dick to hold a relationship together. But I will admit that having a good source of vitamin D is important for my dietary needs."

"Mine too." Aunt Connie's voice came from behind. "It certainly does the body good."

***

Later that night, Sylvia smiled as she peeked out of her bedroom window at the Cadillac parked across the street from their house. Why her aunt was so stubborn, she didn't know, but Sylvia was certain she had her reasons.

"Aunt Connie with her boo again?" Garry, who'd been lounging in the sitting area, put down the iPad he'd been looking at. Sylvia still hadn't allowed him back into their bed, but he somehow always ended up in their room lately.

"Yep. They're out there talking." As soon as the words escaped her mouth, she began laughing hysterically as she thought about the conversation they'd all had earlier.

"What's so funny?"

Sylvia was laughing so hard that it took a moment for her to compose herself enough to answer. "Something we were talking about earlier, that's all."

"Well, tell me so I can laugh too," Garry said.

Sylvia told him about Lynne contemplating reconnecting with Hampton, and how Aunt Connie, in true fashion, somehow turned the conversation to sex. Garry laughed, and Sylvia sat on the opposite end of the love seat. Their eyes met, and whether it was the way he was looking at her, the fresh haircut and shave he had, the scent of his sexy-ass Sauvage cologne, or the fact that she was horny after semi-bragging about the vitamin D he provided, Sylvia was turned on. However, she really didn't want to make the first move. So instead of hopping up and straddling him like she wanted to, she simply twisted her body and placed her feet in his lap. He smiled, and without hesitation, his fingers massaged her arches and caressed her ankles.

"Damn." She leaned her head back and sighed.

"You like that, huh?" He grinned.

"You always did give the best foot massages, and after trekking all day looking for your daughter's prom dress, I deserve this."

"My daughter, huh?" He laughed.

"Yep." She nodded.

"Interesting." His hands moved up to her calves, and he slid closer to her. "What else do you think you deserve?"

Sylvia playfully bit her bottom lip, her eyebrows raised. "I can think of a few things I deserve."

In one swift movement, Garry shifted her body so that she faced forward, and he kneeled in front, her legs over his shoulder. Sylvia didn't even need to assist him in slipping her leggings or panties off. He handled everything, and all she needed to do was lie back and enjoy the pleasure of his tongue as it explored her welcoming wetness. It had been a while since he'd tasted her, and he made sure to show her just how much he missed the dish she enjoyed serving him. Sylvia gripped the edge of the sofa as he pushed her legs open wider in order to go deeper and find exactly what he was looking for: her clitoris, which now throbbed. The sound of his moans turned her on even more, and she tried to hold on as long as she could.

"Oh shit, Garry, baby, stop," she whispered as she grabbed the top of his head. "I don't want to. Not yet."

Garry ignored her pleas and couldn't answer her even if he wanted to. His mouth was occupied, and he was too focused on savoring each and every drop that was now erupting from within her. Sylvia's legs began shaking as she climaxed, and although she was finished, Garry didn't stop until he knew she was satisfied.

"Is that what you were thinking you deserved?" He smiled when he finally came up for air.

"Definitely." She panted as she tried to catch her breath. "But I'm still thinking I deserve a little more."

Garry unfastened his jeans as he stood, and then he stepped out of them. Sylvia's eyes went from the remnants of her wetness that were on his face and scanned down to the large bulge peeking from his boxer briefs, the sight of it turning her on all over again. She reached to grab it, but before she could reach it, Garry quickly slipped her oversized T-shirt over her head and fondled her hardened nipples through the lace of her bra.

"Your turn." Sylvia went to touch his manhood again, now ready to reciprocate the oral gesture he'd given her.

"Nope." He shook his head, then commanded, "Turn over."

Sylvia didn't hesitate to comply, and as she turned her back to her husband, she smiled at the thought of the good old vitamin D she was about to get. Besides, their marriage could use a little glue these days, and she had no problem helping to add some stickiness.

Chapter 27

Janelle

This is the last time, I swear, *Janelle thought as Titus held her by the ankles. She stared into his big brown eyes, hating herself for enjoying this so much. Her arms wrapped around his muscled shoulders and pulled him closer as she arched her back to make sure she felt every inch of him as he entered.*

"Damn, I missed this, Nelle." He moaned. The rhythm of his stroke game took her to higher heights of pleasure. His rhythm was perfect as he slid in and out of her slippery center, slow and sensual at first, then faster.

"Harder." Janelle gasped, her body reacting to the sensation of his hands cupping her breasts. She maneuvered her fingers around his wrist and guided them to her throat. As the pace of their lovemaking increased, so did the tension of his grip. Janelle closed her eyes, repeating her command, louder this time. "Harder."

The passion between them was so intense as she approached what she knew would be a climax like no other that she became lightheaded. The room began spinning, and she could hear a distant ringing in her ears.

"Oh shit." Titus's voice began fading as the ringing became louder.

"Don't stop, Titus. Please don't stop. I'm so close," she warned, but it was as if he couldn't hear her over the

ringing. Then, just before she arrived at her peak, he was gone.

Janelle sat up and looked around her dark living room. Her dream had been so vivid that beads of sweat had formed on her forehead. The ringing in her ears continued, and she realized that it was her cell phone. She stared at it, so discombobulated that she couldn't even answer. Not yet. She had to gather her thoughts and get her mind together before speaking with him.

"Get it together, girl," she told herself. "Titus is your past. Sherrod is your future. You can't move forward if you keep looking back. Onward and upward. Let that shit go."

Fifteen minutes later, after two more pep talks and a large glass of wine, she felt like she was in a headspace clear enough to return his call.

"How was prom shopping?" he asked.

"Tiring, but fun. We found the first dress. I told Peyton she's on her own for the second one because I'm not going with her." Janelle put her cell on speakerphone and stretched out on her sofa. When she arrived home nearly an hour earlier, she'd planned to sit down for fifteen minutes before heading upstairs to take a much-needed shower. But she was too tired to move.

"You say that now, but we both know you're gonna be right back at the mall with her next weekend shopping," he teased.

"You're probably right," Janelle confessed. "But I'm gonna need at least two weeks to recuperate from all the walking I did today, not one. It was a great time, though. Even Jordan enjoyed herself. She's starting to come out of her shell a little bit. I'm glad we were all able to come up with a compromise."

"Me too. You're right. When I picked her up the other day, she was a straight chatterbox like she used to be. And

can you believe there was no mention of a hairbrush?"
Sherrod laughed.

"Thank God. I am glad that entire situation is over, and
she and Peyton are working through their issues, too.
How was your day?"

"Busy, long, typical life of a drug dealer at the end of flu
season."

Janelle laughed at the words "drug dealer." "Hey,
somebody's gotta be the pusher. It may as well be you. I
ain't mad at ya, bruh."

"I know you say you're tired, but I would like to see you.
I need to run home and take a quick shower, and then
maybe we can go grab a late dinner and then come back
to my place, or yours, whichever you prefer."

Janelle's phone beeped, rescuing her from having to
answer. "Hey, this is Natalie. I need to talk to her right
quick, and I'll call you right back."

"Sure, no problem."

She accepted the incoming call from Natalie. "Hey, girl.
Your timing couldn't be more perfect."

"What's going on?" Natalie asked.

"Sherrod wants to see me tonight."

"And that's a problem why?" Natalie said it as if Janelle
were a remedial learner.

"Stop it. You know why." Janelle sighed.

"Just because he wants to see you doesn't mean y'all
have to have sex."

"I know, but still." Janelle picked up the remote and
turned on the TV. "The sad thing is I really like him. He's
a great guy. And how about right before he called, I was
having a dream about Titus. A good dream."

"So, things still weren't right the last time you hung out
with Sherrod?"

"Nope. He stayed over the other night, Nat, and we did
it again, or at least tried. It just wasn't it," Janelle whined,

recalling her and Sherrod's second sexual encounter a few nights prior. She'd convinced herself that it was going to be better than their first attempt, which left her underwhelmed at best. Unfortunately, their encounter was just as disappointing. Sherrod, on the other hand, seemed to enjoy each and every moment. "Maybe this is karma. Being with Titus has ruined me for other men."

"That can't be the case. You've had sex with other men, and it's been fine. You definitely enjoyed Jarvis."

"That's true."

"Maybe you should just talk to Sherrod, Nelle. Tell him what the deal is," Natalie suggested. "Explain your concerns."

"I can't do that." Janelle shook her head.

"Why not? The man's a pharmacist. I'm sure he would be open to hearing it."

"And just how do I start that conversation, Nat? 'Hey, Sherrod, you're a great guy, and I really enjoy hanging out with you, but the truth is you are wack in bed'?"

Natalie giggled. "I would hope you would be a little more tactful than that, but yes. Tell him that you're a very sexual being and the times you've been together have been, um, unfulfilling?"

"Or I can just not say anything and deal with it. I mean, it's just sex. He has so many more important qualities. He's smart, funny, consistent, dependable. Nat, he's everything I've been saying I want in a guy. I'd be crazy to break up with him over something so trivial as sex, right?"

"Are you asking or telling?"

"You're not helping me at all. Where is Nivea? She's more suited to assist me with this situation." Janelle laughed.

"She probably would, but that would first require you to finally fess up about dating Sherrod, now wouldn't it?" Natalie responded. "Which you need to go ahead and do anyway. I honestly don't think she's even gonna care."

"Again, you're not helping me at all, Nat," Janelle groaned. The sound of the doorbell caught her attention. "Hold on, someone's at my door."

"Uh-oh, Sherrod done popped up on you?" Natalie asked.

"Shut up." Janelle checked her reflection in the hallway mirror she passed on the way to the front entrance of her townhouse. She looked through the peephole, expecting to see Sherrod, and nearly dropped her phone. "Nat, I gotta call you back."

"What's wrong?"

"I'll call you back." She ended the call, closing her eyes and taking a deep breath before opening the door. "What are you doing here?"

"I wanted to see you, that's all. Can we talk?" Titus said.

Chapter 28

Sylvia

The house smelled delicious thanks to Aunt Connie. Peyton's incessant begging had persuaded her to make all of Tank's favorites. Under any other circumstances, their aunt never took requests, but she made an exception and honored the menu suggestion of fried chicken, pork chops, macaroni and cheese, string beans, rice and gravy, and even made homemade rolls. For dessert, there was a choice of pound cake or peach cobbler.

By the time the doorbell rang promptly at seven p.m., everyone's stomachs were growling and mouths were watering. Even Garry was a little excited about their hosting their dinner guest and daughter's beau, whose phenomenal performance at the McDonald's All-American Game now made him an even bigger prospect for colleges and universities. The entire community was buzzing with talk of Tank King and where he would decide to go to school.

"I got it," Peyton screamed as she scurried out of her room so fast she nearly slipped on the freshly Swiffered hardwood floors.

"Peyton," Sylvia said as she caught her just in time, "calm down. Your father will get the door."

"Oh God, he's going to do or say something embarrassing." Peyton exhaled.

"No, he's not. Relax, everything is going to be fine," she said with a reassuring smile.

Peyton nodded and took a deep breath. Sylvia listened for the door to close, and then after a few moments, she motioned for her daughter to continue down the steps. She followed Peyton into the den where Garry and Tank were now sitting.

"Hi, Tank." Peyton grinned as soon as they entered the room.

"Hey, P. I mean, good evening, Peyton." Tank wasted no time hopping to his feet, forgetting about the bouquet of flowers in his lap, which fell to the floor. He quickly grabbed them. "Oh, sorry."

Sylvia found his nervousness just as amusing as Peyton's. "How are you, Tarik? It's nice to finally meet you."

"Nice to meet you too, Mrs. Blackwell. These are for you." Tarik held the bouquet out.

"Why, thank you, Tarik. How thoughtful." Sylvia smiled.

"Oh, and please call me Tank."

"Thank you, Tank." Sylvia nodded as she admired the colorful bouquet. "Calla lilies are my favorite."

"Thank you so much for inviting me. Your home is lovely."

Peyton sat on the sofa beside Tank, making sure to leave enough distance between them that would be considered safe in front of her parents. Sylvia sat next to Garry on the love seat.

"Well, Tank, I must say, you are one helluva basketball player. I caught that All-American Game the other week. Congratulations," Garry said.

"Thank you, sir. It's been a great year." Tank nodded.

"Dinner is ready when you all are," Aunt Connie came into the living room and announced.

"Tank, this is my Aunt Connie," Peyton said.

Again, Tank stood, this time walking over to the doorway where Aunt Connie was standing and giving her a hug. "Nice to meet you, ma'am. P—I mean, Peyton—talks about you so much I feel like you're my aunt."

"It's about time we met you too. Peyton wasn't lying when she said you were tall and handsome, and you smell good, too," Aunt Connie told him. "Now y'all get washed up so this young man can eat this food I prepared especially for him."

By the time they washed up and went into the dining room, the food was on the table, and Jordan and Aunt Connie were both sitting and waiting.

"What's up, Jordan?" Tank spoke as he held Peyton's chair out.

Sylvia glanced over at Garry to make sure he noticed how well-mannered Tank was. So far, she'd been impressed with him and saw why Peyton liked him so much. He was very much like his father: personable, handsome, polite, and smart. As they ate dinner, it was as if Titus were there with them. Even their voices were similar.

"This food is amazing," Tank commented as he devoured his second plate. "I can't remember the last time I had real home-cooked food, let alone soul food."

"That's because you're never home. You're always at practice." Peyton laughed.

"Nah, that's because there's no one in my home to cook, especially like this. I mean, my dad grills, and he makes decent spaghetti, but nothing like this."

"What about your mother?" Garry asked. Sylvia kicked him under the table. They'd agreed that there would be no discussion of Tricia, for several reasons, and now here he was asking about her cooking abilities.

"No, sir, my mother does not cook anything at all. The only thing she knows how to make is an order for takeout." Tank shook his head.

"Sounds a lot like my mom." Jordan laughed. "She was an expert on pairing wine with food, but couldn't cook a meal at all."

It was the first time Sylvia had heard Jordan share a pleasant memory about her mother. Usually, she would clam up whenever Randi's name was brought up, so hearing her laugh about this was a pleasant surprise.

"Listen, I was excited when I found out Aunt Connie was staying with us because I knew the meals were going to be popping," Peyton added.

"Whoa, whoa, whoa, don't act like I can't cook." Sylvia pretended to be appalled at her daughter's confession. "Garry, tell them."

Garry looked down at his empty plate and reached for the pan of macaroni and cheese. "I mean, you can, babe. But I gotta admit, I was a little excited too."

"Lemme get a little more of that, Mr. B, before you scoop it all up." Tank held his plate out.

Laugher erupted around the table. Aunt Connie smiled. "Well, as pleased as I am to hear that you all enjoy my cooking, I'm gonna need all of y'all to leave room for dessert."

"Don't worry, I'll have room," Tank told her.

"I'll clear the table," Peyton offered, picking up the now-empty macaroni pan.

"No, you have a dinner guest. I got it." Jordan reached to take the pan from her.

"You sure?" Peyton looked shocked.

"Girl, give me the pan." Jordan sighed. "It's fine."

"Thank you, Jordan." Garry smiled and nodded his approval, then turned his attention to Tank. "So, Decision Day is almost here. Are you excited?"

"Daddy." Peyton's tone matched the warning look she gave her father.

"What? I didn't ask what his decision was, Peyton," Garry explained with an innocent shrug. "I just asked if he was excited. I know he can't tell me what school he's picked, or can you?"

"Dad!" Peyton gasped.

"It's okay, Peyton." Tank laughed. "To be honest, I'm still deciding. But I am excited about going to college. You both went to Mission College, right? That's where my dad went too. He didn't finish, but he still loves that school."

"Yeah, both of them did, and so did my aunt Janelle." Peyton spoke before anyone else did. Sylvia gave Garry a look to let him know this was dangerous territory they were entering with this conversation.

"That's dope. When my dad talks about it, he gets this look in his eye and his face lights up as if he's talking about paradise or something."

"As he should." Garry nodded. "I had some of the best days of my life at Mission College, and that's where I met the love of my life."

"The two of them used to turn up together in college. I think that's why they're so strict," Peyton said sarcastically.

"Peach cobbler, pound cake, and vanilla ice cream," Aunt Connie announced as she and Jordan returned to the dining room with dessert. They enjoyed dessert while listening to Garry's and Sylvia's stories of Mission College and other tales of their teenage antics, pledging their respective fraternities and sororities, and the lifelong friendships they'd made. Afterward, they all went back into the den and laughed and talked some more until it was time for Tank to leave.

"Thank you guys for this," Tank said. "It was amazing, and I'm just grateful."

"Well, I'm sure Aunt Connie would be willing to cook for you again," Sylvia told him.

"I would love that, but honestly, it was more than the food, Mrs. Blackwell." He looked around the room.

"What do you mean?" Garry asked.

"I know this sounds crazy, but tonight, I felt like, well, family. I don't get to feel like this, so it was cool." For a second, it looked as if the young man was gonna cry, and Sylvia couldn't help but pull him into an embrace.

"Well, Tank, you are family, so you are welcome." Sylvia sighed. After she released him, Aunt Connie hugged him just as hard.

"Can't wait to have you over again." Garry nodded as he shook Tank's hand.

"Can Tank and I hang out for a little while?" Peyton asked her father. All eyes turned to Garry as they waited for his answer.

To her surprise, Garry looked over at Sylvia and said, "If your mother doesn't have a problem with you guys going out for a while, then I don't."

It was a simple response, but it meant so much more, and Sylvia nodded. "Be home before eleven. You're still under punishment, remember?"

"Thanks, Mom," Peyton exclaimed, throwing her arms around both of her parents, then heading out the door with Tank behind her.

"Well, that was real nice." Aunt Connie commented, "He's a nice fella."

"He really is," Sylvia agreed.

"He's cool. He and Peyton make a cute couple," Jordan commented, surprising everyone.

"You think so?" Garry asked.

"Yeah, and I get what he was saying. Tonight was kinda dope. It really did feel like family," Jordan told them. "Thanks from me too, for everything."

Sylvia was unable to hold back the tears she'd been fighting since the hug she shared with Tank moments earlier. She pulled Jordan into her arms, and within seconds, Aunt Connie joined, and Garry. As she stood in the midst of the group hug, she felt that there may be hope for her family after all.

Chapter 29

Tricia

"I'm sorry to keep you waiting, Mrs. King. My last client went over their time," Dr. Guyser said when he walked into his office.

Tricia was smiling at something on her phone, which she was holding. She glanced up as she put it into her purse. "It's okay, I understand."

From the look on his face, Dr. Guyser was surprised by her response. After taking a seat at his desk, he said, "Well, you seem to be in a good mood today."

Tricia's head tilted. "Good mood?"

"Yeah, your voice is pleasant, and you're smiling," Dr. Guyser pointed out. "I take it things have gotten better since our last session."

"A little," Tricia told him. It had been two weeks since her last appointment.

"So, did you start taking the meds I prescribed? Are they helping?"

"No," Tricia said. "I told you I didn't want to take them."

The antidepressants he'd prescribed on the day of her first appointment were still in the glove compartment of her car. She had no intention of taking them no matter how much he claimed they'd help. The blood pressure and anxiety medicine she took was enough, but she drew the line at what her mother referred to as "drugs for crazy people." She wasn't that damn depressed.

"That's your choice, and I still think you should recon-
sider. But you seem to be better," Dr. Guyser told her.
"I'm sure this is a pretty exciting time for you all. Your son
is choosing what school he's attending soon, right?"

"Actually, today is Decision Day. I have to go straight
to the school when I leave here for his announcement."
Tricia sighed.

"And are you going to be okay with that? I know being
in crowds at Tank's events are bothersome for you." Dr.
Guyser leaned forward.

"I'm actually okay. It shouldn't take that long. He'll just
pick a hat off the table and take a pic, then we can leave.
Well, I can. His dad does the press stuff," Tricia told him.
The fact that she wasn't anxious about attending Tank's
Decision Day announcement was surprising even to her.
Maybe Dr. Guyser was right. She was in a great mood.

"Have things improved at home between you and Titus?
How is the communication between the two of you? Your
son's basketball season is over, right? So the two of them
should be spending a little more time at home."

"Yes, basketball season is done, thank God. They're not
gone as much, but Tank is still in training and condition-
ing. He still needs to be in top shape to play college ball."
Tricia repeated the words she heard Titus say on some
news interview after Tank's All-American Game. Even
though the season was over and her family was home
a bit more, things between her and her husband hadn't
improved, but they hadn't gotten worse either. As far as
she could tell, they were back to normal. "We haven't
argued, if that's what you're asking. We haven't had a
fight since the day we were in here, so that's a good thing."

"Good. And how's the sexual relationship? Are we still
utilizing the calendar, or are you working on spontaneity,
which we talked about last time?"

Instead of answering, Tricia cleared her throat. She couldn't remember the last time she and Titus even had sex. She really wasn't able to work on her sexual spontaneity because not only had he stopped badgering her to have sex, most nights, he barely slept in their bedroom. Her husband had been more distant than usual. Between his job and everything their son now had going on with his newfound fame, prom, graduation, and college Decision Day, Tricia decided to allow him some space. Besides, she had a distraction of her own occupying her time, so she wasn't concerned.

"Tricia?" Dr. Guyser said softly.

"No, no changes in the bedroom," she finally said. "Not yet."

"Well, what do you think has brought about this change of attitude?"

"So, remember you suggested I open up and become a little more social?" Tricia asked.

"Yes."

"Well, I did. I started a friendship, and I'm really enjoying it."

"Really? That's great to hear, Tricia. I told you being open and not so closed off to others would be beneficial." He nodded.

"Yeah, it's nice having someone to talk and laugh with. We have a lot in common, and it's like our conversation just flows." Tricia smiled. "It's like, refreshing. I know that sounds cliched, but that's the only way to describe it."

"And is this friend one of your coworkers? A neighbor?"

"No, he doesn't live in the area." Tricia laughed.

Dr. Guyser frowned slightly. "He?"

"Yes, my new friend is a he. His name is Everett. We actually met when he tried to recruit Tank for Burke University, but Tank wasn't interested."

"He's a coach?" Dr. Guyser asked.

"No, he's actually the president of the black alumni association for Burke. He's really cool."

"And you talk to him frequently?"

"We talk quite a bit." Tricia thought about the number of calls and texts she'd exchanged over the past couple of weeks. Since having dinner, she and Everett Matthews had become quite close. They talked daily, and she enjoyed their conversations, which could be about anything from current events to the latest episode of *Downton Abbey,* which they both watched. It felt good to discuss something other than basketball or sports. Everett was smart, and he took the time to explain things to her if she didn't understand. She hadn't seen him since the last time he was in town, and she looked forward to him visiting soon. They'd already planned a coffee date, and he promised to bring her more Burke swag: blue, of course.

"Tricia, are these conversations more in-depth than the ones you have with Titus?"

"I mean, yeah, Everett is easier for me to talk to, and he's way funnier."

Dr. Guyser stood and walked around to the front of the desk. "Tricia, are you developing feelings for this man?"

Tricia gasped as she stared at him, shocked at his question. "What? Why would you ask me that?"

"It's a valid question. Are you attracted to him?"

"I told you he's my friend."

"You're evading the questions. Is your friend single?" Dr. Guyser continued.

"I don't know what you're getting at, Dr. Guyser, but you're wrong. First of all, he doesn't even live here, and you're making it sound like he's out here seducing me and trying to get me into bed, which he's not. We're just friends. It's not some sordid affair." Tricia's face became hot, and had her complexion been shades lighter, she was sure she'd be blushing. "You are the one who told me to get a friend, and now that I met one, you're insinuating that it's something else."

"That's not what I'm doing at all. I'm just making sure you're not going down a slippery slope of being intimate with someone outside of your marriage."

"Intimate? Did you hear anything I said? We hardly see one another, and I've never had sex with him. He's a nice guy, that's all." Tricia shook her head and reached for her purse. As far as she was concerned, this session was over, and she was going to have to think long and hard before deciding to come back.

"Tricia, calm down, there's no need for you to become so defensive. Just listen to what I'm trying to tell you, please." Dr. Guyser's voice was calm as he pleaded with her.

Tricia hesitated, then said, "What?"

"Intimacy and sex are two different things. You're sitting here telling me how you're having detailed conversations with this man—"

"We aren't having phone sex."

"Let me finish. Again, this isn't about sex. Sex is the physical act of intercourse."

"Which we've never had."

"Understood. But intimacy is something much deeper. It's having an emotional connection with someone. It's developed through talking and laughter and something as simple as a 'thinking about you' text from someone you're close to," Dr. Guyser said. "It's holding hands, a lingering hug, something simple and affectionate."

Tricia thought about the random "hey, you" texts Everett would send her that made her smile. She enjoyed them, but they didn't automatically make her want to have sex with him. They were just friends. He was the one person who made her feel like hearing about her day mattered. They hadn't crossed any lines, and she didn't plan on crossing any. But now it sounded as if Dr. Guyser was about to tell her that she shouldn't talk to him anymore.

"We're just cool, that's it. Men and women can be just friends, you know. It happens all the time. We're not having an affair."

"It does, and you're right. But if you're not careful, you'll end up in an emotional affair with this guy, and that can be worse than a physical one. And if one of your goals is to eventually improve your marriage, then you need to avoid any potential outside distractions and work on your intimacy with your husband if it's not there."

Tricia stood up and picked up her purse. "I'm not gonna stop being friends with Everett."

"Does Titus know about your new friend? Because if it's as innocent as you say it is, then you shouldn't have a problem telling him all about it, right?"

Tricia opened her mouth but decided not to justify his question with an answer. Instead, she walked out of the small office, slamming the door behind her.

The parking lot of Tank's high school was jam-packed by the time Tricia arrived. She sat in her SUV for a few moments. The anxiety she bragged about not having earlier was now in full effect, especially after her session with Dr. Guyser. She was a grown woman and capable of maintaining a platonic friendship with a male. His suggesting otherwise was the main reason Tricia left his office without making her next appointment. There was no point in coming back. She was done. The whole reason behind going to therapy was to have Titus admit to being in love with her, and that hadn't happened. Hell, he hadn't even been back. The only help Dr. Guyser gave was showing that she needed a friendship in her life, and now that she'd found it, he acted as if it was a problem. It wasn't making a difference in her marriage anyway, which was the reason she'd started seeing him in the first place.

Her phone vibrated and notified her that a text was waiting to be read. She tried to resist the urge to open it, but then opened it anyway.

Good luck and congrats again, Mom. Remember to breathe deeply, and don't focus on the crowd. Tell Tank it's not too late to throw Burke in the running.

The message was just what she needed, as usual. She replied with a smiley face before turning the phone off, smiling as she took a deep breath and walked inside. Titus and Tank were on stage, along with a few other players who were also announcing their decision and their parents. Tricia made her way to the front, and the coach waved for her to join them.

"Glad you could make it," Titus told her.

"This is important," Tricia told him, then looked over at Tank. "You ready?"

"Yep." He nodded.

The ceremony began, and as the coach made his remarks at the podium, Titus, Tricia, and the other parents moved to the side while they waited their turn. She spotted Peyton and her parents in the crowd. Two other players went before Tank, both of whom selected top-tier schools, but neither had the Ivy League or NCAA choices that Tank did.

"Which one did he choose?" Tricia whispered to Titus while they set three hats on the table in front of Tank.

"I don't know. He said I'd find out when everyone else did." Titus shrugged. "Probably Duke."

Duke was also one of the schools Everett felt that Tank would choose. If he did, Tricia smiled at the thought of having to tell him he was right. He would no doubt enjoy that phone call. She frowned as she thought about what Dr. Guyser said. She looked at Titus, who seemed nervous. Tank cleared his throat in the microphone, and a hush fell over the crowd.

"I'd like to thank everyone for being here. It's been an incredible four years playing here and an outstanding season. I want to thank Coach Darby for everything and my teammates for always having my back. I couldn't do it without any of y'all. I also want to thank my parents, especially my dad." Tank's voice cracked, and he looked over at his father.

Titus dabbed at the corner of his eye, and in that moment, Tricia saw one of the cameras pointed at them. Thinking there was a chance that her sisters were watching and this could be an opportunity to show just how united she and her husband were, she mustered an awkward smile and reached over to take Titus's hand. Instead of holding hers, Titus flinched and shifted slightly in the opposite direction. If she did go back to Dr. Guyser, at least she could say she attempted to work on intimacy but was rejected. Her attention turned back to her son, anticipating what he was going to say about her.

"Dad, you have always been my best friend, and I can depend on you for everything. You've taught me to be the best in everything I do: on the court, in the classroom, no matter what. I pray that I continue to make you proud. And it is now with great pride that I announce that I will be attending . . ." Instead of reaching for one of the three hats in front of him, Tank reached under the table. It sounded as if everyone in the room gasped at the same time and held their breath. "Mission College in the fall on a full athletic scholarship."

The stunned look on Tricia's face matched everyone else's, including Titus's. After the initial shock wore off, people began to applaud. Tank stood up and put the hat on his head, beaming with pride. Cameras flashed, and his teammates congratulated him.

"What the hell? Did you have anything to do with this?" Tricia hissed, livid at Tank's decision.

Titus looked at her and said, "No, I had no idea. I can't believe it myself."

Tank came over and hugged his dad. "What you think, Pop?"

"I mean, wow. You picked Mission." Titus still seemed shocked.

"I picked Mission." Tank nodded.

"Mission? Why the hell would he choose some bottom-of-the-barrel black school?" Tricia scowled, horrified at the spectacle of her son's announcement in front of the entire world. She couldn't believe he would embarrass her like this, and had she known prior, she damn sure wouldn't have been there. Her sisters were probably going to have a field day after seeing this. Not only had Tank not even mentioned her in his speech, but he'd failed to make the right choice.

"Hold up, Ma," Tank stopped her. "This was my decision, and Mission is far from being some bottom-of-the-barrel school. It's one of the top HBCUs in the country. Not only that, I picked it because the people I respect and know who attended Mission, including Dad, all say that it was the place that changed their life."

"Do they even have an engineering program?" Tricia asked.

"Doesn't matter if they do. That's not my major."

"What?" Tricia frowned.

"I'm majoring in Recreation Therapy. I want to open my own community center and help kids." Tank high-fived his father, then disappeared into the crowd of reporters waiting to speak with him.

"This is what you called yourself working so hard for?" Tricia looked at Titus. "Your son could've gone to any school in the country for free, and this is what he picks, huh? This is an embarrassment, Titus."

"Embarrassment for who? I don't think I've ever been prouder in my life," Titus said before walking away and leaving her alone.

Tricia's anxiety returned, and she pushed her way through the crowd toward the nearest door. As soon as she got to her SUV, she took out her phone and hit the last number dialed. She needed a friend now more than ever, and for once, she was grateful she had one to call.

Chapter 30

Janelle

Drinks tonight. Eight p.m. Copeland's. First round and appetizers on me. I miss my girls. We need to catch up, and I have some tea to spill.

Janelle stared at the cryptic message she'd received earlier and checked her watch to make sure she had gotten the time right. It was eight thirty, and she'd been waiting in the lobby of the restaurant for almost fifteen minutes. Neither one of her friends had arrived. It had already been a long day filled with nonstop meetings at work, and she didn't get the chance to have lunch. She was tired, irritated, and the only thing that kept her from grabbing her bag and going home was the fact that she was hungry as hell, and she really did want to hang out with her girls. Between dealing with the reality of Sherrod's lackluster sexual performance, and Titus showing up on her doorstep, she needed some girl time.

"I know, I know, I'm late," Natalie said as she walked over and hugged Janelle.

"You're not the only one." Janelle shook her head and slid over so her friend could sit beside her.

"Wait, she's not here? How the hell are you gonna invite us somewhere and not be on time?"

"Hey, that's our girl. That's why I wasn't pressed about being on time."

They decided to go ahead and get a table while they waited for their host, and they ordered their first round of drinks and appetizers that Nivea had so graciously offered to pay for.

"Okay, what's this about?" Janelle turned and asked. She and Nivea barely talked these days, and they hadn't hung out since they were at the nail spa weeks ago. Any other time her boisterous friend would be chock-full of information about her daily life that she shared in their group chat, but Nivea had become radio silent, and other than a simple "good morning" or "hey, besties," she hadn't had too much to say and seemed busy these days. Janelle and Natalie knew something was up and it most definitely had to do with a guy. Putting her friends on the back burner was usually what happened whenever Nivea became boo'd up, but this time, she'd been oddly secretive. Truthfully, Janelle had been relieved that her friend had been distracted these days because of her own situation that she'd been hiding that she planned to reveal tonight.

"I don't know. I told you I haven't talked to her in a while, so your guess is as good as mine," Natalie responded. "You think she's gonna finally introduce us to her latest victim? I wonder who it is."

"I have no idea. She's keeping this one quite private. Something's up, that's for sure. Maybe he's unattractive," Janelle suggested.

"Nah, she's dated ugly guys before. I'm thinking he's white."

"Oh, hell no. She would never date a white guy. You know how woke she claims to be." Janelle laughed.

"That's true, but I believe she'd date a white guy if he was fine enough. And I'm talking Jason Momoa fine."

"True," Janelle agreed. "Hmmm, maybe he's short."

"She'd definitely date a white man before she dated a short one." Natalie laughed.

"Wait, maybe he's an ex-con who's just been released."

"She does like them thuggish-ruggish dudes. Lord, our friend about to be on the next season of *Love After Lockup*. We can't let her publicly embarrass herself like that, Nelle. Wait, I got it."

Janelle, now laughing so hard that she was in tears, composed herself enough to say, "What?"

"Nelle, what if he's married?"

"Hell no." Janelle gasped. "That can't be it. As much shit as she's talked about me and my situation with Titus? She wouldn't never."

"I think that might be it. Think about it. She hasn't posted him on social media or even sent us a pic of them together. She hasn't even mentioned his name."

"You think she's dating a married guy?" Janelle lowered her voice and glanced around, now suddenly concerned about others hearing what they were discussing. Never in a million years would she think Nivea would be someone's mistress. Then again, never in a million years would she think she'd ever be one either. But her girlfriend had always been so condescending and judgmental when it came to Janelle's situation in a subtle, shady way that let it be known that she certainly didn't approve. If Natalie indeed was dating someone married, the tables would be turned.

"Could be. Then again, we may be looking at this all wrong, and maybe this impromptu invite is to tell us that she's no longer dating whoever this dude was she's been kicking it with."

"So soon? If that's the case, it definitely ain't last long."

"Speaking of lasting long, what's up with you and your boo? Did you give it another try?"

Janelle leaned back in her chair and inhaled deeply, thinking about the answer to Natalie's question. "No, we didn't."

"I thought he came over the other night."

"No, it wasn't him at the door. It was Titus."

"Oh shit." Natalie's reaction had been the same as Janelle's when she opened the door and saw Titus. They hadn't spoken since the flower incident, and it was the longest they'd gone with no communication. She missed him but was determined to sever the soul tie they shared and stay away from him. His number was blocked from her phone, and so was his email address.

"Titus." Janelle's heart began pounding as she stared at him. "There's nothing to talk about. You shouldn't even be here."

"I know, but I miss you. I miss us. And I know you're pissed that I pulled up at your crib like this, but I just wanted to see you. To tell you—"

"Tell me what, Titus? There's nothing to tell. I can't do this anymore. Don't you know how hard it is for me to get you out of my head without you doing shit like this? I'm trying to move on."

"Maybe you can't get me out of your head because that's not the only place I'm in. We both know I'm in your heart, Nelle. The same way you're in mine. That's how it's always been with us. That's how it's meant to be." Titus went to reach for her, but she stepped back.

"No, that's not. You're right, you are in my heart, and that's why I gotta stay away from you, because as long as you're there, I don't have room for anyone else." Her voice trembled.

"You don't need anybody else."

"You can't be this selfish, Titus. Don't you think I deserve to be with a man who loves me and cares for me? A man who wants to build a future with me? Don't I deserve to be happy?" Janelle didn't even try to wipe the tears that fell from her eyes.

"I love you and care for you. You're not happy with me?" Titus frowned.

"So, I'm just supposed to be your mistress for the rest of my life and be happy with that? That's all you think I'm worthy of? I want to have a family."

"We can have a family, Janelle." Titus reached for her again. "You want a baby, we can have one. I want another child."

"Do you know how crazy you sound right now? You want another child, go and have one with your wife. I'm finished with this . . . this relationship, friendship, whatever you want to call it. Leave me alone, Titus. If you love me, please leave me alone," Janelle pleaded.

"Is that truly what you want?" Titus said, his eyes now filled with as many tears as Janelle's.

"Yes, Titus, that's what I want." She nodded.

He kissed his fingertips and placed them on her forehead. This time she didn't move away.

"You deserve to be happy," he whispered. "Bye, Nelle."

"So, you're really done with him?" Natalie's voice had a hint of sadness, as if she was disappointed to hear that the forbidden love affair that consumed the last three years of her friend's life was over.

"Yes, I'm done. It's time I settle down with someone that I can build a future with." Janelle nodded.

"And that's Sherrod?"

"Yes."

"Despite the shortcomings? No pun intended, Nelle. I'm just making sure." Natalie smiled.

"Nobody's perfect, Nat. Not even me. And if Sherrod's willing to accept my flaws, then I can accept his. He's a decent guy, and sex isn't the only thing that holds a relationship together." Janelle prayed that she was right.

"To new beginnings." Natalie raised her glass.

"I know y'all heffas ain't start drinking without me."

Janelle's head turned toward Nivea, who stood a few feet away from the table, her arms folded and her head shaking in disbelief.

"Heffa, we know you ain't rolling up in here forty-five minutes late like you're on time." Natalie smirked.

"Hell, we about to start eating without you," Janelle said.

"Greedy asses." Nivea kissed both of their cheeks before sitting.

Janelle noticed the large Gucci purse she hung on the back of her chair. "Whoa, whoa, whoa, what do we have here?"

"Oh, this?" Nivea looked at the bag and shrugged. "Just a little treat I got from someone special."

Janelle's eyes met Natalie's across the table, and they gave one another a knowing look. They were right. She had a new boo, and clearly, he was paid. They'd been invited for the big reveal of the boo and the bag.

"And who is this someone special?" Natalie asked.

"Let me get a drink and I'll explain, because well, it's kinda funny, actually," Nivea said.

"Funny how?" Janelle asked. "Is he a comedian?"

"No, he ain't a comedian, smart ass," Nivea replied and ordered a drink from the waitress who was delivering their appetizers to the table. She picked up one of the coconut shrimp, and before popping it into her mouth, said, "Before we talk about my someone special, how about we talk about yours?"

Her statement was directed at Janelle, who was stunned for a second, and didn't answer right away. "What do you mean?"

"Well, I know you haven't been hanging out with Jarvis these days, but you've been hanging with someone," Nivea said after chewing. "So, spill it."

Again, Janelle looked over at Natalie, who avoided her stare as she grabbed one of the potato skins from the middle of the table and popped it into her mouth. Her friend obviously had mentioned something to Nivea. But how much, she didn't know. Instead of denying it, or avoiding the conversation, Janelle decided to just tell her.

"There's nothing really to spill. I've been seeing someone for a couple of weeks now, and I mean, it's cool. I like him a lot." She wished she'd ordered another drink for herself.

"Interesting. Well, you like him enough to stop dealing with Jarvis?" Nivea asked.

"Yeah." She hadn't spoken with Jarvis or gone out with him since she started seeing Sherrod. "You do realize Jarvis and I weren't a thing, right? He wasn't my man. We weren't in a relationship."

"That's true. But Jarvis was fine," Natalie pointed out, suddenly contributing to the conversation.

"Yes, God, he is," Nivea agreed. "Well, let me ask you this: this new guy, do you like him enough to leave Titus alone?"

"How did this conversation turn to be about who I'm dating? We're here for you to spill the tea about your new man, remember?" Janelle asked.

"Oh, trust, I'm going to spill it. But answer the damn question, Nelle. You like him enough to stop messing with Titus?"

"Yes, I do." Janelle nodded.

"Damn, okay, now I gotta know. Who the hell is he?" Nivea asked. "I never thought I'd hear you say that."

Janelle paused for a few seconds, then said, "It's Sherrod."

Nivea's eyes widened. "Rod? My Rod? My ex? That Sherrod?"

"Now, Niv, you know that's a stretch. You messed with him for a couple of months in high school. I wouldn't call him your ex," Natalie said.

"Sherrod Crawford." Janelle nodded.

"Well, damn." Nivea sat back, a look of shock on her face.

Janelle waited for the loud outburst and plethora of profane words she knew her friend was about to release, but there weren't any. To her surprise, Nivea slowly smiled, then started giggling.

"What's funny?" Janelle gave her a strange look. She'd expected some kind of reaction, but this definitely wasn't it.

"I'm sorry, I don't mean to laugh." Nivea dabbed at the tears in her eyes. "My bad. I just wasn't expecting you to say Rod. But that's really nice though, Nelle. He's a good dude. I'm happy for you guys."

"You are?" Natalie asked.

"Yes, I am. Why wouldn't I be?" Nivea shrugged.

"Because the first thing you said was, 'My Rod? My ex?' That may be why," Janelle reminded her.

"Okay, true. But I guess I was kind of surprised to hear that's who you were talking about. Real talk, I thought it was someone else."

"Who?" Janelle asked.

"I thought you were gonna say Kenny."

"Kenny?" Janelle and Natalie said simultaneously.

"Now we all know Kenny is a man whore. Hell, he's tried to holler at everyone at this damn table," Natalie pointed out. "Probably everyone female in this restaurant." They laughed.

"No, I'm not dating Kenny," Janelle said. "So, now that I've spilled my tea, it's time for you to spill yours. Who is this someone special monopolizing all your time these days and buying you Gucci bags?"

"And belts." Nivea leaned back to display the belt she was wearing that matched her purse.

"Well, damn," Natalie said.

"Okay, well, like I said, it's kind of funny, especially since now I know you're dating someone I know. He's actually someone you know." Nivea exhaled. Her eyes went from Natalie to Janelle. "Someone you've known for a while, actually."

"Someone I know? Who?" Janelle frowned as she began to wonder who Nivea could possibly be talking about. Her mental Rolodex went through all the possible guys Nivea could date, but no one in particular stood out.

"Damn, I gotta take this call. I'll be right back," Nivea stood up and said.

"Wait, we're in the middle of a conversation," Janelle told her.

"Nivea," Natalie called after her, but it was too late. Nivea had walked away.

"Who the hell is she talking about?" Janelle asked.

"Maybe she's using reverse psychology and she's the one dating Kenny."

"Nah, if Kenny was dating Nivea, he'd tell Syl, and she would tell me. The two of them have no secrets between them." Janelle shook her head. "It damn sure better not be who I'm thinking about."

"Who?"

"How does she know I don't deal with Jarvis?" Janelle pointed out. Granted, she and Jarvis were never in a committed relationship, but the thought of one of her best friends dating him made her uncomfortable. Could she really say anything though? After all, wasn't she dating Nivea's old high school boyfriend, and to make matters worse, the guy she'd lost her virginity to? But she'd dealt with Jarvis a couple of months ago, and it had been decades for Nivea and Sherrod. There was a big difference, wasn't it?

"What? Hell no. You don't think she'd be with him. Nah, she wouldn't do that." Natalie's head shook back and forth so hard her long braids fell out of their bun.

"Okay, I'm back." Nivea returned.

"Great, now sit your ass down and tell us who this dude is," Janelle told her.

"How about I show him to you instead?" Nivea gushed.

"He's here?" Natalie began looking around.

"He is. He's walking over here now."

Janelle turned around, silently praying she wouldn't see Jarvis. She blinked at the man walking toward them. A lump formed in her throat, and she slowly inhaled.

"Oh shit," Natalie murmured.

"Be nice. I promise I'll explain everything later," Nivea warned just before welcoming her guest with a big hug and a kiss that left both Janelle and Natalie stunned.

"What's up, ladies?" He grinned.

Janelle didn't say anything as she stared at him. It wasn't Jarvis. The man standing at their table with his arm around her best friend was Hampton Davis. The same Hampton Davis who'd been married to Lynne, Sylvia's best friend. The same Hampton who Lynne had been excitedly bragging and talking nonstop about the weekend before while they were out shopping for Peyton's prom dress.

"You guys know Hamp, right?" Nivea smiled.

"Uh, yeah," Natalie answered for both of them.

"I think they're kinda in shock, baby," Nivea told him. "Look at their faces."

"I understand. That's how I reacted when you told me you were pregnant too, remember?" Hampton said.

Janelle's mouth gaped open, and Natalie made a noise that sounded like the squawk of a bird.

"You need to stop playing." Nivea laughed. "Now y'all know I ain't pregnant."

Finding out that Hampton was joking about Nivea being pregnant was a little relieving, but Janelle was still a bit disturbed. She couldn't believe Nivea was dating Hampton Davis. Not that Nivea and Lynne were friends, but they knew one another. They'd all hung out on more than one occasion both before Lynne's divorce and after. Hell, if Janelle recalled, Nivea had been at Sylvia's house one night for a girls' night when Lynne broke down crying about her divorce after having a few too many drinks. This was messy, and Janelle wanted no part of it, especially after the conversation she and Lynne had days before. Was Hampton cheating on Nivea or Lynne? Because from what she saw, he damn sure was sleeping with both of them.

"It's good seeing you again, Janelle. How's Syl and Garry?" Hampton had the nerve to ask.

"They're good." Janelle's voice was noticeably flat, but she didn't care. She stood up and said. "Excuse me."

Janelle went into the restroom and began pacing back and forth as she tried to think. A few seconds later, Natalie and Nivea walked in.

"I know this is kinda funny, and I tried to prepare you, Nelle, but he just popped up," Nivea explained.

"Funny? You think this is funny?" Janelle looked at her as if she were crazy.

"Okay, maybe not ha-ha funny, but funny as in unusual or unexpected," Nivea told her.

"Niv, this is not cool. We all know Lynne, and she's really nice," Natalie said.

"Yes, we do, and you're right, she's good people. But this has nothing to do with Lynne, and for the record, they've been divorced for years. Don't act like I'm some kind of side . . ." Nivea's eyes met Janelle's, and she stopped.

"I'm leaving. I'm not staying here for this." Janelle shook her head. "Nat, can you pay my portion of the bill? I'll Cash App you."

"No doubt." Natalie nodded.

"I said tonight was my treat," Nivea said.

"Nah, I'm good," Janelle told her.

"So, you're just gonna dip? Really, Nelle? You can't stay and at least have one drink? That's messed up."

"What? You think I'm gonna go back out there and pour it up with the ex-husband of a woman I consider a sister? Nah, that's what's messed up. You can't expect that shit to happen, because it ain't."

"I expect my best friend to at least spend fifteen minutes with me and the guy I'm in love with. But whatever."

"In love? Nivea, you've only been dating him for a couple of weeks," Janelle told her.

"About the same amount of time you've been seeing Rod, huh? Aren't you in love with him?"

"This isn't about me."

"That's my point. All of a sudden, because I'm dating someone you don't agree with, it's a problem? That's what we do now? I never thought you of all people would be this damn hypocritical," Nivea said as they faced off. Janelle, who was slightly taller, looked down at her, determined not to be intimidated. Nivea had a lot of mouth, but Janelle knew that's all that it was.

"Niv, hold up," Natalie tried to intervene. "Let's all take a step back."

"What the hell are you getting at?" Janelle's eyes became small as she stared at Nivea.

"For years, we've sat back and watched you play your position with Titus, and even though we voice our opinions on occasion, we let you do you. Now you wanna leave, then fine. All I wanna say is I don't need you running to Syl and saying shit about me and Hampton. I mean it."

"Oh, so it's a secret?" Janelle was baffled by her request.

"No, it ain't a secret, but it ain't nobody's business." Nivea shrugged. "And we'd like to keep it that way."

Janelle looked over at Natalie, then back to Nivea. "That's how you know this is some bullshit. Let me guess, Hampton told you to tell me that."

"Actually, he didn't. He just said he'd prefer the opportunity to tell Lynne about us himself, and I agree. So I'm just saying, respect that request."

"And if I choose not to?"

"You won't," Nivea replied. "Because if you do, that huge contract your sister just got from the mayor's office, and the one that's in negotiations right now, won't happen. Trust me, Hampton will make sure that it doesn't. His words, not mine."

Chapter 31

Sylvia

"You look beautiful, Peyton," Sylvia whispered as she stared at her daughter's reflection in the mirror they stood in front of.

"You do," Janelle, who sat on Peyton's bed, agreed.

"Is my hair okay? Do I need to curl it some more?" Peyton asked nervously, touching her flowing waves.

"No, everything is perfect," Janelle responded. "The dress, the shoes, the jewelry, the makeup, everything."

"Thank you, Aunt Nelle." Peyton smiled, then turned around and said, "And thanks, Mom. I know I blew through my budget, but I'm gonna get a summer job and—"

"Stop lying, girl." Sylvia laughed and shook her head. "It was worth every penny."

The budget she'd given Peyton for prom was forgotten the moment she'd seen her in the dress she wore. Somehow, they'd also found another dress for Tank's prom that was just as perfect and cost as much. But the accessories they'd purchased would be worn to both proms.

"Well, at least my going to Mission is gonna save you some coins, right?" Peyton winked.

Janelle hopped up. "Wait, are you serious? You decided?"

Sylvia gasped. "You're going to Mission? Since when? I thought you were choosing Spelman."

"Shhhhh, I don't want Dad to hear. I want it to be a surprise," Peyton whispered.

"Wait, it this because Tank chose Mission?" Sylvia peered and folded her arms.

"No, Mom. I chose before he did. See?" Peyton walked over to her desk and handed Sylvia a paper.

Sylvia took it and saw it was a receipt from Mission College for Peyton's enrollment fees and housing dated months before. She turned to Janelle. "Did you pay this?"

Janelle shook her head. "No, it wasn't me."

"Aunt Connie gave me most of it," Peyton said.

"Lord, that woman, I swear." Sylvia sighed. Her aunt never ceased to amaze her. "She ain't said nothing."

"It was our little secret." Peyton giggled. "She's still not back home?"

"Not yet." Sylvia shook her head. Aunt Connie left over an hour ago, saying she had an important errand to run, but promised she would be back before Peyton headed to the prom.

"Well, I am so happy you chose my alma mater. It's the best school in the world, but I'm sure you already know that." Janelle hugged Peyton. "It's the school I picked."

"Our alma mater," Sylvia corrected her. "And I picked it first, and she followed."

"Touché." Janelle took out her phone and began taking selfies of the three of them. "Well, my beautiful niece and future Mission maiden, I want you to be safe tonight and have fun."

"You're leaving?" Peyton gasped. "But Tank hasn't even gotten here yet. Don't you want to see him and take pictures of us together?"

Sylvia glanced at her sister, and they gave one another a knowing look. Janelle had already said she would be leaving right after Peyton was dressed so she wouldn't run into Tank's parents. She was happy to hear that Janelle decided to cut off all ties with Titus once and for all. And she understood Janelle wanting to avoid him.

"I'll make sure to take plenty of pics and send them to her," Sylvia promised.

"Fine." Peyton accepted her aunt's decision to leave with a pout.

Sylvia walked her sister downstairs. Janelle said goodbye to Garry and Jordan, who were sitting in the den watching television while waiting for Peyton's date to arrive.

"Thanks for coming to help her get dressed." Sylvia hugged her just before she went out the door. "I'm sorry you can't stay, but I understand."

"I wouldn't have missed it for the world. She looks gorgeous. I can't believe she's going to prom," Janelle told her. "She's all grown up."

"And heading to Mission. Garry's going to be ecstatic," Sylvia whispered. "And to be honest, I am too. A sister can get her retail therapy on with that contract money."

"Syl, I need to talk to you about something." Janelle became serious.

"What is it? What's wrong?" Sylvia could tell something had been bothering Janelle all afternoon, but she thought it had to do with possibly seeing Titus and his wife. But she realized it was something else.

The doorbell rang, causing both of them to suck in air. Gypsy ran into the foyer where they were standing and began barking.

"Gypsy, calm down!" Jordan ran behind the dog.

"I'll call you later," Janelle said and headed toward the kitchen to slip out the side door.

Once her sister disappeared, Sylvia opened the front door. Tank stood in the doorway, looking like a model in his custom tuxedo with a tie that matched Peyton's dress. In his hand was a beautiful wrist corsage, and behind him was Titus.

"Good evening, Mrs. Blackwell," Tank greeted her.

"Tarik, you look so nice." Sylvia gave him a brief hug as she welcomed him inside. She paused and politely said, "How are you, Titus?"

"I'm well, Sylvia," Titus replied.

"Wait, you two know each other?" Tank looked confused.

Titus quickly answered, "As much as you talk about Peyton's family, I feel like I've known them forever."

Sylvia quickly added, "And as many times as I've seen your father on television bragging on his son, I feel the same way."

"Oh, that's true." Tank shrugged.

As she closed the door, she saw Janelle's car still parked in front of the garage and wondered where her sister went.

"You look nice, Tank," Jordan said, now holding Gypsy in her arms to keep her quiet.

"Thanks, Jordan. Hey, Gypsy." Tank petted the dog's head.

"Your mother's not here?" Sylvia noticed Tricia's absence, which was odd, but a bit relieving. She had not been looking forward to seeing her.

Tank looked over at his father then back to her. "Uh, no. She was supposed to meet us here, but I guess she's running a little behind."

"Well, there's my future Mission man!" Garry strolled in and announced.

"How ya doing, Mr. B?" Tank smiled and shook Garry's hand.

A few moments later, Sylvia escorted her anxious daughter down the steps to her date. Tank nervously fumbled to place the corsage on her wrist while they all, including a very emotional Garry, took pictures. After Peyton pinned a boutonniere to Tank's jacket, Titus adjusted his son's bowtie, and Sylvia saw him slip some folded bills into his hand before telling him he loved him and to have fun.

"You ready?" Tank asked Peyton.

"Wait, we can't leave yet," Peyton exclaimed. "Aunt Connie's not here yet."

"Baby, y'all have to get going," Sylvia told her.

"Yeah, we have dinner reservations at seven, remember?" Tank said.

"I'll make sure she gets the pictures, and Aunt Janelle," Sylvia promised, immediately glancing to see if Titus reacted to her sister's name.

The door opened, and Aunt Connie stepped inside. "Well, hello, everyone."

"Aunt Connie, I thought you were gonna miss us." Peyton hugged her. "We were just about to leave."

"Of course I wasn't gonna miss y'all. And you can't leave before your limo arrives," Aunt Connie announced.

"Limo? We didn't rent a limo." Peyton laughed.

"Well, not exactly a limo. But something a little better." She beckoned for them to follow her as she stepped back out the front door.

"Oh, snap!" Tank yelled.

"Is this for us?" Peyton squealed.

"Oh my God." Sylvia gasped as she saw what had them so excited. Sitting in the driveway was a beautiful vintage Rolls-Royce Phantom in pristine condition. Standing beside it with the door open was Deacon Barnett, decked out in a tux, top hat, and gloves.

"Now, y'all go and have fun." Aunt Connie hugged Peyton then Tank as they rushed off to get into the classic automobile.

As soon as they drove off, Titus turned and said, "Thank you all for everything. I appreciate y'all."

Garry shook his hand. "It's no problem. It was good seeing you, Titus. You raised a fine young man."

"He's a good kid. Thanks." Titus turned to Sylvia, pointed at Janelle's car, and said, "Give her my love, Syl."

When he was gone, they all went inside. Sylvia went upstairs to her room to finally relax. She was about to call Janelle and ask where she disappeared to when Garry walked in.

"Syl, can we talk?"

Sylvia put her phone down and said, "Sure."

Garry sat beside her. "First, you did an amazing job with Peyton and all of this prom stuff. She looked beautiful. I know it took a lot of time and energy, but you pulled it off, so thank you."

"She's our daughter, Garry. I just did what any mother would. You don't have to thank me."

"No, you've done way more, and not just with her, but with everything. You have pretty much been a single parent in a lot of ways and done a hell of a job raising our daughter while I've been away for most of the time. And now, despite the circumstances, you've started parenting Jordan. You are amazing, and I appreciate your willingness to do that. You have always been one of the most selfless women I know. But I can't let you do this anymore. It's not fair."

"Garry, what are you talking about?" Sylvia frowned. "What's not fair?"

"Me expecting you to single-handedly raise a child you never expected to raise, especially at the moment that the business you and your partner have worked so hard to create is taking off. It's not fair for you to put your dreams on hold to take care of a responsibility I created. So I want you to know that you don't have to, Syl. I get it,"

Garry said. "I thought me being a great provider meant that I was a good partner, and that's not what I am, or was."

"Are you leaving me, Garry?" Sylvia asked.

"No, Syl, that's not what I'm doing at all. As a matter of fact, I'm doing the opposite, I'm joining you." Garry told her, "That is, if you agree."

"What do you mean?"

"I want to quit my job, Syl, and be home. I want to be home for you, for us, for our family. To help with whatever you need me to do," Garry said.

For years, Sylvia had been waiting for him to finally decide it was time for him to slow down and spend more time with her and Peyton. Now Peyton was graduating, and he was having an epiphany. She then remembered his admitting how he hated his job, and even after telling her, he still continued working. Sylvia didn't know how to respond. Having him home full-time would allow them more time to work on their marriage and help with Jordan, and she would be able to grow their company. All the things she'd been trying to figure out over the past few months.

"Are you sure about this, Garry?" Sylvia asked.

"Only if you think it's a good idea. It's not up to me. It's up to us," Garry said. "You don't have to answer right now. Just think about it."

He leaned over and kissed her cheek, then said, "Let me see if I can convince Aunt Connie to make some hot wings for dinner."

"You know she doesn't take requests," Sylvia reminded him.

"I'll tell her they're for Tank. Better yet, Deacon Barnett." He laughed as he walked out of the room.

Chapter 32

Janelle

"When exactly are you going to tell her?"

"I don't know," Janelle said to Sherrod as she finally pulled out of Sylvia's driveway. She'd hidden on the side of the house and watched Peyton and Tank as they got into a Rolls-Royce driven by Deacon Barnett, of all people. Then, once Titus left, she was able to get into her car. "I told her I had something to tell her, but there was so much going on with Peyton, tonight wasn't the time to say anything. If I even say anything at all."

"So, you're not going to tell her?"

"I don't know. What if Hampton is bluffing? I mean, he could just be saying that because he's playing Lynne and doesn't want to get busted." She was grateful that the conversation was about Nivea's threat. The last thing she wanted to think about was having to watch Titus outside of her sister's house. Or the fact that he kept looking at her car in the driveway. No doubt he wondered where she was, and from the way he kept looking around, maybe he could somehow sense that she was less than 500 feet away. She forced the image of how great he looked out of her head and focused her attention back to Sherrod.

"Or Nivea may be bluffing and Hamp didn't say that at all," Sherrod suggested. "This may be her way of protecting whatever it is she's got going on with him."

"Do you think she would do that?" Janelle thought out loud.

"She's your best friend. You know better than I do. But when it comes to guys, I wouldn't put anything past Nivea," Sherrod answered. "Are you on your way over?"

"I am."

"Good. I've got a surprise for you."

"What is it?" Janelle couldn't help but ask.

"Something you'll like, I hope," Sherrod said. "See you when you get here."

Janelle wondered what it was that he had for her. She'd somehow managed to avoid sleeping with him again, but she knew that it would have to happen soon or he would sense something was up. It wasn't as if she didn't want to have sex with him, because she was attracted to him. It was just that she had to figure out a way to enjoy it. If she could do that, things would be great. The problem was she didn't know how. Not only that, but she wasn't speaking to the one person who she thought would even be able to help: Nivea. Janelle would have to figure this one out on her own. And she was determined to do so.

You can do this, she told herself as she waited outside the door to his townhouse. As soon as he opened it, she stepped inside and put her arms around his neck, pulling him into a passionate kiss, one that she hoped would be hot enough to ignite a passion that would stay lit and not fizzle in the middle of their interaction. Sherrod's excitement from her action turned her on even more, and their kiss continued as they made their way inside and into his living room and onto the sofa.

"Damn," he paused long enough to say. "Hello to you too."

Janelle didn't say anything. She just removed her sweater, then pulled him back to her. She had one goal, and one goal only, and didn't want to waste any time. She kissed Sherrod's neck and whispered in his ear, "I want you."

"Oh, really?" He smiled.

"I do." She nodded, fumbling to unfasten his belt.

"Janelle, hold up. Wait, just a sec." He grabbed her wrists.

"What's wrong?" She frowned and stared at him.

"I was wondering the same thing. What is going on with you?" Sherrod sat beside her.

"Nothing's wrong. I'm just in the mood, that's all. Is there something wrong with that?" she said, confused by his question.

"I guess I'm wondering why you're in the mood all of a sudden. I mean, don't get me wrong, I'm glad, but I was under the impression that you wanted to slow things down." He held her hand in his.

"Why would you think that?" She frowned.

"Because for the past couple of weeks when I hint that I wanna be with you, you haven't seemed interested. So I thought we were taking a step back from that part of our relationship for a while."

"No, that's not, I mean . . ." Janelle shook her head.

"Janelle, it's cool. I just wanna make sure this isn't about your seeing Titus today."

Janelle's back straightened. "I didn't see him."

"No, you saw him. He didn't see you. There's a difference."

"Sherrod, this has nothing to do with Titus, okay? It has to do with me, us. You're right, I've been kinda off for a few days, but now I'm good, and I want this." She reached for him.

"Janelle, are you sure you're ready for this?" Sherrod asked.

"I just told you I was ready for it," she said with a sexy grin.

"Not just that, but all of this." He stared into her eyes. "Look, you know how much I'm feeling you. You are everything I'm looking for in a woman. I'm certain of that. I can see myself being with you and enjoying life together. But I'm not sure you're ready for that. And if you're not, that's fine. I'm ready to take this thing to the next level, but I want to be sure that that's something you even want from me."

Janelle's heart raced as she listened to Sherrod's words. Words that she'd always wanted to hear but never expected. Until now, she'd thought he was the cause of her frustration, but she realized that she had become her own worst enemy and had been selfish.

"Sherrod, you are just as much of a total package for me that you say I am for you. I need you to know that I do want you, and I am ready." She nodded.

Sherrod smiled and stood up. "I'm glad. Don't move."

"Where are you going?" Janelle asked.

"Just wait here, I'll be right back." He walked out of the living room.

Janelle's cell phone rang, and Sylvia's name flashed on the screen. "Hey, I got my car and left."

"I know. I've got Lynne here on three-way. She says she has something to tell us."

"Hey, Nelle," Lynne said.

Janelle became nervous, knowing exactly what Lynne was about to say. "Hey, Lynne. Listen, I'm with Sherrod, and we're in the middle of something."

"This will only take a minute," Lynne said.

"Okay, talk fast," Janelle whispered.

"So, I was at a workshop tonight for my job at the Westin Downtown. That's why I missed Peyton leaving for prom, but I promised I would see her when she went to the other one."

"I said talk fast," Janelle reminded her.

"Okay, well, as I was leaving, I saw this couple all hugged up," Lynne told her. "I damn near fainted."

"Look, I already know, and I was gonna tell you about Nivea after I talked to Sylvia first," Janelle admitted.

"Nivea? What the hell does she have to do with this?" Lynne asked.

"Huh? Oh, never mind." Janelle realized she'd misspoken and tried to clean it up.

"Lynne, who the hell did you see?" Sylvia demanded.

"Girl, it was Tricia, and the guy she was hugged up with damn sure wasn't Titus." Lynne cackled. "She got a boo too."

Sherrod walked in, carrying a small velvet box. Janelle's jaw dropped open, and she quickly said, "I gotta go."

Chapter 33

Tricia

Missing her son picking up his date for prom wasn't something Tricia had purposely done. She had every intention to be at the Blackwell home, but her day had been filled with unexpected delays, starting with a call from Everett, who sent a text telling her he was in town for a turnaround trip. She was already running late for her hair appointment and then had promised to pick up the corsage Titus ordered for Tank to give Peyton. It was going to be cutting it close, but there was no way Tricia was going to not go and see him. She quickly agreed to a late lunch at his hotel.

"We gotta be at the Blackwells' at six fifteen," Titus told her when he called to remind her about the corsage.

"I know that, Titus. I'll meet y'all there."

"Meet us?" Titus asked.

"Yes, meet you. I have a lot to do today, so I'll just pick it up while I'm out."

"Tricia, are you sure you're gonna do this and be there on time? I would do it myself, but I got some stuff to handle here at work, and then I'm picking up the tux while Tank gets a haircut."

"If I wasn't gonna do it, I woulda said I couldn't. It's just picking up a damn flower. I may not be some great influence in his life like he told the world you are, but I can pick up a corsage for his prom. Or don't you think I'm capable of doing that?" she snapped.

"Fine, I'll see you at six fifteen. And, Tricia?"

"What?" she moaned.

"Thanks."

She was surprised to hear him say thank you. Not that she did a lot that warranted his gratitude, but it was nice to hear. "You're welcome."

Tricia's hair stylist had inadvertently double booked and took longer than anticipated. By the time she walked out of the salon, she looked good but was almost an hour behind schedule. There was bumper-to-bumper traffic leading to downtown, then when she finally arrived, Everett sent a text letting her know the hotel shuttle had just picked them up and he would be another fifteen minutes. She looked at her watch and had to decide whether to leave or wait it out. It was already after four o'clock. But she was already at the hotel, and she could at least stay long enough to see him, even if they didn't eat.

"Tank," Tricia said when her son answered the phone. "I'm gonna need for you to go pick up your corsage. My hair appointment is taking longer than I thought."

"Ma, I'm at the barber shop, and I still ain't got my hair cut yet. I ain't gonna be able to go get it," he snapped.

"Who are you talking to like that?"

"Nobody. It's all good. I'll get it," Tank said and hung up.

Tricia was about to call him and lay him out for hanging up on her, but she looked up and saw Everett walking into the hotel lobby. She smiled as she walked over, and he hugged her.

"Look at you, lady in blue. I like your hair. It's nice."

"Thank you." She blushed.

"I'm sorry it took so long. I'm starving." He hugged her again. "I'm glad you came to see me."

"Me too." Tricia nodded, promising herself that she would leave in an hour. But time slipped away as they talked and ate. Before she knew it, it was almost six

o'clock as she rushed out of the hotel parking lot, promising Everett that she'd call him later. Despite breaking all
types of speeding laws, she knew it was too late. Instead
of going to the Blackwells', she went straight home.

"How did it go?" she asked Titus as soon as he walked
in. He glared as he walked past her without saying anything. She continued behind him. "I'm so sorry I missed
it. Traffic was horrible, and my stylist took forever. It was
a mess. That's why I called Tank and told him I was going
to be late."

Titus remained silent. She was right on his heels as
he went into his man cave, turning on the light and TV
before sitting on the sofa.

"Titus, it's not my fault," Tricia said. "Talk to me. Say
something."

"I don't have nothing to say."

"You want me to order us some food?" she offered even
though she was already full.

"No."

Tricia had never seen him this upset and knew she had
to do something. She sat and leaned against him. "I'm
sorry. Come upstairs and let me make it up to you."

"I'm good," Titus murmured.

Tricia sat up. "You're good? What the hell is that supposed to mean? You don't want to come upstairs with me?"

"Nope," Titus told her, his eyes still on the TV.

"That's how you're gonna act? Really?" Tricia snapped.
"Here I am apologizing and trying to make it up to you,
and you don't even care?"

"I don't," Titus said. "I really don't care."

Tricia was unnerved by his cold demeanor, and she
realized he really did not care. She walked out and stood
in the kitchen for a few minutes before grabbing her
purse and keys. If he didn't want her, that was fine.

She returned to the Westin and had the valet park her
car in the overnight lot.

What room are you in? she texted Everett.

1512, he sent back. Why? Are you sending me room service?

No, something better.

She got on the elevator and hit the button. She took a deep breath as she knocked on his room door.

"Tricia, what in the world?" he said when he opened the door.

"I came back. Told you it was better than room service." She shrugged.

"I thought you had to go see Tank and his prom date."

"Are you going to ask me inside or just play twenty questions while I'm standing in the hallway?"

He moved so she could enter his room. He'd taken off the dress shirt he'd had on earlier, and the white T-shirt he wore clung to his potbelly, reminding her of Winnie the Pooh. Even his physique was the opposite of her husband, whose body was muscled and athletic. The two men were like night and day in every aspect. Titus was hard and cold. Everett was warm and caring.

"Would you like to sit down?" Everett offered, pointing to one of the empty chairs near the large bed.

"No."

"Well, let me grab my shirt. We can go down to the bar and have a drink." He picked his shirt up from the bed.

"I don't want a drink. I don't want to sit. I want to stay in here and get in bed with you."

Everett's eyes widened, and he looked panicked. "Uh . . ."

"Why does that surprise you? Don't you enjoy being with me?" Tricia asked as she took a step closer.

"I do. I mean, I enjoy our conversations, and I think you're very special. But—"

"But what?" Tricia took another step toward him.

"But you're married."

"So, you're saying you don't want to be with me?" Tricia was now standing directly in front of him.

"Tricia, I'm saying you probably need to leave," Everett stared and said.

Tricia's heart sank. "I, oh, I'm so sorry. I thought, maybe . . ."

"I enjoy you, Tricia, but not in that way. Not now I don't." Everett gave her a sympathetic look that made her even more embarrassed than she already was.

Tricia nearly tripped as she ran out of his hotel room. Had she not been on the fifteenth floor, she would've taken the stairs, but she not only had to endure an elevator full of other guests as they slowly descended, but the valet took forever. By the time she got into the truck, Everett had called five times. She sent a text telling him to leave her alone before blocking him from her phone, and then she allowed the tears she'd been holding to flow. *How could I have been so stupid? All that talk about being his lady in blue. He's a damn clown and probably gay anyway. Fat-ass pooh bear.*

As she turned into her neighborhood, she got a call from an unfamiliar number, which she ignored, thinking it was Everett calling from his hotel room phone. The number called twice more before she answered.

"What!"

"Tricia King?" a woman said.

"Yes? Who the hell is this?" Tricia demanded.

"This is Mercy General hospital. Your husband was just brought in."

"What? Why?" Tricia screamed.

"It appears he's had a heart attack."

Tricia made an illegal U-turn and sped to the hospital, no longer thinking about Everett and the way he rejected her. She ran into the emergency room and was escorted to the triage area, where one of the doctors updated her on Titus's condition.

"Mrs. King, I'm Dr. Baxter, one of the cardiologists here."

"Is he all right?" She trembled.

"Your husband had a heart attack. We're prepping him for surgery."

"Surgery? Oh my God," Tricia wailed.

"He's going to be fine. He's stable, and we're just going to put a stint in to help the blood flow." Dr. Baxter smiled.

"Can I see him?"

"Yes, you can. He's under anesthesia and pretty out of it, but you can go in."

"Thank you." Tricia nodded. She walked into the room.

Titus lay in the hospital bed with his eyes closed. An oxygen tube was in his nostrils, and his body was connected to several machines, including one that monitored his heart rate. A nurse adjusted an IV in his arm. Tricia walked to his side, touching his face. Despite their strained relationship, he was still her husband, and she loved him. Seeing him like this made her realize that now more than ever. *God, please let him be all right. I promise if you pull him through this, I'll be the best wife I can be to him. He won't even need the calendar, and I'll learn to cook. Just save him. I need him.*

"Please, God," Tricia prayed out loud.

Titus's eyes fluttered, but they remained closed. She leaned closer to him, touching his forehead. "Titus, baby, I'm here. You're going to be okay. I love you, do you understand? I love you."

"Yes," Titus murmured. His voice was raspy. "I love you too. I've always loved you, Janelle."

Coming Soon . . .

All in Love Is Fair